Dark Desires

Francesca Quarto

Dark Desires

Printed in the United States of America

For all who dare to cross the threshold to their fantasies, touch their darker desires and fall back unscathed into a safer reality, enter here. Life is not black and white, but many shades of shadows.

Chapter 1

She pulled away from the growing pressure of his mouth, not allowing this to become a long, passionate kiss. She vaguely wondered if she was incapable of a sustained intimacy. Were these subtle rejections of passion a reflection of a deep flaw in her libido?

Maggie Newsome had taken a few casual lovers since she turned seventeen. The question of a healthy sex drive never occurred to her, especially since she was only twenty-five.

But in the arms of this sexually attractive man, she found herself more and more distant and unreceptive to his intimate attentions. She felt herself moving away from him mentally, but unable to make a complete break.

"See you at Isabella's tonight, Collin," Maggie said, while disengaging from his arms and heading toward the staircase.

"Why don't I stay for a while, darling, and we'll drive over there together? Harrison is getting the Rolls spiffed and I'm in no hurry. We can go riding if you'd like, or just walk around the village if you prefer."

Collin Fitzhugh felt put off by Maggie's rebuff of his passion, wondering how much more of his fiancé's odd behavior he would have to endure. The wedding was four months off. Their engagement was barely two weeks old and she'd been withdrawing more and more into herself ever since it was announced.

As the wealthy owner of a large timber processing business, he considered himself landed gentry. Not many dared to cross him. And he surely never expected to encounter any resistance to his romantic overtures from any woman, least of all, his fiancé.

He was talking to her back now, as she moved up the staircase, her slender form, impossibly desirable to him.

She wore her thick black hair in the defiantly short "bob" of the day. Like all her fashions, she reflected the very essence of a modern woman.

Maggie stopped on the landing, turning that glossy dark head to look back at him, fixing her cold, blue-violet eyes on him.

"Walk around the village, so the peasants can view our magnificent selves? Honestly, Collin. There are times I wonder if you've converted to colonial attitudes altogether. Before you start singing Hail Britannia, I can't lazy about here all day. I need to get to my office and prepare the questions for my interview of the Mayor next week."

Maggie felt irritated that Collin seemed dismissive of her work as Publisher and Editor at the Paxton Guardian, a small, but influential paper founded by her grandfather, George Maynard Newsome. Her father, George Jr., ran it until his unexpected death a few months earlier. A disturbing scene flashed in Maggie's mind, of Collin telling her she'd sell more papers if she covered fashion and local gossip. She'd felt tempted to throw her dinner plate in his smug, albeit handsome face.

They were seated at an intimate dinner party at the time, with a number of influential businessmen and the socially prominent guests.

"I don't believe the cut of a woman's skirt is more relevant than the cut to the public monies that support local charitable programs," she had answered quietly. "I also find gossip to be a distasteful and often poisonous form of entertainment. The Paxton Guardian has higher standards than the local pub tittle-tattle!"

A silence descended on the group like a thick fog rolling in from the sea. Collin looked mortified at her response to what he thought as news-worthy material. There was much clearing of throats and forks scratching at bone china, as guests moved their food around, trying to ignore Maggie's social transgression.

All except one guest, she recalled.

Grayson Gerrard, newly introduced to the social scene as an important artist and protégé of the wealthy Isabella Butler. She and her secretary-companion, Leslie Porter-Booth, both turned their eyes to the dashing man as he spoke.

"Your point is well taken, Miss Newsome," his deep, velvety voice cut through the dense silence.

The other eleven guests looked up from their plates at the virile artist, who was handsome enough to grace any painting himself. He had become a local sensation when he suddenly appeared among them a few months earlier. He had a definite aura of mystery about him that seemed obvious even to the most obtuse among them.

No one knew where he came from, but none could deny his chiseled features and charismatic qualities, when he entered their closed society.

The women tittered behind gloved hands to their women friends, about how they were tingling in places they believed long dormant. The men tried to puff up, to look more macho when he stood among them.

His patron, the reclusive and very wealthy, Isabella Butler, insisted that he be invited to any social event she chose to attend, or she refused the invitation. Her companion and, some whispered, paramour, Leslie Porter Booth, was already an assumed guest, along with the mercurial Isabella.

Isabella, a short, stout woman, always dressed in black, looked uncannily like a fat spider, sitting patiently and waiting to pounce on the unwary. Her lineage was impeccable, even if her fashion choices were not.

The Butler line was well-established when Southern Louisiana enjoyed a short-lived separation from the Union and declared for the Confederate side. That ended in disaster when General Benjamin F. Butler marched in at the head of his Union troops and began a campaign of hanging anyone who didn't cooperate in the repatriation under the Stars and Stripes.

The General enjoyed the comforts and luxury of the plantation he occupied so much, that he over-stayed his welcome by three generations as the locals liked to quip. Where he was ruthless in his efforts to show the cost of war was high, Isabella Butler was ruthless in her social dictates.

Her companion, Leslie Porter Booth, was willowy and statuesque. She would never be described as pretty, but she was striking. Her pale, blue eyes were seemed always slightly hooded, as if afraid to take in a complete view of the world. She wore her long blond hair braided and wrapped like a yellow crown on her head. She favored dark colors in her own wardrobe, a drab reflection of her employer. Her only break with that monotone, were the colorful silk scarfs she was never seen without, flowing like liquid rainbows around her neck and washing down the long curve of her back.

The trio made quite the splash entering any gathering.

Grayson Gerrard had gone on to address the stunned dinner guests that evening.

"There are many safety nets that are being systematically dismantled by our governing bodies and the poor are paying the cost every day of their shortened lives."

At the time, Maggie was as surprised to hear such an opinion spoken aloud by this enigmatic man as everyone else in the room. Even his closest confident, Isabella Butler, wore a look of surprise.

Maggie only met Grayson Gerrard once, before that evening's dinner party, but that was enough to have made a lasting impression. He was impeccably dressed both then and at this evening's soirée. His dinner jacket was subtly showing off the pumped-up biceps and well-developed shoulder and back muscles. He stood well over six feet, Maggie observed, when first introduced to him at Isabella's. Her fiancé was six feet and Gerrard was a good three inches taller.

She noticed at the time that Collin looked like he was stretching his neck to compensate for the lack of stature every time he encountered the man throughout the evening.

While they had only exchanged the expected bland small talk, Maggie felt the weight of his lingering gaze on her throughout the evening. At one point, when Collin had to excuse himself from her side to speak to a business acquaintance, Maggie found herself gazing up into the slate-gray eyes of Grayson Gerrard.

He never said a word to her, only stood looking down on her upturned face. She saw a slight smile playing at the corners of his sensual mouth as he watched her. She felt like a speared fish, hooked on the lance of his all-seeing eyes.

As Maggie looked over at Grayson Gerrard this evening, she realized he was addressing his comments to her alone. She felt the same urge to squirm under that steely gaze but forced herself to return the open look.

"I appreciate your support, Mr. Gerrard, and can only wish others shared your insights," she said, directing her response to him, as if the others had vanished.

Maggie had not thought of Grayson Gerrard until they were to dine at Isabella Butler's that evening. Now her memory seemed jerked back to his all-consuming looks.

She was disturbed by her thoughts and turning her back on her fiancé, began to climb the stairs to her room.

Collin stood looking up at her, wondering how he could rekindle that hot flame they once shared.

Without speaking he took the stairs two at a time and before she could resist, swept Maggie into his arms. He carried her, protesting, into her bedroom, kicking the door shut with a bang.

"Collin, what do you think you're doing? I need to…"

Her next words were lost under the hard demand of his kiss. His tongue filled her mouth as he pushed her down on her bed. He was pulling at her clothes, his passion rising with every button pulled open from her blouse. Before she could object, Maggie was swept away with the moment, as Collin found the exact spot that he knew would bring her to complete release.

After she climaxed, he was quick to shudder with pleasure at the moistness between her legs and gave himself over to his own ecstasy.

After several panted breaths, he shifted onto his elbows and looked down at her. Her eyes were closed and there were tears spilling down her cheeks.

"Despite your protests, you enjoyed every second," he said, trying to ignore her turned back and lack of response.

Chiding herself for her body's response to his rough, demanding love-making, she rolled away when he got off her. Going to the bathroom, she closed and locked the door. She felt furious with him. Strangely, she was almost as angry with herself for giving in to his knowing touches.

Both would have been foreign thoughts until recently, and she couldn't begin to understand the changes she was feeling toward the man she was to marry.

Chapter 2

Collin banged on her bathroom door, upset at her rejection of what to his mind was his outpouring of romantic passion.

"You are being totally unreasonable, Maggie! I know you enjoyed our little interlude, so why deny it now?"

When his questions and entreaties were answered with stony silence, except for the running of her bath water, Collin walked away, perplexed and hurt.

"I'll be at Isabella's at eight," he shouted as he left the bedroom. "See you there if you get over whatever is eating away at you these last few weeks."

Maggie sat on the edge of the oval shaped porcelain tub, watching it fill. As the hot water began steaming up the bathroom, the fragrance of the lilac bath oils began to calm her. Her mind drifted with the sweet vapors.

She knew Collin was a skilled lover. He'd undoubtedly had lots of practice with other women. He knew every button, every sensual trick. For a while now, all she felt after their love-making was an unreasonable resentment toward him for using those skills and she didn't understand why.

His demanding treatment of her just now might have led to a physical climax, but it also deepened that bitterness and confusion. Perhaps she was angrier with herself than Collin.

She stepped to the large mirror hanging over the marble sink. Looking at her through the steamed-up glass was the unspoken answer to that question.

She couldn't see herself clearly when she was with Collin. She felt lost; her personality blurred like her reflection.

Maggie used a towel to wipe away the condensation on the mirror.

She was an attractive woman, perhaps even beautiful, though she placed little value on her physical attributes. Her parents had always warned against relying on only her looks to find happiness in life.

Staring at her reflection, she thought back to one of her last conversations with her father, before his heart attack. They were sitting on their patio, sipping fresh lemonade in a sultry twilight. The long slope of the shadowed lawn led down to the muddy rim of Lake Pontchartrain. The sun was gilding the sleepy moss dangling off the Cyprus trees and the night air was filled with the sounds of bats searching their fill of flying insects.

"Maggie, you are a pragmatic and intelligent young women. Don't ever let your looks become your best asset, my dear. I fear your relationship with Collin Fitzhugh may lessen the value you place on your many talents."

When she protested laughingly at her father's concerns, he looked over at her saying, "Always remember, you are a person of intellect and abilities, before you are a woman of beauty. Just like I've told you since you were a little girl, your mother and I were *people* before we were *parents!*"

She sighed, shut off the faucet and turned her back to the mirror. Slipping deeply into the fragrant water she knew she was doing more than bathing. Holding up her left hand, the sparkle of the large diamond on the engagement ring Collin had placed there, jolted her into a realization. *I honestly don't think I love him.*

Toweled off, Maggie sat at her dressing table. As always, she used the barest amount of make-up, her creamy skin, already had a healthy blush. She applied a bit of kohl to her long lashes and eye pencil to highlight the vivid blue of her eyes. She never used lipstick, disliking the traces it left on napkins and glasses. Strangely, it felt as if she was leaving a part of herself behind.

She vigorously brushed her new "Dutch Boy" haircut until it shone, straight, glossy and smoothly edged, to just below her delicate chin line. The heavy bangs covered her thin brows, completing the fine geometric look of the Art Deco with which she filled her house. Retro though it may be, to her mind it looked like modern chic.

After putting on her sheerest hose, she went to her closet, pulling out the newest acquisition to her wardrobe. A bold red, sleeveless chiffon evening dress. Maggie wore what she enjoyed. It didn't bother her if her taste made a fashion statement that didn't mesh with the older, more stogy matrons attending these affairs.

Stepping into the feathery light, chiffon, she pulled down on the hem where it reached her knees and studied herself in the long mirror. The drop waist and soft layers of fabric gave the dress a gently swaying character when she moved. She barely felt the weight of the material on her lithe body.

Choosing a long rope of pearls to loop twice around her neck, she decided to add a matching headband, decorated with tiny pearl beading. She rummaged around the closet to locate a shawl in the creamy color of the beads, grabbing a small beaded clutch, she was ready.

One last look in the full-length mirror showed a beautiful woman with an independent look in her eyes. Maggie felt ready to make herself a free woman, but for this one evening, she resolved silently, she didn't want a scandal. She'd make peace with Collin at least to the point of being civil.

She grabbed the keys to her father's beautiful Packard Roadster. Maggie learned to drive in the "beast" as she referred to it, her father doing the instructing himself. She always felt his presence as she slid across the cool leather upholstery and pressed the starter button on the floor.

The powerful engine seemed to stir some kind of secret place inside her chest, with the vibrations of the smooth rise and fall of the pistons.

She drove slowly out of the circular drive, smiling to herself. Her thoughts were centered on the coming change in her life, a change that would bring her total freedom.

No more engagement, no more expectations of me, no more Collin.

The finality of her thoughts gave Maggie a comfort she hadn't felt since her father was alive. She knew this was the right decision, the only decision, she could make and live with herself.

Strangely though, she had no idea why she had changed so toward the man she'd loved since they were childhood playmates. It seemed an impossible thing to consider just a few months ago.

She pressed down on the accelerator pedal. The sound of the car's engine vibrated in the close space of the roughly carved out road.

The headlights on Maggie's car bounced off the close-knit rows of Cyprus tress, with their heavy burden of wiry gray moss. They formed a tunnel in places, the substantial clumps of moss coming at her windshield like attacking bats.

Maggie shuddered as if a cold hand had touched her bare arm.

She was relieved to see the lights of Butler Plantation loom into view. It's long, white pillars were overgrown with ivy climbing up to the second floor. Isabella Butler loved saying, "Nature is consuming us as we sleep."

Maggie drove under the portico. She smiled at the attendant who opened the door for her, ready to take her seat and park her vehicle.

Taking a deep breath, she moved up the wide skirt of stone steps and into the beginning of a new life.

Chapter 3

The guests at the dinner party were an eclectic group of ten notable residents of Paxton Parrish, most holding lineage back to pre-Civil War days in Louisiana and around New Orleans.

When Maggie entered the echoing, marble foyer, the maid, Annette, escorted her directly to the dining room where the other guests were already gathered. On the way to join the others, the maid kindly pointed out that they had just been seated a few minutes ago.

The maid ushered Maggie into the room by announcing her name to the assembled group.

"Miss Maggie Newsome, Madame."

Maggie felt all eyes rise from their plates and conversations and turn toward her. She stood on the threshold before entering, looking back at the faces of the other guests. The mellow lighting of candelabras, placed at intervals around the room, bathed the setting in a warm, inviting light.

Maggie forced a confident smile, looking around the room briefly and nodding at the seated guests.

She made herself take a deep breath and stepped to Isabella's side at the head of the table, ignoring any questioning looks she was getting from the others.

"Forgive me, Isabella. I had trouble getting myself together, but I didn't want to miss seeing you."

"Give me a kiss child and take your seat. As you can see, it's been left open for you alone."

Isabella was deeply fond of the young woman, admiring her intelligence and independence. She sometimes wondered aloud to her companion, Leslie Porter Booth, about the unlikely pairing of the beautiful, strong Maggie, with the seemingly pleasure-seeking, Collin Fitzhugh.

She felt Collin unworthy of such a remarkable young woman.

Isabella's sharp eyes immediately caught the reserved look Maggie gave her fiancé this evening, when sitting down in the open chair beside him.

She leaned close to Leslie's ear and whispered, "Hmm. I wonder if there is trouble in that paradise?"

She noted the frosty peck Collin placed on Maggie's cheek as she turned away from him.

Maggie had resolved on her drive over, to make the best of the situation, as awkward as it felt for her. She'd already arrived on her own and offered the weakest of excuses and she was certain everyone noticed her aloof posture toward Collin.

Settled into her chair, Maggie looked around at the other guests, speaking to those nearest to her as they murmured their welcome to her. Maggie did see a few raised eyebrows at her obvious social mis-step in coming so late to the party.

Leslie Porter Booth was seated on Isabella's right. She'd been listening to a hushed comment by Isabella.

Her own greeting to Maggie was quickly followed by the deep, velvety voice of Grayson Gerrard.

Maggie hadn't seen the mysterious artist since Collin hosted the "Three Musketeers" as he called them in his usual mocking fashion, a few weeks back. While she might have laughed at his description then, for some reason it seemed petty and vulgar to her now. She had begun to see her fiancé in a different light. Collin never displayed any loyalty to anyone, but his own ambitions, Maggie began to see that evening.

While Maggie picked at her food, ignoring the hum of chatter around her, Collin's presence so nearby, felt almost suffocating.

Her mind wandered back to what happened after the dinner party he'd hosted and the guests were all gone.

Collin had scolded her like a four-year old, for her lack of manners during a dinner discussion.

"Politics are not a proper conversation over a filet mignon my dear, especially for a woman to be espousing."

Maggie recalled bridling at the ignorance of the remark and the blatant sexism it displayed. She had stormed off and left him standing in his bedroom, where he had begun to unzip her dress, expecting her full compliance with his intentions.

Maggie had slapped his hands away and slammed his bedroom door in his face.

Driving home that night, she knew something had changed inside her, something that was irreversible and she felt it again only sharper in her mind.

Following that blow-up, Collin had showered her with flowers, jewelry and notes, and finally, after she agreed to see him, apologized for his pig-headedness and begged her forgiveness.

She relented and they resumed their engagement, love-making and planning, but Maggie felt a wall had gone up between them, she knew he could never penetrate.

Now, sitting stiffly beside him, their argument burned like a cinder in Maggie's mind and they carefully ignored each other, while Collin charmed the woman beside him.

Maggie was certain her decision to break the engagement was long overdue and smiled back at the handsome Grayson Gerrard whenever he caught her eye.

Dinner over, they all followed the squat hostess to her Solarium where she announced they would be entertained with a fireworks display.

"We'll celebrate the end of a long summer and the coming of autumn, my favorite season," she declared enthusiastically.

Ruth Rydall looked pleased with the attentions of the rich and dashing, Collin Fitzhugh, throughout the dinner. He had totally ignored his fiancé, which encouraged Ruth's own flirtations, several times placing her small hand on his muscular thigh under the table.

With the coming entertainment, she was quick to occupy the chair next to Collin, brushing his hand as she sat down as close as possible without being on his lap. He smiled and she knew he understood all her subtle messages.

Maggie loved fireworks and hoped, somehow, they cheered her darkening mood. Being close to Collin all evening was beginning to wear on her nerves and she wanted desperately for it to be over.

She realized Grayson Gerrard had taken the chair next to hers and felt his eyes intently studying her profile.

"You look enchanting this evening, Miss Newsome, but I couldn't help noticing the reserve, in your normally frank gaze. I hope all is well with you."

"You are very observant, Mr. Gerrard, but then I'd expect as an artist, that would be part of your talent."

They were sitting within touching distance of one another. Maggie found herself drawn into his probing gray eyes, letting her own eyes drift down to the fullness of his lips.

The mood was broken when a booming sound and multi-colored lights filled the room.   Surrounded by windows the Solarium offered perfect viewing to all the guests, of the colorful display against the ebony sky. They were expressing their enjoyment like an assembly of children, to Isabella's great delight.

She reached for Leslie's hand and intertwined the long fingers with her own stubby ones.

With the shadows of the room and everyone peering upward, this affectionate gesture went unnoticed. Except by one guest.

Grayson Gerrard had become acquainted with Leslie Porter Booth long before any of these guests were even born, long before this house of one hundred-plus years, had been built, and long before Louisiana even existed on an American map.

Grayson and Leslie found a common history back in the bleak days, just after the French revolted from the greedy tyranny of the crown. They stood and watched together, as the heads of the beautiful and privileged, rolled down into wicker baskets, wet with the blood of many.

Grayson watched as Leslie's eyes slid over in his direction. A small smile played on her thin lips as she caught his look in the burst of the next spray of color. He gave her an imperceptible nod in return.

Life was good for them here and it had just become even better for her Maker, Grayson Gerrard.

<h1 style="text-align:center">Chapter 4</h1>

The dinner guests began gathering at the front door, saying goodbye to their hostess. The word *delightful* was repeated often, many giving the stout woman a perfunctory peck on her round, powdered cheek.

Maggie hung back until the end, wanting to invite Isabella over the following Sunday for brunch. She was quite fond of this woman the locals called "The Dark Bayou Queen" because of her vast wealth and black dresses she always wore.

Maggie looked upon Isabella as an honorary aunt, having known her all of her life. When she met Isabella's companion, she felt an undercurrent in her greeting, a hard reserve. Though Leslie was always cordial, Maggie felt a subtle agenda existed in the outwardly dotting companion. An agenda that was set with some kind of self-serving goal.

But the invitation had another purpose. She hoped the mysterious Grayson Gerrard would be in attendance. There was an allure to the man's very presence that she wanted to explore, if only to satisfy her natural curiosity.

Maggie was a born journalist and could sniff out an obscure story, like a coon dog on scent.

She already found out the artist had taken up residence in a small guest cottage on Isabella's vast plantation, several months earlier. She'd heard gossip from some local workmen, it had been restored for his use. This, after years of sitting empty and vulnerable to the ever-encroaching woods.

She had seen it often as a child, wandering around the property while her father visited with Isabella. The cottage was built solidly of brick, located off a long path leading down from the big house and set deep in the flourishing gardens.

Its windows were boarded up back then, but the young Maggie managed to loosen the rotting plywood at the front of the house, climbing through, into the main room. It was dark, with only a thin, greenish light filtering through the surrounding trees.

Maggie was never a skittish child and this was an adventure! She let her eyes adjust to the gloom and poked about in the four rooms, finding only musty smelling furnishings and rotted carpeting. There was a full length mirror in the bedroom, with the veiny look of an old man, sitting in one corner.

Maggie left off her search that day when her father's voice penetrated the darkened rooms, calling her name. Isabella was with him, but instead of chiding the little girl, she promised to restore the cottage one day, so Maggie could have her own playhouse. This was never done. Until the artist appeared.

Maggie's memories were interrupted by people moving about as they got ready to end the evening.

As the first of the guests began gathering their things, Maggie waited in the Solarium. She stood in front of a wide window, her slim back to the room. She stared out, scanning over the dark lawns leading down a long slope and eventually melding with damp earth of the sultry swamp. This small part of the bayou at least, was totally tamed.

She had a sudden vision of the swamp as a beast, its mouth open wide, showing hundreds of moss covered teeth, waiting for the next unwary footfall.

She shuddered at the sinister feeling that came over her. She'd never looked at the bayou as evil or menacing. It was just a part of her life. A life it permitted to co-exist with it.

Collin approached her from behind, touching her elbow and making her jump.

"Forgive me, Maggie. I didn't realize you were so lost in thought. I know you drove here, but I think we need to clear the air between us and put to rest any misunderstandings. I'd like to come over tonight. I can follow you back home, after we leave here."

Maggie was touched by his pleading, contrite tone. He did seem anxious to get back in her good graces but had just unwittingly provided her an opportunity to tell him she was breaking off the engagement.

"Collin, I do think we need to talk, but I'm tired now. Come by in the morning. I want to speak with Isabella before I leave. I'll see you around eight."

She felt a twinge of guilt at the look of relief that came over his face as he leaned down to kiss her cheek. Knowing him well, she knew he had been playing at ignoring her all evening, because of his hurt pride. Now, she saw how vulnerable he could be in the face of her rejection.

Does he truly love me? she thought as he walked away.

She watched him as he went to say his goodbyes to their hostess.

Just as Maggie stepped toward the foyer, Grayson Gerrard seemed to materialize out of nowhere to stand in front of her.

"Miss Newsome, would you allow me to walk you to your car? It's gotten rather dark, even with the light coming from the house."

"Thank you, but that won't be necessary. Around these parts, we're all part human and part bayou," she joked, smiling up at him.

His own smile in return left her weak in the knees. She would have gone on staring into the endless depths of his dark eyes, if Isabella hadn't broken the spell.

"I suppose you'll be deserting me for home too, Maggie."

Maggie took in a deep breath, trying madly to collect herself. She invited Isabella and Leslie to brunch the following Sunday and turned to Grayson.

"I'd very much enjoy your joining our little group, Mr. Gerrard. Just don't expect the lavish fare Isabella is famous for laying out. I'm a mediocre cook and will have to rely on my gram's old recipes to produce anything edible!"

"I would be delighted to test your home-cooking and will bring something special to toast the occasion."

After setting a time, Maggie kissed Isabella, saying good night to Leslie. Forgetting her objections to his offer, she let Grayson take her elbow to guide her down the wide, stone-staircase.

The young man hired away from the stables for the evening, ran to get her car, parked in the shadows of the large, antebellum style house.

The pair stood next to the gently burbling fountain in the center of the circular drive.

While they waited, Maggie found Grayson's nearness made her feel like an inexperienced teen, trying to act grown-up around the man of her dreams.

She pulled the pale shawl tighter around her bare arms, throwing one end over her left shoulder to hold it in place.

"Would you have any objection to my addressing you by your first name, Miss Newsome? I feel such formality puts an unwelcome distance between people, wouldn't you agree?"

"I don't hold to many traditions ...Grayson," she answered with a self-assurance she wasn't feeling.

"You are indeed both exquisite and emancipated...Maggie. A most desirable and rare combination in a woman."

The big Packard came to a jolting stop in front of them. Grayson subtly slipped a

five-dollar bill in the young man's hand, while Maggie got behind the wheel. He walked around to the driver's side as she started the engine.

"I'm looking forward to seeing you this next Sunday, Maggie. I hope you'll allow me the honor of showing you some of the work Isabella has commissioned from me, in the coming days. As the daughter of an artist, I'm sure you'll appreciate my need for some praise." He laughed easily at this little vanity.

"That would be wonderful. See you next week."

How did he know mom was an artist? she wondered. It was quickly forgotten when he smiled once more at her and stepped back from the car.

He stood watching her taillights until they were pin pricks and finally swallowed by the night.

"I believe I'll be seeing quite a lot of Miss Maggie Newsome in the coming days," he said as the willowy woman stepped out of the shadows to stand beside him.

"Yes, much, much more of her will be revealed to me before her time comes."

Leslie Porter Booth gave a soft laugh, keeping her thoughts wrapped as tightly as her golden crown.

Chapter 5

Maggie relished these early hours. The sun crept into the morning sky, burnishing the clustered stands of swamp dogwood growing at the edges of her property. Her father told her they were among her mom's favorite wild plants. Maggie admired their tenacity to be beautiful, though surrounded by the murky, foul smelling swamp.

She was curled deeply into an over-sized leather chair in her mother's old art studio, newly converted into a home office. It was her favorite room in the rambling house, with three walls of windows and views of the back gardens and surrounding lawn. The view ran like her mom's wet watercolor paintings, down to the eternal bayou.

It all butted up against a stiff wire fence her father had installed when Maggie was just a toddler. Her mother said the little girl had gypsy urges, loving to wander and the dangers of the swamps were all too real.

Maggie tucked the sky-blue, silk robe under her legs, enjoying the feel of the fabric as it wrapped around her snuggly. She had begun to sleep naked after her father died, preferring the texture of the sheets on her body. His death emphasized the lack of freedom she actually had in her life, but she understood his protectiveness was rooted in his love for her. She never resented him for trying to keep her safe, but saw clearly, his strong personality would eventually have crushed her free spirit if she allowed.

Coming home from college after graduation was not her original plan, but her mother's illness turned everything upside down. She put her life on hold to help care for her and to support her father, as they prepared for the final goodbye.

She took another sip of Earl Grey tea from one of her mother's delicate china cups, sighing deeply. Her thoughts wandered to her fiancé and how Collin preferred his mornings to start with coffee, dark and strong.

That reminded her he was coming by later in the morning. The prospect of handing him his engagement ring weighed heavily upon her mind and her tired state from lack of sleep only made her feel more anxious. She had to admit to herself that her restless sleep didn't entirely have to do with her tiff with Collin.

The enigmatic Grayson Garrard kept making appearances in her scattered dreams.

She could still feel the weight of Grayson's penetrating dark eyes. He had held her in his appreciative gaze like a butterfly collector who came upon a rare specimen. She had experienced an irresistible urge to linger forever under their spell. Only her resentment at being in the thrall of any other person helped her shake off the mesmerizing effect of his hypnotic eyes.

But now, recalling it, she smiled with a new resolve. Collin would no longer dictate her thoughts or actions. Her tea finished, she left the studio. It was early, but there would be a long day ahead of her.

A while later, the front door opened with Collin's key and he stepped quietly into the foyer. His arms were loaded down with two dozen fresh-cut roses. A long velvet box, stuck out of his jacket pocket.

He crept as quietly as he could into Maggie's kitchen, hunting down a vase for the flowers and arranging them in a splash of deep red, walked through to the dining room. Placing them in the center of the sideboard, they filled the room with their heady fragrance.

He removed the box from his jacket, laying it under the bower of heavy blooms.

As soon as he was certain he'd not been heard, he exited the house and walked back to his car to wait until he was certain Maggie had found his surprise.

Back upstairs in her bedroom, Maggie was slipping into a pair of jodhpurs. She'd been invited to return to the Butler Plantation, to go horseback riding with Leslie.

Not having many friends around her age since leaving school, Maggie welcomed the offer from the rather elusive Miss Parsons Booth, hoping to get to know her better under less formal circumstances.

Maggie sorely missed the female companionship her mother provided when she was home on school breaks, and now, she had very little contact of that nature.

While she rummaged in her closet for the jacket that went with her riding outfit, her thoughts circled back to Leslie. She had to admit; she was something of an enigma.

Her arrival at the Butler Plantation as companion to the reclusive Isabella Butler had the locals full of speculation. Random gossip made its way to Maggie's ear.

She'd been with Isabella for a few months before Maggie met her, when they attended her father's funeral. Isabella sat beside Maggie since they'd always looked upon her as close family. Her new companion stood attentively, slightly behind the older woman's chair.

Maggie had a clear recollection of the tall, slender woman, about her age, standing as stiff as a fashion mannequin, in a dark tailored suit, belted at her slim waist, a golden circlet of braids encircling her head. A long black scarf at her neck moved gently in the breeze, bringing attention to the lovely figure of the reserved woman.

Looking through her closet, she chuckled to herself remembering how her mind, so muddled that day with grief, thought the stranger resembled a mud wasp, hovering around Isabella.

Maggie recalled how once, during that endless day, she caught Leslie's eyes riveted on her. There was a slight smile playing on her mouth, the deep, red lipstick making it hard to miss. It was as if she found it all amusing.

Maggie remembered feeling a chill run down her spine under that frosty gaze.

They met formally after the graveside service, when the small group of twenty or so mourners, returned to Maggie's house for a light buffet luncheon.

Maggie had been speaking with Richard Hammond, the family lawyer and her dad's best friend. He was telling her she'd need to come into his office the following week, to review some important legal matters, when Isabella and Leslie joined their quiet conversation.

The new companion was introduced to her by Isabella, as if she were a lost daughter, something Maggie found odd, considering Isabella's penchant for formality.

As she slipped into her riding jacket and grabbed for her boots, she recalled how she felt drawn to this very singular person, with her vague accent and pale, strangely empty, blue eyes.

Maggie shook herself out of her reveries, wanting nothing to do with thoughts of the day she buried her father.

Why am I being so overemotional?

She raced down the long hallway to the staircase in time to see the front door shutting.

My God, someone's been in the house!

She slipped into her father's old bedroom and retrieved the small handgun he kept beside his bed. She was a crack shot since he made her learn how to shoot before her mother would allow the weapon in the house. The old hay barn had lots of holes riddled in its sides to prove her dedication over the years.

Standing at the top of the stairs, she started down, the gun snug at her side. She wasn't as frightened as she was angry that someone invaded her home.

As her foot made the landing, she was breathing hard. That's when she detected the rich fragrance of roses.

"What on earth…"

She bolted the front door and turned back to the dining room. There, on the side-buffet, sat a glorious array of blood red roses, oozing fragrance like a perfume atomizer.

She spotted the long velvet box beneath the flowers and slid it out. The bracelet was exquisite. Every other gem was a diamond, followed by a ruby. She couldn't resist putting it around her wrist and turning her arm from side to side, marveling at the brilliance of the effect.

Collin was well-aware of her love of both diamonds and rubies and there was no doubt this was his peace offering. She hated to remove it from her arm, but if she meant to return his engagement ring, she could hardly keep his gift. The loud snap of the velvet box felt like the first nail in the coffin that held their love.

Chapter 6

Maggie went out the kitchen door and around to the garage. She would be late to the stables at Isabella's if she didn't hurry.

She gunned the motor and the old Packard roared into life. She'd only driven to the end of the driveway when she saw Collin's beautiful "Gold Bug" Speedster.

Owned by the rich and famous, like boxer Jack Dempsey, Collin had irritated Maggie with his insistence that he had to have one. It was beautiful and ostentatious, his favorite combination.

"I'm not famous like Amelia Earhart, darling," he had said, "but I am rich!"

Maggie found his obvious classism revolting and told him so, starting another of their famous arguments.

"It was you in the house, wasn't it?" she asked pulling alongside his vehicle.

He stood away from the car where he'd been leaning against the driver's door.

"I wanted to surprise you, sweetheart. Did I succeed?" he asked like a young boy seeking approval from his father.

"You're lucky I didn't blow your head off! I'm late but come back at four and we'll talk. I forgot I had an engagement with Leslie to ride."

She roared off before Collin had a chance to ask about the flowers and gift. He watched her auto until it was swallowed up by the cloud of dust she raised, racing down the unpaved road leading out of her property.

Getting back into the Speedster, Collin slammed the door fiercely, angry with himself for appearing like a groveling fool.

"Damn you, Maggie! Damn me for being such a fool for you!"

Collin Fitzhugh was so madly in love with Maggie Newsome, he felt lost inside the swamp of his own passions.

He'd known her since they were small children. They continued to fade in and out of each other's lives, as he left for boarding schools and then went away to attend college.

Maggie shocked some of her family's social circle, insisting on going off to a small college in Pennsylvania, to pursue her own education. Her mother wholeheartedly supported her daughter's goals to become an educated woman of the dawning, modern age.

Collin would inevitably seek out the lovely, independent Maggie, whenever he returned home for holidays. The adventurous tomboy had grown into a beautiful young woman. A woman he desired and longed for during their long separations, over their respective school terms.

He was haunted by a deepening attraction to Maggie that he couldn't deny, and barely understood, when sharing time with her during these vacations. She always welcomed his attention, but never encouraged more than a close friendship based on their shared childhood comradery.

For Collin, home was not the charming, airy house, built by Maggie's great- grandfather. A sturdy, two-story wood structure, dotted throughout with wide windows, wrap-around porches and sitting in a park-like setting.

His family's great-great patriarch, Henry Emerson Fitzhugh, built an opulent manse, with gabled roof, evenly spaced window and Greek-type pillars, or columns. There were balconies at all the bedroom windows, offering impressive views of the estate grounds, maintained by an army of gardeners. The local paper once dubbed Henry Fitzhugh as "the next Louis XIV, the Sun King". In fact, he was not dissimilar in his love of elegance and grandeur, with an outsized ego to match his "Palace in the Bayou," as the people of the area nicknamed the Fitzhugh mansion.

The Fitzhugh legacy was based on Henry's vast holdings as a lumber Baron. In 1845, when the people in his homeland were thrown into the miseries of the Irish Potato Famine, Henry was building his own palace.

He came to America with the swelling tide of Irish immigrants, most of whom worked in the shipyards, laid track for the Pontchartrain Railroad, or sweated in the sultry, fever-ridden air, excavating the New Basin Canal in New Orleans.

Henry Fitzhugh was highly intelligent and quick to recognize the common laborer was considered of less importance than the canals they were building. He convinced two other recent arrivals to trade their picks and shovels for axes and saws and opened his first lumber mill on property they jointly purchased.

With all the building going on in the burgeoning state projects, the three were quick to recoup their investments while hiring workers, to do the back-breaking work. Henry used a large portion of his newly founded fortune to buy out his partners, leaving him sole proprietor of Fitzhugh Lumber Mills.

Collin was the lone heir to the vast estate and fortune built by his grandfather. He had everything money could buy, except the woman he wanted above any other.

As he watched the dust settling behind her car, he made a snap decision. He got behind the wheel, tearing down the dusty road after her. He meant to follow Maggie and confront her immediately about her feelings toward him. He had to know if his love was truly returned, or if he'd made a fool of himself, believing Maggie loved him as completely as he did her.

"No more taking orders from Miss Maggie Newsome!" he mumbled, trying to strengthen his resolve.

He saw her car far ahead, moving toward the Butler Plantation. He hung back, watching as she pulled into the private road and then onto the circular drive. She parked and got out, walking toward the semi-circle of the wide stone steps, leading to the front door. Collin noted her riding outfit as she exited the car and couldn't help admiring how beautifully it fit the curves of her body. He pulled in at an angle, staying unobserved behind a clump of moss-covered Cyprus.

About to leap from his own vehicle, he spotted the tall, muscular figure of Grayson Garrard step from behind a pillar near the top step. He moved with the grace of a panther, fluid and exuding a secret ferocity even at a distance. Collin tried to curb he jealousy. This man was indeed his rival. He had no doubt about that. It was a visceral reaction, coming upon him in a flash.

He watched as Garrard approached Maggie. She looked genuinely startled by his sudden appearance. Collin couldn't hear their conversation clearly, only picking up a few words in the still morning, but enough to put together the gist of it. Something about a riding date with Leslie Porter Booth being cancelled, but Gerrard was stepping in, if she didn't mind.

He felt the power of the other man's attraction toward his fiancé. It radiated like an aura from every gesture and movement of his powerfully built body. As Collin watched from his hidden vantage, Maggie started through the front door.

Just before he followed Maggie into the dark recesses of the foyer, Gerrard turned in Collin's direction. Collin was shaken when he realized Gerrard was fully aware he'd been spying on them. From the distance between them, Collin saw him raise his hand, waiving a greeting.

Collin blinked as the door was shut firmly behind his love and his rival.

Chapter 7

Maggie was surprised to hear Leslie couldn't keep their riding date. The offer by the handsome artist to take her place as a riding partner stirred more than her curiosity.

As he spoke to her, he seemed to be searching her eyes for a truth hidden from him. Maggie felt something decidedly stronger than directness radiating from those dark eyes. She decided there was a subtle power, an irresistible force that radiated from the man. Something mysterious and somehow, dangerous. But to whom?

She wondered about his background for the umpteenth time. As did everyone else apparently. At the dinner the evening before, when questioned by the other guests about his family or travels, he carefully deflected further questioning.

The only hint he gave into his history was to say he was originally from Louisiana, leaving when quite young to study abroad.

"My talents as an artist were nurtured more fully in the salons of Europe."

One instance stood out in her mind. The woman sitting across from him asked if Grayson trained in the studios of any of the greater known painters in Europe. Grayson smiled without any warmth, answering coolly. "There was no need madam, as I *am* one of the great painters."

When the tittering settled, her husband stubbornly took up the questioning, asking why they'd never heard of him before his arrival in Paxton Parrish.

This obvious affront, brought a sharp reply from the artist. "Because, sir, this is not Paris, or Venice. My work hangs in private collections only, commissioned by the great families of the *cultured* world. Which is why I accepted the invitation of our gracious hostess. Coming to the Butler Plantation, to enhance madam's own art collection with my works."

Maggie remembered Isabella adding, "I shall hold a private showing here at Butler House, when Grayson has finished the requisite pieces. He assures me, by New Year's Eve, he'll have completed my collection. You shall all be invited to a grand unveiling and celebration!"

Now, standing in the foyer, the soft light of early morning stroking his chiseled face, Maggie looked back at the enigmatic man. "I'd like to say a quick word to Isabella while you change to your riding clothes, Grayson." Without waiting for him to comment, she turned toward the Solarium where she knew the older woman would be sitting. She felt Gerrard's eyes on her body, the whole time she walked toward the room in the far corner of the house.

Maggie knew how much Isabella loved watching the sun rise.

"Announcing another day of life for me," she'd confided to Maggie long ago. Isabella loved this room, calling it her bit of Paradise on the Bayou.

As Maggie predicted, she found Isabella sitting in a large upholstered chair in her Sunroom. The light poured in through the many wide, floor-to-ceiling windows, warming the air against the ever-present chill Isabella began to complain of in recent months.

"My darling girl," Isabella said as she reached for Maggie's hand and received a peck on her powdered check.

"I thought you'd be gone by now. Is Leslie saddling the horses?"

"She's taken ill, Isabella, but Grayson, Mr. Gerrard, has offered to ride with me."

Maggie saw a look pass over Isabella's face that made her ask, "Is everything all right? I don't need to go riding, I can just visit for a little while."

"No. No. You two young people need the fresh air and I'm quite well, dear girl. I'll want to check in on poor Leslie after you've gone."

"Isabella, you know you can tell me if you needed help with something. Anything!"

The older woman smiled up at her from the deep cushions of the chair. She loved Maggie like the daughter she might have had, if her courage had been as big as her fortune. Speaking softly, she looked into Maggie's eyes. "It's only that Grayson..."

"What *about* me, Isabella?"

Grayson Gerrard entered the room as silently as a dark cloud passes over the moon. He smiled warmly at the women, walking over to stand beside Maggie. His perfectly tailored riding outfit, hugged the contours of his muscular body as he moved. Maggie felt a twinge of naked desire shoot through her body watching him come toward her. She tried to distract herself from that lustful notion, looking back at her dear friend.

Wearing her usual black dress, Isabella momentarily appeared to shrink into its darkness. Maggie noted how the elderly woman seemed more relaxed after Grayson leaned over her, placing a feathery kiss on a plump cheek.

"Did you sleep well, Isabella?" he asked.

"As well as any old lady," she answered.

She turned back to Maggie, "Will you return for a visit, Maggie, after your ride?" she asked her.

Maggie thought she detected a hopeful note to the question.

"I'm so sorry, Isabella. I can't. Collin will be over later. Shall I call Annett to help you to the dining room for breakfast?"

"Thank you, dear. Perhaps you could do that as you leave. Are the horses saddled Grayson?"

"The stable boy attended to that when he saw Miss Newsome arrive. Rather than wait upon Annett, let me assist you to your breakfast."

Grayson moved to the side of her chair. Isabella wrapped a pale hand around his forearm for support. He deftly slipped his other arm around her back and helped her to her feet.

"Thank you, Grayson. I'll be fine now. Just needed that hoist out of this infernal chair. You two run along now. It will be hot enough in a few hours to make the trees sweat!"

Maggie laughed at Isabella's vivid description. Her unfiltered comments and biting wit, made Isabella appear fearless to Maggie as a young girl. As she matured, she appreciated Isabella's indifference to the disapproval of others. This unique freedom was what Maggie so admired in the older woman and was determined to have for herself.

They left Annette to care for her mistress, walking over to the stables side by side. The stable boy, walked out pulling the reins of two horses.

Maggie thanked him and Grayson nodded, taking the reins of a huge thoroughbred, his coat brushed to a gleaming burnished copper.

Maggie deftly swung herself into the saddle of a beautifully built Andalusian. The black mare was slimmer and more agile looking than the larger horse next to her.

"Thanks, Peter," Maggie said looking down at the boy. "We'll be back in an hour, or so."

With that, Maggie put gentle heels to the mare's flanks and they trotted out of the courtyard and down the long road leading away from the grounds.

Maggie was a fine horsewoman. She loved the feel of speed, whether in her auto, or on the back of a fine horse. Now she signaled her mount to a gallop, keeping her legs tightly wrapped around her, pressed to the horse's heaving sides.

The young horse responded immediately to the joy of running and picked up more speed than Maggie had intended. Maggie let her set the faster pace, easing up on the leather reins.

Grayson's big gelding followed behind, matching the young female's strides, but careful not to over-run her. They approached a wide swath of open field after running flat out, down the dirt roads.

Here, Maggie pulled on the reins, signaling her mount to slow, urging her softly to check her speed. When they were trotting, Grayson pulled up next to the hard breathing rider and horse.

"You ride like you were born to it, Maggie!" he said smiling down at her from his taller seat.

"I've ridden since I was big enough to be put into a saddle. My dad used to board my horse at Isabella's, but when she had to be put down, Isabella insisted I ride horses from her stable." Her mind wandering back to happier years, Maggie went on. "Isabella had no children of her own and no real family after both her parents died when she was fairly young. My father and I came over to the plantation every week for a ride and lunch. Before my mother passed, my parents were great friends with Isabella and Dad and I just continued that comfortable relationship."

"She's obviously quite fond of you, Maggie. I haven't known her that long but sense a loneliness in her that seems to lighten when you're around."

The horses nudged each other as they fell into a rhythmic gate, allowing their riders to look over at one another while they talked.

"How long have your known Isabella, Grayson? I don't mean to pry, but when you were introduced at the dinner a few weeks ago, you became something of an instant mystery-celebrity."

Grayson's laugh rewarded her curiosity. It was rich and deep. "I am far from a celebrity, Maggie. I remember you espousing some very forward thinking about social responsibilities and politics that evening. I recall your fiancé being less than pleased with your defiance of, shall I call it, your lack of an expected behavior. Does he often try to rein you in like one of these horses?"

She'd been looking over at him as he spoke, but now stared straight ahead, angry that he would bring up what was an embarrassing exchange between her and Collin. She suddenly felt strangely protective of Collin, blurting out, "Collin is not a mean spirited man, just a product of his class and times." She was too distracted to realize Grayson hadn't answered her question about knowing Isabella. She put heels to the horse and it slipped gracefully into a cantor, leaving Grayson to follow suite to catch up.

After another fifteen minutes of riding, the pair came to a secluded area closer to the swampy waters.

Maggie didn't want to get too near, reining in her mount at the edge of the wooded area they'd passed through. Cotton mouth snakes and gators stalked this territory and she didn't want to expose her horse, or herself, to their swift attacks.

Her horse was beginning to browse among richer grasses growing nearby. She seemed content to stand beside the larger horse when Grayson pulled up beside her, whinnying her greeting.

They sat their horses in silence for a minute, listening to the prodigious swamp life that crawled, buzzed and swam several yards in front of them.

Maggie always viewed the bayou with awe and respect, knowing of its many beauties, as well as its dangers. She was as calm as the mare now, enjoying the heady, rich odors of the verdant wetland spread out before them.

She was feeling silly for taking offense at Grayson's comment about Collin. The fact that she felt compelled to defend him, irritated her even more. After all, she would be breaking their engagement later that morning. This flare of emotion made no sense, even to her.

She knew her relationship with Collin had deeper roots than her political leanings. Had she painted him with the same brush she used in viewing most of the upper class? He had never been anything but kind to his employees at the lumber mills he owned. She knew he even established a type of "widows and orphans" fund for any families of workers killed or hurt on the job. Something none of his predecessors would have dreamt of doing. They took their title as Lumber Barron and wore it like an honor due them.

As she stared across at the swamp, deep in thought, Grayson cleared his throat.

"Maggie, I hope I haven't offended you with a thoughtless comment. I should keep my observations to myself I guess."

"Grayson, I'm the one who needs to apologize. I didn't mean to fly off at you like that. Let's just forget it and enjoy the day, shall we?"

She leaned across to him, offering to shake hands. Her smile was open and lit her face with her naturally sweet nature. He took her small hand, covering it inside his own, smiling back at the beautiful woman.

The contact of her soft skin in his hand, felt as if he held fine silk, as she slipped through his fingers to take hold of her reins again.

"I detected a slight accent in your speech, Grayson. I wondered if you were born out of this country."

"I compliment your impressive ear, Maggie. I was born in a small town in Bavaria. It was known for its marvelous bakeries and heavy drinkers. Unfortunately, my father was a baker who fell into the latter category as well. I left home for America as soon as I could make enough money to book passage over."

"What did you do to earn the money? It must have been an awful lot for a young man to raise."

He looked over at her, seeing the look of curiosity and compassion for his past situation.

"Actually, I worked in my father's bakery. I think that's what sparked my interest in art. Besides shoveling breads into the ovens, I used the draw illustrations for the bakery, of wedding cakes, and other specialty cakes. I designed them for the clients and my father built them. He was a genius as a baker."

Maggie asked if he thought he would have stayed in his boyhood town if his father hadn't been a drinker.

Grayson looked deeply into her vivid blue eyes for a second before answering.

"I believe in fate, Maggie. If I'd have stayed, I would never have shared this moment with you."

Maggie could feel the weight of Grayson's eyes studying her face. She had an incredible impulse to feel this stranger's mouth pressing down on her own. Her mouth opened slightly, invitingly, to fulfill that rush of desire. Only the jostling of her horse's head, pulling on the reins, drew her attention from Grayson's hungry eyes.

"Look, by that stand of hardwoods," she said pointing toward the swamp and the source of her horse's skittishness.

A large alligator lumbered out of the gray-brown waters, finding a sunny patch on the bank to stretch out and sun himself.

"Don't be fooled by his sleepy-head appearance. That big boy is just waiting for something to cross his path," Maggie said.

She began pulling on the reins to turn the mare for the trip back to toward Butler Plantation.

Grayson commented on the stealth the gator used in his hunting technique.

"Not unlike some humans, I believe," Maggie added smiling coolly at him.

She knew he received her message loud and clear. She may not be ready to marry Collin Fitzhugh, but she surely wasn't interested in being swept off her feet by this baker's boy.

Chapter 8

"It was a delightful ride, Maggie. I enjoyed your company very much. Perhaps you'll allow me to accompany you again?"

"That would be nice, Grayson. I'll just pop in to tell Isabella we've returned her horses safe and sound. See you soon."

She walked off without another word.

Grayson smiled thinly, sensing her discomfort while he watched the natural sway of her hips and slight bounce to her breasts as she moved away.

He had a sharp pang of need and desire that he knew he could not satisfy. *Not yet. But soon, very soon Miss Maggie Newsome.*

Maggie went straight back to the Solarium, unannounced. Though she wasn't trying to sneak up on them, Leslie Porter Booth stood over Isabella, her back to the doorway, unaware of Maggie's presence.

Leslie's complexion was always very pale, but she seemed healthy enough now as she spoke firmly to Isabella.

"Isabella, it's time for your medication," Leslie was saying, holding out a spoon filled with a dark liquid to the elderly woman.

"Leslie, I detest that foul tasting stuff! I'm not even certain why I need to take it. When did the doctor prescribe it to me?"

"At his last visit here, dear, remember? It's to enrich your blood and give you energy," Leslie answered, more or less stuffing the spoon, into Isabella's protesting mouth.

"Good morning ladies," Maggie announced herself lightly, trying to erase the look of concern that she knew had crossed her face at the scene.

"I'm glad to see you're up and about Leslie."

Leslie spun around at the sound of Maggie's voice. In that split second, Maggie saw a look of annoyance pass over the pale face of the hovering woman.

"Good morning, Maggie! I'm really sorry to have missed our ride, but there was no way I could have bounced along on horseback this morning. I actually slept until a short while ago. I'm going back to bed in a few minutes, I just needed to make sure Isabella was alright."

Isabella spoke up from her deep chair. "Leslie was just dosing me with some sludge from the swamp, Maggie," she said with a grimace on her plump face.

Maggie was unaware of Isabella's doctor prescribing medicine for a blood condition, wondering if this was something newly developed in the older woman. She thought she knew her ailments and complaints pretty well, in light of her close family relationship with her over the years.

The old housekeeper, Mrs. Hodges , had been with Isabella Butler for over twenty-five years when she died. She acted as nurse, personal secretary and companion, to Isabella, until her own, quite unexpected death.

She often filled Maggie in on the latest news around the Butler household, including any significant medical changes with her employer.

The maid, Annette, told Maggie how the efficient housekeeper succumbed to a fast acting illness. She'd become progressively weaker, until she couldn't lift her head off her pillow. She was dead before the end of the fourth day, leaving Isabella nearly inconsolable with grief, for her trusted friend.

Months before her sudden passing, Mrs. Hodges had taken Maggie aside saying, "If I'm no longer able to see to the Mistress, you need to know what ails her, Miss Maggie. I don't trust her well-being to anyone other than family and that would be you!"

Maggie had taken this directive from Mrs. Hodges to heart and was suddenly suspicious of this new medication.

She needed to question Leslie subtlety, so as not to offend her.

After Leslie excused herself to return to her bedroom, Maggie decided to find out more about Isabella's companion, without her curiosity being too obvious.

"Did Leslie have to move far, before you hired her to replace Mrs. Hodges as your companion?"

"Not unless you count five miles from downtown Paxton, to my front door as a long way. Lucky for me, Leslie happened to hear of poor Mrs. Hodges from the boarding house landlady and came out to inquire about the newly available position.

I wasn't certain we'd get on, but, Leslie has a talent for keeping me pain-free most days. Must be that horrid stuff she insists I choke down."

Maggie acted as if this was news to her and asked what the medication was for.

"Leslie says I have some kind of blood disorder. It helps build it up I suppose."

All Maggie said in response to this assumption was, "Oh."

Isabella insisted Maggie stay for a bite of breakfast since she hadn't eaten before leaving for her ride.

"I'll have my third cup of coffee and annoy Leslie!" Isabella said with a chuckle.

"I'm not exactly dressed for the table, Isabella," she laughed looking down at her riding pants and jacket.

"Nonsense! This isn't a time for fashion to take precedence over a good meal!"

Maggie was sipping her second cup of coffee when Annette, returned to the dining room.

"Mr. Grayson asked if he might join you, mam."

Grayson filled the doorway to the dining room, moving gracefully to Isabella's side. He was no longer wearing the beautifully tailored riding outfit but had changed into dark slacks and a dark red shirt, open at the neck. He held a slim leather portfolio at his side.

Maggie wondered how he managed to get back to his small cottage on the estate, to change and make it back to the main house in less than the forty-five minutes she'd been with Isabella.

Her riding jacket was hung on the back of her tall chair, showing off the fine material of her silk blouse. There was a matching scarf tied loosely about her throat.

Maggie looked over at Grayson as he leaned down to kiss Isabella's cheek. She saw a broad smile appear on the older woman's face. She clearly enjoyed the attention of the dashing man.

Maggie felt an unreasonable irritation at what looked like a scene contrived for her benefit. She got to her feet, taking her jacket off the back of her chair. She went to Isabella's other side, kissing her quickly and thanking her for the use of her horse and breakfast.

"Why are you bolting out the door, Maggie?"

"I have a meeting at ten and will likely be late as it is. And Collin is still to meet with me later."

Looking back over her shoulder as she left the room, she said, "Goodbye Grayson and thanks for the company on the ride."

The artist smiled as he took the seat Maggie had vacated.

Maggie heard him address Isabella. "Well, dear lady, after that whirlwind departure, I expect we might enjoy a quiet cup of coffee together. I wanted to show you a few pieces I've planned to add to our exhibition."

Isabella perked up, agreeing enthusiastically. Grayson produced the artist sketch pad he carried with him. While Isabella perused the sketches, making sounds of admiration for the work, Grayson's mind was free to wander.

He wondered what Isabella was about to say about him to Maggie when he entered the Solarium earlier. More importantly, he wanted to know what Maggie's future relationship with Collin Fitzhugh would be.

He was taken aback by Maggie's whip- sharp defense of her fiancé, hoping to see more of a wedge between them where he could step in.

It was Grayson Gerrard's intention to fill any void left between the engaged couple. His attraction to Maggie was more intense than he wanted to admit, even to himself.

He heard the pages of the sketch pad turning slowly, where Isabella had come to the last one.

It was a beautiful rendition of a male nude, lying on a chaise longue, his long, muscular legs crossed at the ankles. The man had his back turned to the viewer, his broad, well-defined shoulders, supported on his elbows. The figure was lying in front of French doors, opened to a garden, mostly hidden in the shadows of night. A watery moonlight fell across his taught body, stroking the arm, lying relaxed, along his side and thigh. The rounded buttocks invited the eye to linger a second longer, searching for some subtle movement in the perfection of firmness.

"He is exquisite," Isabella breathed out, admiration softened her voice and face.

"Who is he, Grayson? I must know!"

"You know very well, Isabella, an artist is never at liberty to divulge the identity of his models. Just as a priest cannot break the Confessional seal, I cannot tell you his name."

"Oh, I know you lot are a secretive bunch, Grayson," she teased. "But this sketch is too beautiful. In fact, it should be framed and hung just as it is."

"I have already begun a painting based upon this subject. I believe you'll be pleased when you see the finished piece."

He stood up and leaned close to her steel gray head, speaking softly.

"This is an Adonis who will steal more than a lover's heart. He'll steal her body and soul. I shall give you this pathetic doodle for your bedroom, Isabella, if that would please you."

Isabella dropped the pad on the dark surface of the table. Her face a mask of distress and confusion. She reached over for the small silver bell that would summon Annette from another room. "I do believe I need some fresh air, Grayson. Take your "Adonis" and ask Leslie to see to a proper frame. I shall enjoy it at my leisure. I hope to see the more refined version soon."

Annette answered her mistress's bell ring, helping Isabella slowly exit the dining room.

Grayson watched as they made measured progress around the lush gardens, Isabella leaning heavily on the young girl's sturdy arm.

He had to admire the old girl's effort to live as fully as she was able, in spite of her many infirmities, real and imagined.

He retook his place at the table and waited for his expected visitor. Another minute passed before Leslie Porter Booth entered the dining room. Her face was radiant with a soft blush. The thick golden braid wrapped around her head, highlighted a newly vibrant blue of her hooded eyes. She wore a sleeveless, summer frock in bright yellow, showing off firm arms and smooth, rounded shoulders. The dress had a scoop neck, exposing just enough of her breasts to invite more than a casual look. As usual, she had chosen a long silk scarf as an accent, the color of her eyes, shot through with the yellow of the dress.

Grayson didn't stand when she came into the room. He sat staring silently at her. She moved to his side. He took an end of the scarf in his hands and pulled it gently until it unwound from her neck and fell to the floor.

The same healthy blush of her cheeks colored the rest of her body as far as he could see. She looked almost ethereal in her beauty.

"It would appear you've eaten my dear, Leslie," he said taking her hand. Kissing the palm, he grazed the delicate skin with the sharp incisors protruding from his open mouth.

She shuddered, sighing when he wound his arm around her waist, pulling her closer to those fangs.

Chapter 9

By the time Maggie reached home from the Butler Plantation, she felt tense and confused. Tense, because she knew Collin would be over in two hours. Confused, because her feelings regarding Collin Fitzhugh were far from clear to her. *Why did she suddenly feel as though she didn't even know him? How could she have gotten engaged to a man for whom she now felt disgust?*

She ran a deep tub and while she soaked away some of the tenseness from her shoulders, her mind drifted with the steam, rising up, swirling around her.

He drives me mad with his frivolous attitude toward life. But yet, he works so hard to keep his yards open and his men employed. Even in slow periods, he makes sure his workers are kept on. I know he has never let anyone go, even in down turns in orders.

She sank deeper into the water. She added oil of lilac as the bath filled, one of Collin's favorite fragrances. She did it without thinking, but the soft floral fragrance reminded her she did this to please him.

Why can't he understand the world has changed, women have changed? I want more than my mother. I need more than my mother. I'm NOT my mother!

Maggie knew she was fortunate indeed to have inherited the family newspaper business. The Paxton Guardian was her father's pride and joy and now it was hers.

Some of the old-timers on staff raised eyebrows and she raised salaries which had the immediate effect of squelching any complaints. Her father was an outstanding editor, but a penny-pincher when it came to rewarding the newsroom team and the few support personnel working at the Guardian.

Maggie understood the value of building bridges with people by showing appreciation and rewarding good work. The paper had a relatively small circulation of seventy-five hundred but encompassed the whole of Paxton Parrish in its reach and influence. Maggie had already written as a columnist there for a few years, using a pen name, so the staff didn't think she was taking advantage of her position as the boss's daughter.

Her father enjoyed her work and encouraged her to dig deeper into social issues, until she felt comfortable doing that without his nod of approval.

She only went into the press room late at night, when the staff were gone for the day. The cleaning people were told she was working on school "stuff", not far from the truth, since she often wrote about the obstacles faced by young women away from home for schooling, or their difficulty finding jobs rather than husbands.

She smiled, remembering the cry of outrage from women's church groups. They sold lots more papers that week. She continued to write, "The Modern Woman," using her closed door at the paper to keep her secret role from prying eyes.

One day Collin had come early to pick her up for their luncheon date. Maggie forgot what she was working on and asked for a minute to freshen up before they left. While she was gone he sat behind her desk and perused the story on her typewriter.

"Do Poor Women Have Too Many Babies?" lay beneath his gaze.

When she returned to find him reading her column, she rushed over pulling the sheet out with a jerk. She saw a perplexed look cross Collin's face.

And now he'll hate me even more, after I break off with him, she thought rousing herself out of her daydreaming. Feeling the water chilling around her, Maggie got out of the tub and began drying off.

Collin's words that afternoon came back to her, as she toweled her hair. "I hope you aren't going to suggest illegal means of avoiding having a child, Maggie."

She remembered answering that these women were not only poor, but in many cases, ill-educated, or illiterate.

"Ah! So you're referring only to the lower classes?" She sighed as she thought back on his naïve comment, but so like him and most of the wealthy people she knew.

Her father had given her a good piece of advice once, after reading one of her columns.

"Your job as a journalist, Maggie, is to educate the public with facts. You never get preachy, or judgmental. Every challenge to your observations and findings, is an opportunity."

She took a deep breath and went into her bedroom. Her riding outfit was scattered around the floor.

She was pushing hangers around in her walk-in closet when she felt a rippling feeling run along her spine. Someone was watching her.

Spinning around she was looking into Collins clear, brown eyes.

"Collin! You nearly gave me a heart attack!"

"I'm sorry, Maggie. I called out to you, darling, but I guess you didn't hear me in here."

She unconsciously held a gauzy white chemise in front of her like a shield.

Collin studied her like a piece of art, a look of desire in his intent eyes.

"Maggie, I've seen you naked a thousand times and you look more beautiful each time."

He moved to stand close to her, looking into her eyes, while his fingers stroked the side of her face. She loved the way Collin always knew when she needed his gentleness and responded to his touch, dropping her arms and the top.

Collin used only his fingertips, running them down from her cheeks to the soft mound of her firm breast. He kneaded them gently, until Maggie closed her eyes, making a soft moaning sound.

He dropped to his knees and pushing on her leg slightly, Maggie opened them wider to his roaming fingers until she was panting with anticipation. Suddenly, wrapping his arm around her, he carried her to the bed where he laid her down carefully. He began stripping until he was as naked as the woman lying there, watching him with hungry anticipation.

A minute later he was pushing his throbbing member into her, carried away with her moans and demanding urges, bringing them both to a screaming release from the pangs of passion.

Collin lay heavily on Maggie's body, exhausted by the intensity of their love-making, but even in his satisfaction, wanting to have her again. He knew in that moment his lifetime of knowing Maggie Newsome had been a lifetime of loving her.

Maggie gave him a little shove, her signal for him to move. He rolled off of her, watching as she walked toward the bathroom. Her body was moist with the light sheen of their heated love-making,

He dozed off just as he heard the bath water running. Twenty minutes later, Maggie was sitting next to him on the bed, dressed in a light top and a pair of linen trousers.

She brushed his thick brown hair off his damp forehead. His eyes flashed open and he pulled her down to his mouth. They kissed, but this time, their passions fed, it wasn't an urgent act of need.

Maggie decided during her second bath that morning, she could not break off her engagement to Collin Fitzhugh. She loved him and had always loved him, whatever their differences.

She would use her father's tactic to educate him to the truths that mattered to her most in life.

The first certainty was clear. She needed her freedom in the form of a career. Nothing less than that. The Guardian was more than her family's newspaper. It was her legacy and she needed to do its important work.

It was 1920, the world was still recovering from "the war to end all wars." Life, in every social strata of society, was becoming more complex. Important changes were coming and needed to be understood. The Paxton Guardian's mission was to clarify, define and interpret those changes.

Maggie's second ardent desire was to have Collin understand her commitment to a better quality of life for all residents of Paxton Parrish. He'd lived away from the local poverty and struggles of so many residents, cosseted in his private schools and social circles.

The Paxton Guardian reported on every sector of life in the community, recognizing how they were all inter-related. This often led Maggie's parents to become personally involved in local charities and efforts to improve the lives of the local poor.

Maggie saw Collin's wealth as an invisible barrier between him and those who struggled around him, even those employed at his lumber yards. Unlike other companies, however, feelings of unjust treatment had not begun to surface among his workers. Maggie knew his reputation for fairness in dealing with any grievances was rock-solid.

Though she viewed his money as an impediment to understanding the working class and the poor, his workers didn't view Collin as the snob she sometimes did herself.

Could she have it all wrong?

She pulled away from their kiss and he laid back on the pillow, smiling up at her.

"Time to get up sleepy-head. Did I wear you out, poor boy?"

Collin made a lunge for her. She laughed, jumping off the bed and out of reach.

"OK, beautiful lady. Let me freshen up and then you can tell me what we needed to discuss today. Then it's off to work for me."

Maggie went down to the kitchen, grabbing a glass and filling it with lemonade. She returned to the bedroom, gathering Collin's clothes as she went. She neatly laid his things out, placing the lemonade on the nightstand nearby.

Returning to the kitchen she opened the door onto the patio, going outside to enjoy the sounds of morning on the bayou.

There was a hum in the air and a verdant fragrance in the sultry breezes, filling her head with pictures of moss-laden trees, the silky movement of alligators through brown water, lush tropical flowers, clinging like survivors of a shipwreck, on the sides of rocks and muddy banks.

She loved this place above any she'd ever visited or lived. With a twinge, it occurred to her that she'd have to leave it for good, after she wed Collin Fitzhugh.

Though she always saw her house as cozy, with its many nooks and crannies, it was the airiness created by the many large windows that gave her the feel of being part of the untamed bayou.

She was into her daydreaming, when she heard Collin call out to her.

Returning to the kitchen she asked if he wanted a bite before he left for his office.

"Actually darling, I'd rather just gulp down another glass of your wonderful lemonade while we talk. I assume this is about wedding plans?"

They spent the next forty-five minutes going over their guest list which Collin produced from his jacket.

"I figured you might want to see this, so I shoved it into my pocket before leaving home."

Smiling into his eager eyes, Maggie was scanning it, when her eye stopped on the name Grayson Gerrard.

"But, I thought you disliked him, Collin," she said.

He looked at her beautiful face, reaching out to touch the curve of her cheek.

"I do, but Isabella won't come without him, or her secretary. Besides, I believe in that old adage about keeping your friends close and your enemies closer."

Maggie saw the seriousness in his dark eyes in spite of his joking manner. Something inside her was glad, no, relieved, that he was being cautious.

The mysterious Grayson Gerrard set off some kind of internal alarm bells in her. And she couldn't deny, when he was near her, that alarm was vibrating throughout her body.

$$\textbf{Chapter 10}$$

Maggie decided to go into the Guardian office to get her mind back to business and off thoughts of Collin and the mysterious Grayson Gerrard.

Something about him was nettling her since their horseback ride. He was almost secretive about his personal history, even where he was from originally. Her keen ears picked up an almost invisible shadow of an accent and she couldn't place its origin. Grayson's explanation sounded reasonable but lacked much by way of family history.

She walked into the offices of the Paxton Guardian with pride. It gave her a feeling of power, something new to her. Since she replaced her father as the paper's head, everyone deferred to her as if her word was law, which it was, at least at the paper. *I could really get used to this this,* she thought, smiling to one and all as she passed through to her office.

She carried her dad's battered leather briefcase, refusing to substitute it with the luxurious black leather one Collin had given her as a gift. She told him she was "saving it" for when they broke the biggest story in the country! He understood her attachment and laughed at her not-so-subtle subterfuge.

Alma Payne, Maggie's personal secretary, opened the door to her office when she heard her passing through the outer offices.

"Good morning, Miss. I was wondering if we'd be seeing you today."

This was Alma's way of suggesting she was keeping a banker's hours rather than a proper newspaper publisher's. Her dad had relied on Alma for the day to day minutia that kept the Guardian running smoothly. "Like a clock," he'd brag of her abilities.

Maggie knew Alma was completely devoted to George Newsome, Jr. and she suspected it morphed into love over their many years of working as a team. There was a ten year difference between their ages her dad confided one day. That made Alma near 55, but still, an attractive woman.

Alma showed Maggie the same respect and loyalty she did her father, often offering important advice while Maggie found her footing. They had a perfect working relationship. It was as though Alma anticipated what Maggie needed and knew where to put her hands on it. Maggie knew she'd be lost without the older woman's support.

Once seated behind her desk with a fragrant cup of English Breakfast Tea, brought in by Alma, Maggie began to plough through the stack of phone messages, mail and news articles that needed her review before going to print.

She was deep in thought, making changes to an editorial piece written for that evening's edition, when a shadow blocked the light coming from the hallway.

She looked up and into the depthless, dark gray eyes of Grayson Gerrard.

"Good morning again, Maggie. I have an interview with one of your reporters on my upcoming, private exhibit and thought I'd stop by to say a quick hello."

"Oh? You didn't mention an interview earlier, during our ride."

"Quite truthfully, I think I was so absorbed in the pleasure of the company, it slipped my mind," he answered smoothly.

Staring at the tall, well-muscled body framed in her doorway, Maggie felt a hot, tingling sensation shoot through her body. She felt compelled to study him like one of his paintings.

He wore a perfectly tailored, dark blue suit, with thin strips and matching vest. His white shirt had the same thin blue stripe, with a round, white collar. His black patent leather shoes were buffed to a high gloss, as if he floated above ground. He was impeccable, not a dark hair disturbed, combed back from a high forehead.

"I hope you'll forgive my interruption. You were clearly busy."

He turned to go when she said, "Please, forgive my rudeness, Grayson. I'm not used to visitors. What time is your interview? Would you have enough time to look around the paper?"

After a brief tour, Maggie brought Grayson to the messy office of Jeff Flowers, one of the two reporters at the Guardian,

"Thank you for the tour, Maggie. You have an impressive media operation here," Grayson was saying while Flowers tried to unearth a chair from under the piles of books and stacks of papers.

"Thanks. I always like to hear compliments for my hard-working staff. I'll leave you to your interview with Jeff."

She turned to leave when Grayson placed a cool hand on her arm.

"Maggie, I'm riding over to look around the old Abby in Beaumont, tomorrow morning. Care to join me?"

She felt as if she was swimming against the pull of a rip tide, while he looked deeply into her wide eyes.

She barely managed to say, "I have to work, Grayson, but thank you. Have a good interview."

The handsome figure had every woman in the office and some of the men, riveted to his every casual movement or gesture. Typewriters became silent as he passed secretaries, coffee sloshed over mugs while being poured, the hum of conversation ceased.

As closely as they scrutinized this dark Adonis, no one noticed the flare of red deepen the near black of his eyes. His gaze was riveted to the lithe figure of Maggie Newsome. The gentle sway of her hips was an unconscious sexual allure. She reached up to fluff her short bob, her arms firm and graceful in their movement.

He followed her with his eyes until she got to her office.

Just as she reached for the doorknob, something made her hesitate and look back. Grayson stood in front of the reporter's office, staring back at her.

She had a nearly overpowering impulse to return to his side.

It took all her willpower to abruptly break off visual contact. Entering her office, she shut the door firmly, the sound seemed loud and final. Strangely, this barrier between her and the artist, made her feel better.

Before long she was lost in her work and only stopped when Alma peeked in to say goodnight.

"Alma, what time is it? I think I've lost track with all this work to catch up on."

"It's nearly eight-thirty, Maggie. I stayed to keep you company as I don't like to see you working here alone."

"Alma, you are a prize! You run along and I'll lock up right behind you. I have one more story to check and then I'm through."

An hour later, Maggie still sat in her office, the shadows filling in the parts of the room, outside the small hallo of light cast by her desk lamp.

Glancing out her window, she saw a thin sliver of moon, claiming a tenuous place in the over-cast night-sky.

She yawned and rubbed the crick in the back of her neck. She went to the window to draw down the shade, just as movement in front of the building caught her eye.

She stood there a minute longer, trying to decide if it was just a stray dog or raccoon, making a garbage raid at the nearby Step 'N Café.

Seeing nothing stir on the shadowy street where the big Packard was parked, Maggie grabbed her briefcase and turned off lights as she made her way to the front door.

What began as a balmy morning had cooled off with hints of rain in the air. Maggie was glad she'd chosen to wear pants into the office. That made her think back to her time in bed with Collin and she almost missed seeing the figure standing near her car.

She stopped several feet away. Her father had always taught her to act sure of herself, especially when she was most afraid. The theory was it would make her appear stronger than the threat.

"Step out of the shadows where I can see you better," Maggie called out sharply.

There was a slight shift in the patch of darkness and Maggie realized the figure was gone.

She began to move toward the car, its pale body outlined against the backdrop of the empty street.

Her briefcase was her only defense, that, and getting into the car and driving away as quickly as possible. She quickened her steps.

As she reached for the door handle, someone sprang out of the shadows behind her.

With the speed and strength of a hunting gator, a long arm grabbed Maggie around the waist, pinning her arm to her side. The attacker's other hand grabbed a handful of thick, black hair, forcing Maggie's head back and to the side, so Maggie couldn't see the assailant.

Maggie still clutched the briefcase, swinging it wildly with one hand. It connected with something soft and she heard a deep growl near her ear. This was no normal human. This was a demon from her worst childhood nightmares.

Chapter 11

Growing up on the Louisiana Bayou, Maggie naturally heard many of the legends and folk lore surrounding the moss-encrusted swamps.

The *Rougarou of the Bayou* was one such creature. A man who was capable of shape-shifting into a werewolf.

Another folktale, whispered among Bayou folk living deep in the swamps, surfaced from time to time. It was even more fanciful to her logical mind than the wolf-man stories.

Vampires, who lived incredibly normal lives among humans, but for unmeasurable years. Surviving on the blood drained from man and beast alike. It was believed they roamed the bayou, even frightening wraiths, on haunted grounds.

As Maggie struggled with the attacker, visions of these monsters flashed across her mind. The fear nearly paralyzing her.

She felt herself weakening in the strong grip around her waist and upper body. Her head was pulled back hard, exposing the soft hollow of her throat.

She felt drops of moisture dripping onto her skin during her struggle, realizing her assailant's mouth was open and very close to her vulnerable neck. Her peripheral vision picked up a flash of long, very white teeth.

Into the depths of her fear, a high scream pierced the emptiness around her.

Her body was suddenly jarred as if whoever held her was rammed from behind. The grip around her waist was broken, the thick locks of hair were released and she felt a sharp pain in her scalp as she fell face forward onto the street. Her briefcase cushioned her face, but she landed hard on it, cutting her forehead on the lock.

Maggie lay stunned and disoriented. She was vaguely aware of two voices above her sprawled body.

"There's blood. I smell it! I need it!" someone hissed.

This was followed by a deep, commanding voice saying, "Too soon, you fool."

Maggie wanted to open her eyes, but instinctively knew, whoever they were, they would kill her if she discovered their identities.

Listening as intently as her pounding head allowed, she heard a rush of air, as if someone had turned on a large fan. She stayed down for another minute until the stillness filled with the natural sounds of night.

Pushing herself onto her knees, she searched her pocket for a handkerchief to stop the free flowing cut on her forehead. Holding it in place, the blood was stopped enough to remove the pressure. Holding onto the side of the car, she got back onto her feet.

She was wobbly and wanted to get home to do a thorough check for any bruising, or other injuries. She would ring up Collin as soon as she locked the door behind herself.

Driving as fast as she dared on the rough cut roads back to her house, she tried to think about the incident like a detective would. She was a fair hand at investigative reporting and she wanted to examine this frightening occurrence as dispassionately as possible, to better solve the questions in her mind.

Who was her attacker? And who stopped the attack?

She drove with her window rolled down, needing the cool air to revive her fully. She felt battered over every inch of her body. The idea of a hot bath was as important now as contacting her fiancé. She'd let him handle the Sheriff's office, to report the frightening assault.

As she drove, she noticed the wind stirred a scent around the auto that was vaguely familiar. It wasn't her own perfume, which she used sparingly, but a heavier, floral fragrance. She tucked her head down slightly and the smell was stronger on her top. She stopped wondering about it she pulled into her drive with relief.

When she climbed out of the car, she realized her muscles felt sore and achy. No doubt from her strenuous efforts to free herself from the assailant's incredibly strong embrace. She carefully locked and bolted the front door, then checked every other door and window. Nothing was getting in that was bigger than a puff of smoke.

Satisfied with her security, but still greatly unnerved, she dialed Collin's home. She knew it would take him close to an hour to get there, but she could bath and try to collect herself until then.

It was now close to eleven and she knew Collin would likely be in bed as he was a very early riser too.

The phone was in a small study off the bedroom and rang several times before he picked up, sounding drugged with sleep.

"Hello? Collin Fitzhugh speaking."

Maggie took a deep breath, not knowing how much to share with him on the phone.

"Collin, its Maggie. Something has happened and I need you to come over."

"Maggie, are you alright, darling? Are you injured?" he asked, sudden concern making him sound wide awake.

"I'm alright, but I think I need to see you. Someone attacked me in the parking lot tonight. I'm...afraid."

"Are you hurt? I'm getting dressed as we speak. I'll be there in forty minutes, Maggie. Are all your doors locked?"

After assuring him she was bruised but nothing broken, and that she'd taken precautions, Maggie hung up and went up to her bedroom. She stripped off her clothes and studied herself in the long, oval mirror by her closet.

There were red marks around her ribcage and the sides of her arms. The top of her head was sore to the touch where a handful of hair was pulled hard.

She got close to the mirror to look at the gash on her forehead from hitting the metal lock on her briefcase. It had clotted over and was slightly swollen.

She went into the bathroom and ran a hot bath, stepping into the deep water and submerging up to her neck. She bolted upright.

The teeth…I saw long, white teeth near my throat!

The stories of the most famous bayou vampire, Jacques Saint Germain, flashed like those teeth through Maggie's mind.

She learned about Saint Germain from a Cajun cleaning lady who worked at the Guardian since her grandfather's time but was long gone by the time Maggie left for college.

She remembered, as an inquisitive five or six-year-old, the yellow skinned, old woman, telling her fantastic tales, while they sat together, sharing small cakes and sweet tea in the tiny kitchenette.

The old woman's voice had a raspy edge to it, likely from the thin, black cigars always hanging from her slack mouth. A fog of smoke would float around Maggie's dark head like a cloud of incense as the old woman began her ritual of story-telling.

"Legend says, he's a most handsome man, with blackest hair, and eyes dark as a deep hole. Few can turn away from his gaze. He has many talents to boast of. Some stories say he's a master at piano, and violin and can speak many languages from far-away countries. They say he is charming and has sat at the tables of Kings and Queens, who have fallen under his spell."

Maggie would pepper the woman with questions, ignoring the fact that the old crone was as scary in her way, as the tales she shared.

Lying back in the warm bath, she thought back to one question in particular.

"Was he a good man, or a bad man?" the young Maggie asked about St. Germain.

The old Cajun woman shivered. Maggie thought that odd, as hot as the day was. She didn't understand half of what the woman told her but was drawn into her stories like a compass to the north.

"He weren't always a bad man, no child. But now he walks wrapped in an evil known only to the Devil himself. You see child, he must live by drinking the life blood of others and our bayou is littered with the bones he's left in his wake."

Breaking off these gruesome daydreams, Maggie stood up from the water, standing like an alabaster goddess, while the rivulets silently returned to their source.

She stepped over the high lip of the claw-footed tub, and onto the round bath rug. She automatically began toweling off, as she continued unpacking the stories from her childhood, about the vampire, Saint Germain.

Wrapped in the large Turkish bath towel, she was using her hand to wipe the steam from the mirror over the sink. She stopped when a rush of air stirred her damp bangs. A memory of that same whooshing sound, flashed through her mind.

Maggie froze with terror.

While she looked on, the mirror covered over with a thicker film of condensation. Peering into its foggy surface, she saw a tall, broad shouldered man standing behind her. His face was a blur, lost in the gray mist of reflection.

 She didn't scream, she barely breathed.

His voice felt like velvet inside her head. "Do not turn around, Maggie. I will not satisfy your curiosity, just yet. But I can no longer deny myself a small taste of the woman you are. Close your eyes quickly and let me show you a glimpse into my Paradise."

"Collin is coming and he'll…"

"I have arranged a small delay for your fiancé along the road, Maggie. He will experience a flat tire and be too late to stop us."

Maggie began to protest, but found her words drowned in an ocean of curiosity and dread.

She closed her eyes, as he ordered, half believing she'd hallucinated the moment and was merely exhibiting extreme stress after the attack on her. She barely finished that thought when she felt herself airborne, the same whooshing sound filling her ears.

"You may open your eyes, my dear," the smooth voice said.

Maggie was standing in a candle-lit room with a large bed at its center. There were dark curtains at the windows and the candles gave little light for close scrutiny of the place.

"Where am I? Why am I here?" she demanded.

But the force behind her question betrayed her rising fear.

Am I becoming delusional?

Her stomach knotted with dread. She began to shiver in the ice-cold air of the room, the damp bath towel giving little warmth.

It feels like a mausoleum in here, she thought frantically. *Maybe that's where he's taken me, but why? Dear God, let me be dreaming!*

Despite her denial, she still saw the man's figure.

He was standing in the shadows clinging to the area around a high, canopy bed. Maggie caught the muted reflection of candlelight off the smooth surface of silk sheets.

Her eyes felt a sudden stab of bright light when the stranger raised a hand. The flash of his ring brought an immediate response and she moved unthinkingly, to the bed.

The bath towel dropped to the floor.

She became vaguely aware of the coolness of silk sheets under her.

Why am I laying here? Have I fainted?

She desperately tried to grasp her situation.

She was staring at the red folds of the canopy over-head, trying to make sense of her nightmare.

Suddenly, she became aware of a feathery soft touch along her cheek, fingers traced the outline of her jaw line, dropping to the slender curve of her neck and throat. The fingers stopped moving at the slight depression of the throat. Maggie heard a distinct intake of breath.

"I must have my taste, or I will go mad with desire and destroy you. I do not wish that for you, Maggie. My feelings for you are much deeper than I wished, but I cannot fight my needs to have you, right now."

She was listening to his voice, little understanding what he was saying, when he bent his dark head over her. She couldn't see his face as he moved his arm under her shoulder, tipping her head backward above the pillows.

Without another word, he fell upon her exposed throat and sank two long fangs into its living pulse.

Maggie gasped with the sharp pain, but her next breath came in a pant. She felt the stranger gripping a breast, its nipple, already hard and erect with desire. His hand dropped lower, as he began stroking the dark, tender mound. She moaned with pleasure as he continued to suck at her throat with loud, suckling sounds. She was delirious with need, pushing his large hand firmly on the incessant throbbing between her open legs.

Just as suddenly as he attacked her, he pulled back. Maggie was still squirming with the pleasure of his touch and groaned for more.

"Not now, my sweet, but soon. Very soon. Then, I'll make you mine forever."

Maggie realized her eyes had been squeezed shut. He had ignited a crazed longing in her with his touch and his hard, demanding mouth. She turned her face dreamily to see his face.

Her eyes were blinded by another flash of his ring and she went limp.

The feeling of floating, with strong arms wrapped around her body, took over and Maggie fell into a quiet sleep. She was lying on her own bed when she heard her name called out from the hallway.

"Maggie!" Collin was tearing up the stairs.

It was just a dream after all.

Chapter 12

Collin burst into Maggie's bedroom, panicking to see her lying on the bed. He rushed over, sitting beside her on the edge.

"Maggie, I'm here, darling!" he said taking a hand.

Maggie struggled to open her eyes when she felt pressure on her fingers. She knew she was still in the grip of an incredible dream, brought on by something she couldn't quite recall.

"Collin? I...I'm feeling very groggy. Why are you here, it's very late?"

"Sweetheart, don't you remember calling me to come? My damned automobile had a flat, or I would have arrived sooner, my love. Maggie, you were going to tell me what happened to you earlier tonight."

Concentrating on the effort, Maggie pushed herself onto her elbows. Looking down at her body, she realized she was wrapped in her bath towel.

"I must have fallen asleep after my bath."

She gave her damp head a little shake as if to dislodge the memory and float it to the surface.

"Collin, I remember what happened! I was leaving the paper when someone grabbed me from behind. I'm not certain how I managed to get away, but I think someone helped me."

"Are you hurt, darling? Should I drive you to the clinic in Paxton before we contact the police?"

"I think I'm alright, but my head hurts like mad! Whoever it was, took hold of a handful of my hair and pulled hard! Let's not call the police yet Collin, I'm just too tired."

She slumped back onto the pillows and closed her eyes. Within a few minutes, she'd drifted off.

Collin sat perfectly still not wanting to wake her again. He reached down and stroked her forehead, then gently pulled the damp towel out from around and under her. He looked longingly for a moment at her desirable body, forcing himself to cover her with the chenille spread.

He walked over to the rocker in the corner of the room. Picking it up, he placed it close to his sleeping fiancé, watching over her. He dozed off and on, until the sky lightened with the coming dawn.

Knowing Maggie's habit of rising by six, he left her, deeply asleep and went down to the kitchen to start coffee.

He'd just lit the pilot light on the small gas stove, putting the percolator on the flame, when he heard movement from above.

He looked into the bedroom in time to see Maggie, her back to him, slipping into a sleeveless lavender shift, with small pearl buttons in back, running from a scoop neck to her waist. It hung open while she searched through her scarfs for an appropriate accessory.

He watched her for a moment longer, the pinks and subtle oranges of the sunrise, softly lighting her room.

Collin knocked, not wanting to startle her.

Turning in his direction, Maggie smiled warmly back at him. The dress swayed gently as she moved to go to him, showing off long legs to their best advantage.

"You look beautiful, Maggie," Collin said as he studied her with hungry eyes.

She stood on tiptoe to kiss his mouth firmly. Collin felt himself respond with a need that had been gnawing at him for months.

They used to have an agreeably spontaneous love life. When he tried to trace the cool change settling in, he kept coming back to an insignificant argument at one of Isabella's dinner parties a while back.

Before he could think more closely about the circumstances of their fight, Maggie took his hand, looking deeply into his eyes.

"Thank you, Collin, for coming and for staying with me. I've begun to remember a few things about last night that I'd like to tell you, before we make any report."

"I will always be here for you, Maggie," he said seriously.

He took her face between his hands, kissing her soft lips as hungrily as he dared. He needed to wait for her to signal when she was ready for lovemaking. He understood that now. Maggie was her own woman and he loved her for that strength of character.

"I've put the coffee on darling, let's talk over a cup so we're both more awake," Collin suggested, taking her shoulders and gently turning her around so he could button her dress.

After fastening the last pearl button, he leaned down to kiss the slender stem of her neck. His eyes were immediately drawn to what looked like two small puncture wounds, red and irritated looking against the fair skin surrounding them.

"Maggie, you've been bitten, sweetheart!"

"Bitten? Where? I haven't noticed any itching?"

"It doesn't look like any kind of bug bite I've ever seen."

He took her over to her full length mirror and placed her hand over the tiny wounds.

When she dropped her hand, the marks stood out vividly on her neck.

"Dear lord, Collin! Whoever attacked me last night, must have done this. I don't remember."

She shuddered, trying to picture her attacker.

Collin took her into his arms, holding her tightly until she seemed to calm inside his embrace.

"Let's go downstairs sweetheart, so you can sit and we'll talk," Collin suggested as he firmly took her elbow.

They went down to the kitchen where the aroma of fresh brewed coffee gave off a comforting normalcy.

Maggie tried to distract herself by gathering up the cups and saucers, while Collin went to the new refrigerator he bought as a present for her. The condenser motor on top, was humming like a choir director. He opened the heavy white door, spotting the cream and little else.

They poured their cups, moving to the small table in the breakfast nook off the kitchen. The sun was beginning to take hold of its morning rule, lighting the corners of the cozy room.

Maggie gazed across the expanse of lawn and flower gardens, tended lovingly by her mother and now, by a local workman. She peered into the ever-shadowy boundary she shared with the bayou. Even with over two acres between her home and the swamp, Maggie could still feel the weight of moist air pressing back on the borders.

Collin's voice broke into her thoughts.

"Are you ready to talk about last night, darling? You'll need to make a statement at the police station this morning about the attack."

"Yes, I know Collin and if you're not too busy, I wanted you to come with me."

"I planned on it, sweetheart. We're the same "bayou brats" that always saw things through together, right?" he asked.

They both smiled at his reference to them when they were playmates, building forts, while their parents visited. This memory jolted Collin to another recollection.

Collin had been bitten by a non-venomous Ribbon Snake, on one those visits. He knew firsthand the look of a puncture wound. The marks on Maggie's neck were so similar, it was difficult to conceal his concern.

Maggie could see he was getting anxious to have her make her report.

"Let's go, Collin. I want to get this over with. I have to be in the office this morning. I'm doing a story on unsolved crime in Paxton Parrish. I think my attacker might be responsible for more than my mugging."

She was out of her chair before Collin had a chance to object. He quickly followed her to the foyer where she collected her keys to the Packard, the small clutch she had brought down with her and her briefcase.

Collin snatched the brown leather bag from her hand saying, "Let me clean this up a bit, Mags."

He had used his pet name for her and it sounded as natural as the morning sun to her.

She relinquished her grip on the handle and spotted the blood that had dried over the front of the bag.

"I forgot about my briefcase," she said quietly.

Collin gave her shoulder a squeeze and took the bag into the kitchen.

While he was gone, Maggie went over to the hall mirror and studied the bites on her neck in a better light. They were clearly puncture marks.

The journalist in her made a mental note to check into the rash of unsolved murders in Paxton Parrish and other towns along the bayou.

Maybe this is a common thread in those cases, she mused to herself. *The police might not have put that into their reports to the public.*

Collin held out the briefcase to her, wiped clean of any traces of her blood. Her hand went automatically to her forehead, feeling a slight lump under the bandage she put over the wound before dressing. The last thing she wanted was any publicity about the incident and was grateful for the camouflage of her heavy bangs.

Maggie parked across from the Paxton Police Station, with Collin pulling in behind. He was pleased when Maggie reached for his hand as they walked toward the glass doors.

Forty minutes later, the couple stepped back into what had become, a balmy spring day. The sky was cloudless and the air soft on Maggie's arms. The only hint of a storm warning was on her face. Collin had seen it enough times over the years, to know trouble was brewing.

"Maggie, Detective Morton can't just give out information, or names of suspects, willy-nilly. He needs to keep some of his clues unreported, so he can follow up on them without alerting the perpetrator."

"I understand his motives, Collin. It's just that I can do my own digging around and might actually uncover something he's not aware of yet. I have a vested interest in this case. You saw his face when I told him about the puncture marks."

"Yes, he did go pretty pale, especially when you removed your scarf to show him."

They were talking in front of their parked cars, heads close together, when another automobile pulled up beside them. They looked over at Isabella Butler's sleek Rolls-Royce Phantom, just as her side window was lowered.

"Good morning to you both! How is it I find you in front of the Paxton Police Station, pray tell?"

Isabella had a way of cutting right to the chase. Her directness usually disarmed anyone bold enough to try to keep a secret after her probing questions. Her reputation for prying information, from even the most reluctant, earned her the nick-name of "Royal Inquisitor," among the residents of Paxton Parrish who had fallen under her discerning gaze. Something Isabella privately relished.

Within certain social strata of the community, Isabella Butler was looked upon as mysterious and even sinister. Because of her almost reclusive lifestyle, she was viewed with suspicion by many outside her closed circle and with outright animosity, by those fearing her continued hold over the social elite. A circle few could enter without Isabella Butler's express consent.

Sitting with her ankle length black skirt spread around her plump form, Isabella was raised up by three inches on a special pillow designed for rides in her automobile. Her hands were gloved, in a soft kid, died black. Her fingers sparkled with diamond and ruby rings, worn over the gloves and providing flashes of light to the somber ensemble.

Isabella never complied with the necessity of wearing any kind of hat, scoffing at all head covers as superfluous to "…what's already on top!"

She had wrapped herself in an intricately patterned shawl with symbols of an indeterminate origin, stitched in black and red. No matter how hot the weather was, Isabella always dressed warmly as if awaiting an unnatural snow fall.

She was looking closely at the pair of young people who moved closer to her vehicle to speak with her.

"I can see there's been trouble, so you might as well give me the details."

Maggie stepped closer to the car and caught sight of Leslie Porter Booth sitting beside her employer.

"Hello, Isabella, Leslie. What brings you out so early in the day, Isabella?" Maggie asked coolly.

"I have business at my bank, dear, but don't ty to deflect my interest with casual conversation. I've known you since you were born, so get on with it. What's happened that I find you in front of our constabulary?"

Maggie glanced over at Collin, her look pleading for him to jump in with his own comments.

"Isabella, Maggie was working late last evening and was attacked when she was going to her automobile."

Maggie wasn't pleased that he was so blunt in describing her incident, but there was no other way to tell the story short of lying.

Leslie leaned forward .

"Maggie, that's just terrible! You weren't injured I hope?" Leslie blurted out.

Maggie was looking at Leslie and missed the glaring look Isabella flashed at the young woman.

But Collin hadn't. He wondered why the old woman looked like she wanted to throttle the slender neck of her pretty companion. He also noticed how quickly Isabella covered over that spark of animosity.

Maggie gave a rough account of the mugging, confirming she wasn't injured, only shaken up a bit. She purposely didn't mention the puncture wound.

Isabella gave her an appraising look.

"Maggie, dear, you must both come over this evening at eight for a small dinner party I'm hosting for other art collectors. There may be some interest in my coming exhibit. We'll talk then dear."

Tapping the window between her and her driver, she rolled her window back up and waved goodbye as the sleek, black car moved away as smoothly as a shark plies the waters.

"Well," Collin said, smiling in the direction of the disappearing Rolls and its enigmatic occupants.

"That was odd. It was almost as if Isabella didn't want you to say too much in front of Leslie for some reason. She gave her some strange looks. But I think we should take her up on her invitation sweetheart, what do you say?"

It was agreed that after work, Collin would pick Maggie up at home and they could drive to the Butler Plantation together.

"I'm not letting you out of my sight, lovely lady," he said taking her into his arms for a kiss.

It wasn't lost on him that she was kissing him back like she used to and not just going through the motions of love. He genuinely felt her desire for him again. *Tonight my love*, he thought to himself. *Tonight you'll be mine again.*

Chapter 13

Somehow, Maggie got through her day at the office, though her head ached and she was glad to leave early.

When she was getting ready for their dinner date, brushing her hair, made her wince. She studied the gash on her forehead after taking off the small bandage. It had closed nicely and she left it uncovered.

Standing in front of her oval mirror, she held up the pearl-gray, silk dress she would wear to Isabella's intimate dinner party.

It had an off-shoulder cap sleeve, with layers of delicate fabric creating a slight fullness to the drop waist. Slipping it on, Maggie smiled to herself, pleased with the shimmering effect of every movement and how nicely it complimented her legs.

Taking a pair of black dress-shoes off the rack, she sat at the dressing table to fasten the straps. As she was bent over adjusting the strap at her heel, a flash of heat brought her head up with a jerk.

The puncture marks on her neck suddenly throbbed like a branding site. Maggie touched them lightly, surprised at the heat around the area. Turning, so she could study them in the mirror, she gasped in alarm at their enflamed appearance.

Staring into the dressing mirror, she felt a slight breeze on her bare shoulders, stirring her hair, as if a fan turned above her head. It brought a whiff of something that smelled like it crawled out of the swamp water.

The bedroom windows were both open, but the evening air was still, without the slightest breeze. Maggie got up, crossing to a window to look outside into the gathering dusk.

The wiry, gray moss dangled undisturbed off the bald cypress and hardwoods at the edge of her lawn and along a rough path leading into the bayou.

The crickets and bull frogs seemed eerily silent. There were no sounds of sudden splashing, where a gator might have entered the still waters. There were no calls from the normally gregarious waterfowl that plunged into the murky brown waters for fish or frogs.

All was dead silent, as if the swamp life held its collective breath.

Not wanting good sense to give way to her overly-active imagination, Maggie went back to the closet, grabbing her favorite fringed shawl from its hanger. Walking to her jewelry box, she pulled out a lacey choker decorated with tiny sea pearls to cover up the marks on her neck. She wanted to avoid any probing questions, especially by her keen-sighted friend, Isabella. The wound on her neck felt less irritated but chaffed slightly under the pearl collar.

Before she left, she couldn't resist taking a look at the ceiling of her room. Beside the gathering shadows filling the corners, she saw nothing. Only the vague smell lingered, but it was still putrid and disturbing. Convinced something large and long-dead must have floated back to the surface of the swamp, she shivered and rubbed her arms. She heard Collin's big auto roll onto the circular drive in front and snatched her clutch.

The front doorbell rang out like the bugle of a rescuing cavalry and Maggie ran like a newly escaping prisoner.

Chapter 14

Four vehicles were already parked in front of the half circle of wide steps when Collin and Maggie arrived at Isabella's. From the number of brightly lit rooms shining from the expanse of the house, it appeared Isabella was throwing a fete, instead of an intimate dinner party. Maggie was glad she had chosen to wear the pearl-gray silk. Her hand went automatically to the pearl choker.

She took Collin's arm after he helped her from the automobile. He leaned down, kissing her lips softly.

"You look stunning this evening, Maggie. But then, I've thought you the most beautiful girl on earth since we were building forts in your backyard."

Maggie smiled up at him warmly. He looked very handsome in his dark gray suit. The double-breasted cut, emphasized his broad shoulders and trim waist. It was as if she saw him more clearly. His deep brown eyes, his sandy blond hair. He was indeed a dreamboat!

"Thanks for being so sweet, Collin. I'm so glad we out lasted our forts, darling."

She brought his head down to her mouth. Kissing him deeply seemed to release a building sexual tension, which was odd. Had she been unconsciously repressing her desire for Collin? When did that begin?

She'd loved him all her life. What made her question that? She held his arm tighter.

The maid opened the door before they had to ring. She showed them to the drawing room, where the other guests were scattered around the softly lit room. Isabella always preferred candles to electricity for her intimate affairs. Guests were sipping cocktails and chatting in hushed voices among themselves.

Maggie thought it looked more like a wake from the somber faces that greeted them.

A quick look around and she realized their hostess was missing as was Leslie Porter Booth. Grayson Gerrard stood in front of the unused fireplace. His dark features looked relaxed and confident. He obviously didn't share whatever concern had invaded the other dinner guests.

Collin spoke up clearly, addressing the pensive group, all old acquaintances, if not friends.

"Good evening all. Where's our hostess?" he asked casually, looking around at the expectant faces.

The soft babble of voice stopped immediately. Maggie noticed how some of the guests cut quick glances at the others. All seemed hesitant to be the first to speak.

The deep, velvety voice of Grayson Gerrard wove its way through the group like a warm current of water between unyielding rocks.

"Good evening, Maggie, Collin. Our dear hostess has been taken ill and has sent word that we should proceed to dinner without her. The maid should be calling us to be seated momentarily.

I believe Miss Porter Booth has made herself available to join us for the rest of the evening. As soon as she's seen to Isabella's comfort."

Collin thanked him for letting them know. He turned away from Grayson's slight look of superiority and toward Maggie.

Speaking close to her ear, he whispered, "Maggie, I think we should check up on the old girl. She never liked being fussed over, but let's slip out of here and scoot upstairs."

He and Maggie waited until the maid came to tell everyone they could be seated for dinner.

"Just need a moment," Maggie was careful to speak loud enough to Collin that a few heard her as she and Collin fell behind the group moving toward the dining room.

As soon as the hallway was clear, they hurried up the ornate wooden staircase and straight to Isabella's room.

There was a bond between the two young people and Isabella that was rooted in both the Fitzhugh and Newsome families. More like a great aunt to both Collin and Maggie, they both felt comfortable enough to go directly to her bedroom.

They padded silently along the beautiful Persian carpet runner, leading down the hallway. The light from the master bedroom at the end, displayed a silhouette on the wall across from it. For a second, both Maggie and Collin froze when the shadow seemed to move up the wall unnaturally.

Approaching the doorway they saw Isabella lying on the white duvet covering her four poster bed. Even across the room they could see Isabella's face was as pale as the comforter.

Oddly, she was still wearing her black evening dress, her black shoes poking out from beneath.

They entered the room, approaching her quietly, when Leslie's voice came from behind.

"She just needed a little lie-down, no need to be alarmed."

Maggie had taken up one of Isabella's small, veiny hands and held it in hers.

"Isabella, Collin and I are here. Are you in need of your doctor?"

Maggie turned to Collin standing close to her side.

"Her hand is so cold, Collin," she said, her voice filled with concern.

"Leslie," Collin said, looking directly at her now, "How long has Isabella been feeling off and why haven't you rung up her doctor?"

"Mr. Fitzhugh, I only discovered Isabella was ill a short while ago, when I came to collect her to go down to her guests. Believe me, she is not in need of her physician, only a little…"

She stopped speaking when Isabella's eyes fluttered open. Collin was looking directly at Leslie and noted an odd look pass over her lovely face.

She looks angry, he thought, studying her a moment longer.

Isabella's voice brought Collin's attention back to his friend.

"Why ever are you two in my bedroom and not with the others at dinner?" she said, struggling to a sitting position with Maggie's help.

Collin answered for them, "We heard you were not feeling your usual tip-top and you know how Mags worries."

Isabella turned so her legs dangled over the side of the bed, telling Collin to get her to her feet while she scooted forward. Maggie tried to object, but Isabella was standing in the next minute.

Leslie hadn't spoken again, but neatly inserted herself between Maggie and the old woman. Taking an elbow, she helped her walk from the room toward the elevator.

Isabella had the lift installed at George Newsome's insistence, when Maggie was away at college. He was concerned that as she advanced in age his old friend would find the stairs difficult and dangerous.

"You young people go ahead; Leslie will see me down."

Isabella and her companion got into the tiny elevator compartment and Leslie pulled the grating shut and hit the button. It began its slow, creaky descent.

Collin told Maggie about the odd look he'd seen come over Leslie's face when Isabella came awake.

"You must have seen relief, darling. Leslie's devoted to Isabella."

They walked into the dining room behind their hostess, hearing the scraping of chairs as the other guests jumped to their feet to greet her with cheers and questions.

Collin steered Maggie over to chairs left open to Grayson's left.

He sat at the end of the table, facing the others as if he was lord of the manor. One elbow on the table edge, a hand gracefully holding a crystal glass of dark, red wine. Collin felt unreasonably annoyed at this position taking, but quickly shook off what he admitted was the bite of jealousy.

Grayson smiled warmly at them both as he and the other men, all got to their feet, greeting the arriving mistress of the manse.

Chapter 15

Isabella settled into her large Captain's chair with the soft rustle of silks. She appeared shrunken, almost swamped in the dark dress, as she sank down into the chair's cushion.

There were thirteen sitting at the beautifully set table, including Isabella.

The gentleman to Maggie's right observed, "Guess you have disproven the old superstition about thirteen being an unlucky number, Isabella. I have to admit, when you left the group earlier, you looked like you were never coming back!" His rather tactless comment, fueled by a few glasses of wine on an empty stomach, caused some uncomfortable chuckles and a swift look of annoyance from his wife.

Isabella cleared the air, coolly commenting that she was too irascible to be put down by a case of mild heartburn. "Should never have eaten that last scone at breakfast. Far too rich for me, right Leslie?" she added.

Leslie leaned over patting Isabella's blue-veined hand, where it rested on her chair arm. Isabella held her wine glass in her other hand.

Maggie saw her elderly friend draw back from the touch so quickly that a few drops of the heavy red wine, splashed onto the ivory linen cloth. Leslie deftly blotted it with her napkin, smiling at Isabella as if they shared a secret.

She began watching Leslie furtively throughout the meal. She noticed that she merely went through the motions of eating, moving the food around her plate with delicate motions.

Maggie observed as Leslie took delicate sips from her wine glass, reminding her of an elusive blue and green Parula at a birdbath, barely wetting her lips, already a dark red.

Watching Collin from time to time throughout diner, Maggie noticed that he too was watching Leslie and guessed he shared her unease. It felt to Maggie as if something ugly had attached itself to their friend. Something unseen and unnatural. She looked forward to speaking to Collin about it.

After a subdued diner, with a smattering of conversation about the upcoming art exhibit, James Hopper, the bore who commented on Isabella's look of death, decided on one more Port before "tearing up the road " as he indelicately phrased his drive home.

Maggie was relieved when his wife squelched this idea, emphatically saying goodnight to the others and taking his arm.

As the last to arrive at table, Maggie and Collin were hoping to be the last to leave, giving them a moment alone with Isabella.

Grayson Gerrard left ten minutes earlier, claiming an early day of finishing up some pieces for his upcoming show, only two months away.

Collin stood close to Maggie, their arms interlaced as they followed Isabella back to the elevator. Leslie waited patiently for her employer to shuffle up to the heavy grate.

Maggie stepped over to Isabella and leaned down to kiss her doughy cheek. "Goodnight, Isabella, and thanks so much for another wonderful dinner. If we keep eating here, I'll never be ever to practice my cooking before I marry poor Collin!""

Collin laughed, bending down to give her a warm peck on the other cheek when she said, "Not so fast you two, I've questions that need answers."

She turned toward the waiting elevator, telling Leslie she'd have the maid help her back to her rooms and she should retire for the evening.

Her attitude signaled discussion would not be welcome.

Leslie answered, "As you wish, Isabella. I'll be in my room if you need me. Goodnight, Mr. Fitzhugh. Maggie."

She stepped into the lift and the three watched as it ascended like a grousing child, screeching metallic protests.

"Now," Isabella said firmly, "we shall sit in the Solarium for a bit, while you two tell me what happened to my sweet Maggie." She wrapped her stubby arm through Collin's and they walked slowly into the cozy room at the rear of the house.

The evening was full-dark by then. Without the obstruction of many trees, a large swath of sky showed bright stars, shining like the facets in Isabella's jewels, cold and beautiful. There was a single lamp lit in the room, but it gave a cheery light to the darkness peering in the many windows of the glass-enclosed sunroom.

They arranged themselves on three cushioned chairs and Maggie related her experience of the night before, trying to keep a growing fear out of her voice.

"And Collin, what are your thoughts on this attack?" Isabella asked, searching his eyes.

He was just as direct, telling her he suspected Maggie had been bitten by something, perhaps the attacker used a snake in the assault he theorized, though he admitted that seemed ludicrous.

Isabella said nothing at first, then blurted out, "Remove your collar Maggie, dear. Let's have a gander at this *puncture,* Collin describes."

Maggie raised her hand and reluctantly pulled the pearl-studded choker from around her neck. The wounds hadn't stopped throbbing the whole time she'd been there that evening. In fact, the discomfort became more intense while they sat at the table. The hammer-pulse of pain, lessened now, as they sat with Isabella.

Isabella leaned closer to Maggie, studying the small twin marks. As the two young people watched her, the color drained completely from her plump face leaving it a pasty-white.

Maggie and Collin glanced over at each other, sharing the same thought that Isabella might be taking ill again.

"Isabella, are you quite alright?" Collin said slipping his arm around her quivering shoulders. Maggie didn't speak or move when the old woman reached her index finger toward the punctures, wincing only when she touched them.

"It's true, then," Isabella said, her words nearly inaudible to them.

It was easier to hear her the second time when she uttered her next, dread-filled words.

"They are here. God save us. They are here and they want the blood of the innocent."

Chapter 16

Maggie and Collin exchanged worried looks when they heard Isabella's comment. Her words hung in the air, almost palpable and dripping with dread.

"Isabella," Maggie said softly.

"*Whose* here? What do you mean, they want blood?"

The old woman reached up to her own neck, untying the long kerchief attached to her black silk blouse. She began methodically undoing the row of tiny black pearl buttons at her throat.

When she finished, she held the material back from her neck, exposing the loose, aged skin to her young friends.

At first, Collin looked slightly embarrassed by the old lady's awkward behavior, but then he heard his fiancé gasp. Maggie had her hand up to her mouth. Her eyes were wide with real fear. Collin leaned forward to get a better look at what had Maggie speechless. "My God, Isabella! It's the same puncture wounds that Maggie has! But how can that be? Have you been attacked as well?"

Isabella fumbled with the collar buttons of the blouse. Maggie knelt down in front of her to finish the job, rewinding the kerchief around the neck.

"I wanted to see for myself, but I have had my suspicions, for quite some time. Now I am convinced, St. Germain has returned and is hunting the bayous once more."

Collin asked, "Who's St. Germain and what does he have to do with the attacks on you and Maggie? You say he's a hunter?"

"Oh, he's a hunter alright," Isabella sounded as if every breath was an effort to take.

She was obviously fighting off a deep fatigue. Collin felt guilty asking her to explain herself. She was obviously showing signs of the mental confusion that afflicted many old people.

Maggie shot him a quick look before he could pose any more questions.

"Isabella, Collin and I will look into these two attacks. When we find anything about this man we'll…"

"He's not like other men!" Isabella cut off Maggie's comment. "He's been here for hundreds of years and will remain here, as long as he can drain the life around him. All of your great-great-great grandparents were young babes when St. Germain made his first appearance in Paxton Parrish. By that time, he'd already ravished surrounding Parishes for hundreds of years.

He returned to his old bayou hunting grounds, time and again, only leaving when the locals became suspicious of him and his activities. And now, he has returned yet again, to Paxton."

Isabella slumped back into the cushions of her chair, looking more fragile than ever. After a few minutes of silence, Isabella asked them to help her to her room. Walking on either side of her, they managed to get her into the elevator and back to her bedroom.

Maggie went behind a dressing screen to help Isabella into her nightgown. She looked lost inside the bulky black garment. She resembled a white pearl in a closed clam shell.

Collin busied himself, turning down the bedcovers and mulling over the fantastic story the old lady shared. As he moved a pillow, pulling back the top sheet, he saw rust colored spots on the lace of the pillowcase. He moved the lacey covering aside and saw larger spots on the bottom sheet. Looking back over his shoulder to be sure he wasn't observed by either of the women, he held the pillow closer to the dim bedside lamp. *It looks like blood,* he thought, with growing apprehension.

Isabella's story was outlandish. A man who lived for centuries, hunting people and draining them of life. *That would make him a…* His jumble of thoughts were cut off when the Maggie came up beside him, holding Isabella's arm.

"Help me get Isabella into bed, Collin," she spoke quietly as if the older woman was already asleep.

Without any protests on her part, Isabella sat on the side of the mattress and laid her head down on the pillow as Collin shoved it under her. Her eyes were closed and she appeared to be asleep before they finished covering her.

As they turned to leave, Isabella's voice floated up, dreamy, but clear.

"Be careful, my dears. The night is his domain and he's always hungry."

They were staring back at the shriveled figure in the large four-poster bed as if they'd already seen her ghost.

Maggie said from the doorway, "We'll be fine, Isabella. You rest now."

"I shall rest for eternity, after I know you are both safe. Must keep fighting until then," Isabella said in her dreamy voice.

"The Count St. Germain never sleeps and never lowers his guard. Watch over one another."

They closed her door, leaving the small bedside light on, so her room wasn't filled with the darkness that crept uninvited into their minds.

Walking hand in hand back to Collin's automobile, Maggie finally broke the heavy silence that settled around them like swamp mud. "Collin, her description of St. Germain isn't new to me. When I was quite young, an old Cajun woman at my father's office, told me about him. I still recall her vivid details. She said he came from France, where he "ruled the night" to quote her, in the 1700's. She scared the life out of me, with her morbid stories about him."

"Darling, you described your attacker as being very strong and until something knocked him off you, you were unable to break his grip. While I must admit, the bite marks you and Isabella have look identical, I don't think a man from the 1700s left them. The only tales of men living that long are about…"

"Vampires," Maggie whispered the name of this mythical creature, almost afraid of summoning the monster out of the shadows.

Maggie stopped just before they reached Collin's auto. The moon floated almost directly above them. Its pale light, occasionally dulled by a skittering cloud across its face, adding to the pervasive shadowing of the portico.

Collin took Maggie into his arms and held her a moment under the ethereal glow.

"Maggie, I love you with all my heart and won't let anything harm you while I draw a breath."

She looked up, her blue eyes shining with reflected moonlight. Reaching her hand to his cheek, she felt the beginning of a rough stubble.

"You'll need to shave before you come to bed, darling."

Collin gave a quick laugh and squeezed Maggie closer.

As the automobile pulled away from the dark house, Maggie looked back at it for a minute, seeing the one light in Isabella's bedroom.

It seemed to flicker for an instant, as if someone had passed in front of it.

Just as she began to say something to Collin, he reached over for her hand and brought it to his mouth.

Kissing her palm gently he murmured, "I can't wait to make you mine forever, Maggie Newsome."

Maggie felt the same thrill she always felt around Collin. She realized it was she pulling away from their bond these past weeks. It didn't make any sense. What had happened to make her doubt her feelings?

Like the clouds moving away from the moon's bright face, Maggie felt some impediment had dropped from her eyes. She had only twenty minutes to wait until she could reignite their fire.

Chapter 17

They were lying quietly, tightly wrapped in one another's arms. Collin understood Maggie's need to feel safe and protected. He didn't want to rush this intimacy. His hunger would have to be satisfied slowly and gently, until he was certain it was what Maggie craved as much as he.

Collin was ashamed of his demanding, chauvinistic behavior the time he all but forced himself on her. He manipulated her physical needs until she climaxed, but there was no joy in her after. He wanted desperately to make amends for hurting her. He vowed never to make sexual demands on her. She needed to feel loved, not taken like a common street walker.

Maggie pulled away enough to look into Collin's light brown eyes. "Collin", she spoke softly. "I've missed this and I can't for the life of me understand why I was so...so remote, these past few weeks. Can you ever forgive my foolishness?"

In answer to her question, Collin ran his hand down the smooth curve of her back bringing her body even closer. A faint lilac fragrance filled his head when he nuzzled her thick hair. He hated that she cut it into the popular "bob", but he'd grown used to her more sophisticated look.

He thought how they were both grown up now and he could no longer pull on her ponytail to get her to chase him.

Maggie heard him chuckle.

"What do you find so amusing, sir?" she asked putting on a serious voice.

"Just remembering pulling your hair to get your attention as kids. And now, you're lying in my arms."

Collin pressed his lips to hers, allowing some of the raw need he had to possess her, to flow like liquid heat between them. She instantly responded with her own flaring passion for him, pulling him over so his long body covered every inch of her.

They had no need to rush and he had so much to make up for.

She called out his name and he pressed himself against her thigh. She felt a throbbing need, wrapping both legs around his back, forcing him to shift until he slid inside her.

"I need you Collin, please, now!"

He met her demands, pushing himself deeper, until her moans turned to screams of release. He didn't let himself find the same orgasmic paradise until he was certain she was fully satisfied.

When he was totally spent, he slid to Maggie's side, both of them slippery with the sweat of their love-making.

Words were not needed to describe their shared pleasure and before long, they relaxed into their exhaustion, silently drifting off.

Maggie was slipping into the first deep sleep she had in many weeks. Her dreams had been filled with demon-headed men and women with pendulous breasts who suckled babies with long fangs and tails. She was too embarrassed by these night horrors to mention them to her fiancé. And lately, she felt she had no right to burden him with her problems.

Lying close to Collin, every part of Maggie felt soothed. She let herself drop into the endless abyss of sexual gratification, floating untethered from all external life.

The darkness outside the house seemed to draw completeness from the shadowy bayou, sighing its own fulfillment.

When a slight wind stirred the curtains hanging at an open window, Maggie snuggled closer to Collin, his warm body soothing her nakedness from the chill air.

As the moon glided over the velvet sky in the darkest hours, a figure materialized from the corner of the bedroom. His fine hearing picked up the rhythmic beats of two human hearts, so close to each other they could have been one.

He cocked his head and sniffed the air, evocative with the mingling of sweat and sexual fluids. He felt his mouth begin to salivate. His full lips pulled back, the two long fangs catching on a shaft of moonlight.

It took all of his will power not to lunge at the vulnerable couple, ripping into the man's throat and carrying the woman back to his lair in the heart of the bayou.

He hoped to find her alone. He'd already invaded her dreams, making her more susceptible to his power. He sensed her blood stir while she dreamt of sexual predators, part man, part monster. Like him.

He watched her then as now, as she tossed in her bed, the sheets wrapping as tightly as a shroud about her lithe, exquisite body. He'd been watching her for over a month already, while he worked his charms on others, so he could feed and spare her. The time was nearing, however, his time to possess the beautiful Maggie Newsome, making her his eternal lover and companion.

Maggie sighed deeply in her sleep. The watching figure knew she was lost in her slumber, as innocent as a child. He looked over at Collin, hating to tear his keen eyes away from the sleek curves and voluptuous mounds of the woman.

Collin had proved tenacious in his desire to keep his fiancé. Her strange behavior toward him only made his feelings for her more stubborn to dislodge. This dogged loyalty to the young woman in the face of her growing rejection stirred a long ago memory in the watcher.

He had traveled the world, held the powdered effete royalty of Europe enthralled, dined with beggars sharing their moldy crusts and small beer, before he emptied them of their meager life forever.

But that was many, many, centuries ago, when he was very young, cast out on his own by his creator for an indiscretion that nearly put him on a pyre.

Oh yes, he still remembered the Count walking into his father's blacksmith forge. The bright sun at his back, he stood like a god among the bleakness of his life.

His father was working at the time, on a dueling sword for the Count Gerrard de Gascon. A sword as supple as a dancer and as sturdy as a horse whip. This project was nearing completion and the Count came by to collect the marvelous piece himself.

He remembered how his father nearly keeled over in his deep bow to the Count. For himself, he had stopped hammering the minute he felt the Count's eyes on him, but he never bowed. Glancing over at his father, he was disgusted to see him groveling like a mongrel.

The Count Gerrard de Gascon had a reputation among the villagers as a vile man, whose castle rang with screams in the darkest hours of the night. No one ventured to his manor without being forced by his armed guards. These men usually brought an invitation from their Lord, in the dead of night, banging on a cottager's door. The faces of the Count's guards were as pale as bleached flour and earned them the name of "Death Reapers" by the villagers of the Count's vast holdings.

The figure watching Maggie's soft, firm breasts, rising and falling, had received such a summons, the night after the Count collected his sword from the smithy.

He and his father shared a hovel behind their shop and late that night, the "Death Reapers" banged on its flimsy, wooden door, splintering it before he was able to respond.

He recalled clearly how they worded the summons and while he watched the pulse at Maggie's lovely neck, he mouthed the words that eventually made him what he was.

"The Count Gerrard de Gascone commands you to his presence and into his service."

And serve him he did, for too many years, too many centuries. Time filled with pain and pleasures, hedonistic luxury and the grinding poverty of a dead soul.

Grayson Gerrard was as insubstantial as the wind and as powerful as a hurricane. He'd had everything except his humanity. Now, all he desired lay supine, wrapped in her fiancé's arms. Her very vulnerability made his manhood throb with desire to possess her.

He moved closer to the sleeping couple, a pale hand gently touched the curve of the woman's silky shoulder.

Maggie made a soft purring sound and Grayson's fangs flashed again in the moon's creamy glow.

He bent over her but jerked his head back when Collin's arm pulled her in closer, moving her head onto his broad chest.

"Not now my lovely, Maggie, but soon, very soon."

With another stirring of the air, Grayson evaporated into the shadows of the night, returning to the verdant and deadly Bayou, where he found the harsh, predatory nature of life comforting and familiar.

Chapter 18

"How could we have slept so long?" Maggie was saying, rushing around to get ready for the office. "I have a column to write and need to edit Elizabeth's last piece before we can go to press."

Collin was smiling at her, his head resting on an arm as he lay among the rumpled bedding. "You look beautiful as you are, Maggie. I think the glow about you may be a give-away though, to your recent amorous activities." He was laughing at her when she stepped over to the bed and gave his arm a jab and then a lovely smile.

They had a light breakfast of the chicory flavored coffee they both favored and two of the muffins Maggie was bringing to the office for her small staff. As a boss, she was well-respected, but the sweets she brought in regularly helped to build good morale.

Maggie accepted Collin's offer to drive her to the newspaper office. He'd pick her up around six-thirty, for a quiet dinner at home they decided. It had been ages since they spent time together, just the two of them. It was one of the things Maggie realized she was missing over the past confusing weeks.

They wanted to drop in on Isabella, before going into Paxton. They left her in quite a state the night before and privately, Collin wanted to see how the puncture marks looked. Maggie's had begun to fade, but when they woke that morning they looked irritated again for no obvious reason.

Maggie wore a pair of black linen slacks, topped this with a short-sleeved black sweater. Her impeccable sense of style always impressed Collin.

He slipped into yesterday's shirt and the suit pants from the evening before. Somehow he managed to look like a silent-movie, heart-throb, in the wrinkled shirt, two buttons left gaping in a teasing fashion.

They arrived at the Butler Plantation around eight, giving their elderly friend time to eat a breakfast before seeing her. They found her in the Solarium, with Leslie at her side.

If anything, Isabella looked more drained than the evening before. Her complexion was chalky white. Her eyes were strained and sunken. The dark circles beneath them, giving her a haunted look, replacing the self-assuredness they'd come to expect.

Collin asked if they could speak with her alone for a few minutes, giving Leslie a direct look that meant this was not a request.

This garnered a sharp look from the companion, but she silently rose and exited the bright room.

Leslie brushed Maggie's arm in passing, saying, "You're looking very well, Maggie. Perhaps we could reschedule our ride one day soon. I haven't had any troublesome headaches for days now."

"Of course, Leslie. I'm glad you're feeling better."

As she spoke with her, Maggie noticed that the companion's normally ice-blue eyes, were so bright they almost looked feverish.

Leslie gave Maggie a long piercing look. Maggie felt as if she was searching for any untruths in Maggie's casual comment.

Giving her golden crown of braids a smoothing pat, Leslie glided from the room.

Maggie glanced over at Isabella and saw a look of relief pass over her ashen face.

"Isabella, as lovely as you always are, you look a little peaked this morning," Collin joked.

Earlier, Collin felt a distinct annoyance directed at him in particular, when they entered the room. Leslie was always cool to him and he didn't enjoy being around her. He wondered to himself if he could find a more cheerful companion for the old woman.

Maggie came to Isabella's side, kneeling down beside her chair. Taking her frail hand, she inquired about the puncture wound.

"Is it better today, Isabella?"

"In truth, I fear it has become infected. It continues to burn, though oddly it feels better since your arrival. It could be, I just needed some jolly company, right Collin? As efficient as she is, Leslie is something of an old stick in the swamp mud!"

Maggie laughed at this apt description. Though very attractive, Maggie recalled Collin's impression of Leslie, saying she projected less warmth than a used matchstick.

"Isabella, can we just take a quick peek at your bite mark. I noticed Maggie's seemed inflamed earlier this morning."

After Maggie helped unbutton the high-necked collar of her Isabella's top, she had to turn her face away so Isabella couldn't see her expression. There were two more marks on the loose skin of her neck, both very red.

Collin stepped closed and shot a look at Maggie.

"Isabella, I think your right about a possible infection setting in. I'd suggest you let us contact Doc. Morse for you, so he can nip by and check them over."

"What do you mean, by "them," Collin? Do I have others?" A creeping alarm came into Isabella's voice.

Collin looked over at Maggie. She was still kneeling beside Isabella, holding her collar back from two, clear sets of puncture wounds. She was shocked to see the newest set, still had a few drops of blood, weeping from rather deep holes in the thin, crepe of Isabella's throat.

Maggie had to answer the question about the second bites.

"Isabella, there is another bite and this one seems much deeper. Collin is right. We need to get Doctor Morse to see you today."

The elderly woman raised a hand to touch her neck. Her grimace of pain wasn't lost on the watching pair. But they were shocked by her response to this suggestion.

"No! No doctors! I need you to carry a message into Paxton for me. Give me some paper and pen, Maggie and an envelope if you would, dear."

Maggie got to her feet. She and Collin were looking at one another, both perplexed at this odd request, when Isabella said firmly, "Now girl! No time to waste!"

While Maggie rummaged through a small desk in the adjoining study, Collin stood like a guard over the frail woman. He thought she looked more resolute than he'd seen in a long time. Her jaw was firmly set, while she gripped the sides of her chair as if she'd launch herself into action at any moment.

"Can you redo these buttons, Collin" she said breaking into his thoughts.

He finished the last of them on the collar when Maggie returned with the writing material and handed the lot over to Isabella along with her portable writing desk.

Maggie took Collin's hand as they watched their friend scribble her note.

Maggie was sure Collin felt as uneasy with the situation as she did, but they waited quietly while Isabella finished.

"Collin, I would like you to find a woman for me. She lives in Paxton, along the bayou canal outside of the town. Her name is Mari. You'll only have to inquire of one of the folk living around the river and they'll direct you to her. Give her this letter and tell her it is urgent she come to me immediately."

"Mari? That's her only name?" he asked hoping it was enough to find her.

"Yes. But she's well-known to the bayou community. You'll have no difficulty finding her," Isabella answered firmly.

"I'd like to have you stay with me until Collin returns with her, Maggie. Would that be possible, dear? "

Maggie answered immediately, "Of course I'll stay Isabella, for as long as you need me to."

The pair both saw relief flood the pale face as Isabella fussed with the collar of her black silk blouse, as if it was too snug around her neck. She tried to hide the drop of blood that stained a finger, but both of them saw her fear as clearly as she saw their alarm.

Chapter 19

Collin was only gone a few minutes on his errand to find the mysterious Mari when Leslie returned to the solarium. Isabella stiffened in her chair and Maggie felt an undercurrent pass between the two women.

"It's time for your morning medications, Isabella." Turning her cool, blue eyes on Maggie, she excused them as she helped her elderly employer to her feet. Isabella didn't object, though Maggie saw her face reflect some resistance.

"I'll just take a walk through the gardens, Isabella. I'll be back in twenty minutes if that's alright," Maggie said as they exited the room.

"You may enjoy visiting the small gazebo this morning, Maggie," Isabella said over her shoulder as Leslie gently, but insistently, tugged at her elbow. "It's really quite remarkable there, in the early hours. I always loved going there alone." She looked directly at Leslie after she made the comment. The companion was focused on getting her to the elevator and didn't seem to pick up on the challenging tone, but it wasn't lost on Maggie.

As soon as she heard the lift squealing its way up to the second floor, Maggie searched out the maid, Annette. Though she'd been with Isabella for quite a number of years, Isabella still referred to her as "the new girl," but she knew the grounds better than the gardeners.

Annette drew a quick map of the more remote garden area, where she remembered the Gazebo was built. She warned Maggie, her last visit in the gardens was two years ago.

"Can't do much of the long walking Miss, due to my arthritis. But my recollection is fairly clear of where the summer house was placed for the Mistress, when we were both young and spry," she said laughing.

Armed with the scrawled directions marking statuary for guideposts, Maggie returned to the Solarium, leaving by the garden door. If her instincts were right, there was something Isabella wanted her to find or see at the gazebo, something she wouldn't name in front of her companion.

Maggie hadn't really visited the more remote parts of the Butler Plantation since she was a child. Even garden soirees were confined to the vast terraced patio Isabella had created for such occasions. She continued to reminisce as she walked further into the depth of the gardens, how she and Collin had played hide-and-go-seek here. Looking around, she realized it was more tame back then. Most of the grassy areas were overrun by wiregrass now and the once pristine paths were overhung by cypress and bottomland hardwoods, heavy with stringy mosses. This put many of the trails she was walking into deep shadows, cutting off any sunlight from filtering through.

In the early days of this plantation one of Isabella's ancestors decided to pepper the landscape with statues and fountains. She had already passed the fountain depicting garden nymphs frolicking in the long, dried-up water and various Greek-styled statues of girls carrying urns or lounging on long stone benches, as if waiting for some lover.

The statuary and empty fountains were all covered with green moss and creeping vines, the female forms appearing to be consumed by the tenacious wildness of the invading swamp life.

Coming to a fork in the path, Maggie stopped to orient herself, looking back at the grand mansion. Its top floors appeared to float over the surrounding trees and tall plant stalks, topped with delicate white flowers. She took the left path, remembering they always kept the big house on their left when she was adventuring with Collin as children.

A soft rustling came from the heavy undergrowth near the woods. She paused, alert. This path took her near the swamps. It curved out in a slight bell shape, before heading back toward the gardens. Alligators were very fast on land and known to lie in wait for any unwary prey, looking like logs among the tall grasses. A white-tailed deer stirred from its hiding place and scurried back into thicker cover. She let our her breath. *Lord! I'm getting so jumpy*, she thought as she resumed walking.

She reached the clearing Annette described to her. What the maid failed to mention, Maggie realized, was the small guest house. Set off to the side of the over-grown path, the house was surround by Magnolia trees and wildflowers in all the lush colors of late summer. Maggie breathed in deeply, capturing the fragrance of delicate blooms.

Studying this placid scene, she wondered who was living in this tidy corner of the vast estate. Then she recalled the artist, Grayson Gerrard, was occupying the Guest House. Maggie had all but forgotten the charming Grayson, in the turmoil of the past few days. With the discovery of the attacks on Isabella and herself, and her much rekindled love for Collin, Grayson had been relegated to a passing thought that she was quick to suppress.

She quickly moved on, believing the gazebo was only a few minutes away.

She looked down to check directions. When she raised her head, the tall figure of Grayson Gerrard stood a few feet away, directly in her path.

Chapter 20

"Maggie, I hope I didn't startle you. I was painting in my studio, nearer the windows, when I saw you coming down the pathway."

Grayson Gerrard looked down from his six foot plus height into Maggie's wide eyes. She covered her initial reaction to his sudden appearance with a quick smile, but he'd already registered the flare of fear that showed in the depth of her lovely, blue-violet eyes.

"No, Grayson, I'm fine, just relieved you aren't a gator out for his breakfast."

Grayson smiled at her obvious effort to sound nonchalant.

Maggie wanted to get away from this man. His sudden appearance seemed to trigger her earlier powerful attraction to him. Her legs actually began to feel weak, the longer she stood near to him.

"I won't interrupt your work, Grayson. Just out for a quick turn around the gardens."

"I'm in need of a break from my labors at my easel, Maggie. Would you mind if I joined your amble? I can protect you from any predator," he said, laughing easily.

She had no way of gracefully saying "no" and a strong urge to have him near to her made her not want to. Her feelings were confusing and instead of answering, she began to move down the path.

Grayson obviously took her silence as agreement. He moved smoothly, walking so closely to her, she could smell the musky after-shave he used sparingly. This thought jarred Maggie, when she realized she was becoming aroused by the artist's very nearness. She could feel him watching her with side-long glances.

They picked their way down the increasingly obscured path, littered with tree debris and over the occasional exposed flagstones, spongy with moist, dark moss.

Maggie heard the familiar, rising twitter of the northern parula's mating song and felt something primal, stirring inside her. She tried desperately to hide her rising emotions, relieved when the gazebo loomed ahead. The green and brown structure appeared to have sprung up from the ground, a part of the wild growth surrounding it.

"Here's your destination, I believe, Maggie. Let's sit for a bit, before finishing our walk."

Again, Maggie allowed him to stay with her, guiding her actions. Silently she wondered why. As she walked up the steps, a vague thought occurred to her. *How did he know where I was going?* she wondered. Then, the gazebo claimed her attention.

The gazebo was an artful blend of wood and stone, curved, marble benches were set along the three sides. Maggie noticed how thick vines had been intertwined with the lattice woodwork surrounding the base of the gazebo.

The roof was an intricate weaving-together of natural material from the nearby swamps, including bottomland hardwoods, which gave it a feeling of permanency, reflecting the timeless nature of the bayou.

"It's lovely here," Maggie said dreamily.

The sun was hidden by the cone shaped roof, making the interior of the gazebo very cool, emphasizing the moisture clinging to the thick vegetation around them.

Maggie moved toward the furthest bench and sat down, turning her body slightly to take in the lush surroundings. Canvas pillows covered the length of each bench, reminding Maggie of the rolled sails on her father's favorite sailboat, when he stored them away for the season. They were rough in texture, but preferable to the cold stone of the benches.

Without asking, Grayson joined her, sitting close enough to smell the delicate lilac fragrance he knew she favored. He was acutely aware of the way her skin smelled without that hint of perfume too. It had a richness, an earthiness, as sultry as the bayou that claimed her as one of its children.

"Do you truly find it lovely here, in spite of the dangers that lurk in the bayous, Maggie? It seems to me death waits beneath the dark surface of the swamp waters. But yet, you don't seem to fear its presence."

"I was born and raised in bayou country. I understand how her heart beats better than I do my own."

"I have a deep respect for this rare environment but am still learning its riddles. I must tell you a little secret, Maggie."

He leaned closer to her face and Maggie was caught in the glitter of his dark eyes. She couldn't move or speak, immobilized under Grayson's gaze.

The spell broke when something rustled through a thin patch of wooded area behind the summer house. Maggie's head snapped around to that direction, expecting to see a deer. Instead, staring back at her through the scattered vegetation was the sleek, muscular body of a panther.

Maggie knew there had been reported sightings of this creature, but the only wild cat indigenous to this area was the bobcat. All those accounts of this elusive cat, sleek and powerful, it's muscles rippling under its inky fur, were generally attributed to drinking buddies having one too many beers while hunting gators in the shadowy swamps.

Maggie froze, feeling the panther's golden eyes fasten on her like a trap. She barely breathed as the creature passed slowly out of the gloom of the woods. It moved gracefully, the muscles of its long body fluid with power as it padded silently toward the shelter. Its gaze never left Maggie's own.

Maggie's heart pounded in her chest. She imagined the beast heard every beat, savoring the blood feast to come. When the big cat stepped into the clearing, the sun ignited its black pelt until it looked like molten obsidian.

There was a movement at Maggie's elbow, ever so slight, almost a breath. Then, a sudden explosion of wind and Maggie jumped to her feet, the trance broken.

She watched the panther be caught up in a whirlwind, becoming a dark blur in the vortex, spinning around with the ferocity of a cyclone.

There were high pitched growls and screams of pain, just before the cat catapulted through the sparse trees. The force of the squall hurled the smooth body of the big animal in the direction of the muddy banks at the swamp's edge. From there, it could be heard yowling, angry, making its escape deeper into the wilds of the swamp.

Maggie was gripping a wooden rail, her mouth slighted open, panting with the effort to control her terror.

"What happened to it?" she asked, but the question was only a reaction to what she had just witnessed.

"Maggie, it's alright," a soothing voice penetrated the dull haze of after-shock in her mind.

Maggie spun around at the sound of Grayson's voice.

"I saw...you must have seen it too! It was pulled into some kind of fantastic wind! I know what I saw!"

"Maggie, you're safe now. I will not allow any harm to come to you. You must trust me."

Grayson put a hand under Maggie's chin, gently bringing her face toward him. She wanted to pull away. Something nagged at her, warning her to run from this place, but she felt immobilized under his dark eyes.

Fixed by his mesmerizing gaze, she felt his strong arm lifting her from her feet. Her mind began to calm as Grayson laid her on the rough cushions.

He knelt down beside her, his hand drifting down her blouse. When the cool air touched her skin, she realized he had opened the buttons and pushed the light material aside. His hands moved to the thin belt at her waist. The whisper of the zipper on her linen pants brought a sudden rush of heat shooting down from her stomach to her groin.

She gave a quick intake of breath as a thrill coursed through her in anticipation. Her eyes felt heavy with sleep and drifted shut. Grayson leaned close to her ear, ruffling her hair with his warm breath. "Maggie, I smell the need in you. I feel the tremors of your passion under my hand. My own need to have you, grows with each turn of the earth beneath my feet."

Maggie's eyes fluttered open, looking into the impossibly handsome face of Grayson Gerrard, inches from where she lay.

His mouth was sensuous, the full lips slightly parted. Before she could gather her thoughts to speak, his mouth was devouring hers in a deep kiss. He pulled her into a sitting position, moving his hand over the flat of her stomach.

She groaned out loud, when his fingers searched deeper into her silk panties.

Maggie threw her head back, abandoning herself to his arousing touch.

Grayson had been watching for this moment and a smile played at the corners of his mouth, now distended by two long, ivory fangs.

He lunged forward, never breaking contact with the silky wetness his fingers stroked and inflamed. He pierced the tender flesh at her throat, the sound of his sucking caused Maggie to moan with pleasure.

Grayson's steely will-power stopped him before he drank too deeply of this precious fountain. The wounds began to close up almost immediately. He laid Maggie back down on the canvas cushions, re-buttoning her blouse and fastening her slacks and belt. His hands trembled at these tasks, as he fought the urge to ravish her until she screamed for release from the desire that now possessed them both.

He had been careful to make his bite low down her slender neck, where the high collar of her blouse covered it easily. This wouldn't be like the first bite, where he indulged his cravings for only a few seconds. This was a mixing of his fluids with her own, bringing her closer to his plan of total submission to his will.

Maggie would fall more and more under his sway. Though he knew this was her destiny, he also knew he was experiencing something he never thought possible again since his maker claimed his humanity.

Grayson Gerrard, a five hundred-year old vampire, had fallen in love with Maggie Newsome. But even as he looked upon her with longing, he knew there was another who had staked a claim on his beauty and passion. Another who would own him as he would own Maggie.

Chapter 21

The rougher roads fronting the bayou canals forced Collin to reduce his speed. He passed several shanties, stopping at the ones closest to the swamp. He asked the locals where the woman named Mari lived, adding it was urgent he find her. This comment was generally met with suspicious, or empty looks, but not much help. One man mutely pointed further down the road.

Like most "swamp rats" as the upper classes referred to them, the folks turning toward the sound of his engine made their livelihoods off the bayou, taking gator skins and nutria pelts from the abundant, large rodents that lived in the swamp lands alongside them.

That's probably how these folks came to be called by the derogatory name, Collin thought, as he went in the direction indicted by the only moderately helpful resident.

He steered the large automobile over increasingly bumpy roads until they were no more than dirt paths. He was about to give up his search when a small cottage popped out of the over-hanging Cyprus trees, lengthy tendrils of wiry gray moss stroking the low roof with each breeze.

It had been a long morning and Collin wanted to give up the search, but he recalled the letter in his pocket and the urgency in Isabella's voice.

"This has to be it!" he said to himself, willing it so.

He turned off his engine and sat there a second, listening to the ticking of the cooling engine. Watching the front door of the shack, Collin nearly jumped out of his skin when suddenly a stooped woman was standing in the doorway, beckoning him inside.

Collin didn't move for a second until she turned and went back inside, leaving the door ajar, obviously for him to follow.

Sliding across the fine leather seat, he took a deep breath, mumbling to himself, "Here we go."

Stepping into the shack, Collin was struck by the neatness of the place. Evidently this Mari was not as disheveled as her cottage would indicate from the outside.

There were rows of herbs and wild plants hanging from beams of roofing, drying out he supposed. Small vials of liquids, yellows, reds and very dark browns, were carefully lined up, obviously, according to usage, with small signs in front of each row.

Cough, Back Pain, Teething, Bone Pain and other signs where lettering was long faded from time and handling.

After watching him closely for a few seconds, the bent old woman took a seat in a rocker.

Collin noticed the cane seat and back were well-worn with use, but as insubstantial as she appeared in her thin black dress, he knew it would hold.

Her skinny arms pushed against the elbow length sleeves, like a scarecrow that has lost its stuffing. As diminutive as she was, she had a powerful presence about her that belied any sign of weakness.

The dark eyes peering up at him, were set in a face that looked as if it had been submerged underwater for hours. Colorless and puckered as her face was, her eyes were flashing like beads of oil on parchment.

"My name is Collin Fitzhugh. I'm a friend of Isabella Butler. She sent me here to find Mari…"

"Yes, yes! Just give it here to me, young man."

She held out a claw-like hand, thick, blue veins and dark spots covering the aged skin. Collin didn't think he'd ever met anyone more ancient looking.

"You are the Cajun woman known as Mari, then?"

"What manner of question is that, you fool? Look around yourself, this is a Witch's hut wouldn't you think? And I live in it, so make your judgements!"

Mari had a short fuse and Collin had obviously lit it the moment she laid eyes on him.

He handed her the brief note, which Mari ripped out of its envelope, placing that carefully on the table next to her. It was written on a peachy-colored stationary, the letter "B" embossed at the top in fancy calligraphy.

As Mari scanned the note, Collin looked around himself and it dawned on him what she had called herself. He cleared his throat to get her attention and asked, "Did I hear you correctly, Mari? Did you just claim to be a…"

"A Voodoo Witch? Of course I am and that's exactly why my dear old friend has summoned me to her side. Help me get my things gathered and we'll be off."

"Things?"

Twenty minutes later, Collin loaded the old crone and a stuffed carpet bag into his auto after she had him snatch up several of the dried herbs and an array of bottles and vials from appointed places around the shack. Collin kept waiting for her to bring out the bat eyes, but gratefully her stock-in-trade was mainly vegetation of one sort or another.

It would take him at least forty minutes to get back to Isabella's. Collin grew more and more agitated as the bad roads slowed him down to a crawl.

"Settle yourself, young man. You're sending out all those dark thoughts and I feel battered already by this beast of yours."

"What beast?"

Collin glanced over to see his passenger clinging like a barnacle to the car door handgrip. She looked too paralyzed to answer.

Once he made it back onto smoother roadway, Collin decided he wanted some answers before they reached the Butler Plantation. For one thing, he wanted to know why Isabella felt herself in need of a practicing Voodoo Witch!

The subject of his curiosity sat like a Greek stoic on a mountaintop. That was all well and good, but Collin was determined to break through her wall of silence and get some answers.

"Mari," he said firmly so he'd have her undivided attention. "Before we get to Isabella's, I need to explain a few things of a rather strange nature. There is some kind of wild animal, perhaps a snake, that's already bitten Isabella twice and my fiancé as well." He shot her a quick look to find her beady black eyes riveted to his face.

"I have seen this creature you speak of young man and it is no simple snake or four footed animal. It is a man who has been in our Parrish before, over two-hundred years ago. He has returned to feast upon the new crop of innocents spread out before his hungry eyes like a feast."

This was the most Collin heard the old woman say since finding her. He was still trying to digest the meaning when she continued in a surprisingly strong voice, "You've heard of the 'man who knows everything and who never dies?' The French philosopher, Voltaire, so named him. His infamy began in France in the late 1700s, when the Count St. Germain worked his charms upon the courts of Europe. He was a master of several musical instruments, could speak many languages fluently, was an extraordinary artist, and held audiences mesmerized when he spoke on any topic. His wealth was unmeasurable."

Collin jerked his eyes back to the road with effort. Was the old woman suffering from dementia?

"But his biggest talent was the skill of never aging," she continued as if it were just an ordinary fact. "No one ever knew what his real age was, though he appeared to be forty in his self-portraits. It seems self was his favorite subject! It was reported that though he dined with kings and other royalty at their fine tables, no one ever saw him take more than sips of wine. He covered his lack of appetite by entertaining the other guests with fascinating conversation on any topic."

Collin was himself fascinated by her account of this historic figure but wasn't clear on the point Mari was trying to make.

"Mari, what does this Count St. Germain character have to do with these strange bites?"

She looked like she was in another place when he shot a quick glance at her but seemed to stir herself to answer. "Many, many years ago, a man named Jacques St. Germain, fitting the description of the Count right down to his great wealth, apparent age and mysterious background, became the highlight of every social event and table in New Orleans. He threw lavish parties that drew much of the New Orleans elite. He enthralled his guests with his broad talents and knowledge, but it was noted time and again that this man never ate from his sumptuous table, only sipped his wine as others feasted."

Collin didn't see anything overly odd about that. Perhaps the man was on some strange diet. *Where there as many diets then as there were now?* he wondered.

"On one such occasion, after a fancy dinner hosted by St. Germain, he convinced one of the beautiful women, full of wine and rich food, to stay after the others left. She reported to the police later that after she'd accepted another glass of wine, he grabbed her roughly. She described how she pulled away, running onto the balcony. When he caught her there, he tried to bite her neck, and backed her to the railing. She fell to the ground in her struggle to escape his attack. The police were called by neighbors who found her semi-conscious, her clothing ripped and bloodied. When they took her statement from her hospital bed, the police returned to the attacker's apartments, only to find he had vanished.

"Of course," Collin muttered.

"In the course of their search for St. Germain, they found his kitchen had no food in evidence, only deeply red wines. It was reported that one officer poured some into a glass and sipped it, spitting it out immediately. It was studied and found to be a mixture of wine and human blood."

Collin drove on in the silence that pervaded the car, only the noise of the roadway keeping him in the present moment.

She didn't offer any other information until they were rounding the curve of the driveway and parked under the portico in front of Isabella's mansion. "There will be many questions running through your head young man but know this: Isabella was right to call me to fight this demon and fight him I will."

Chapter 22

Maggie stretched out on the long stone bench in the gazebo. She dreamt about black cats and hands on her body, knowing fingers stimulating her to intimate pleasures. Her hand drifted down to the crotch of her linen trousers. Finding them damp and her body tense, Maggie pressed her hand down on the sensitive area, wanting to find relief, even in this dream state. She began squirming.

"Maggie! Wake up, darling. Maggie, you're having a dream."

Her eyes flew open at the sound of a male voice.

Kneeling beside her, Collin had taken her hand off the throbbing spot against her will.

She shot him an angry look, jerking her hand out of his grip.

"I don't appreciate your spying on me, Collin," she hissed into his startled face.

"I'm sorry, love," he said sheepishly, a little embarrassed at her obvious sexual arousal.

"I didn't mean to frighten you, but you've been gone from the main house for well over two hours. Isabella told me you were walking in the gardens, so I left her with her friend, Mari, to find you before it got dark."

His even tone worked to bring Maggie back to her surroundings.

"I'm at the gazebo? But I don't really remember getting here. And why was I lying down?"

"Maggie, don't upset yourself, darling. I think you probably felt lightheaded from lack of food. You've had nothing since this morning's cup of coffee and it's past three already."

"Past three! My God, Collin! How long did Isabella say I was gone? I can't think clearly," she said, her hand rubbing at her temples.

Collin heard the edge of panic sharpen Maggie's voice. He helped her to her feet and when doing so, noticed her blouse was buttoned incorrectly. He was immediately on alert and began scanning the area around the isolated summer house.

"Maggie, was there anyone with you on your walk? Or did you see someone else on the pathways?"

She let Collin hold her hand to help her down the steps, but now, jerked hers out of his grip.

"Are you accusing me of secretly meeting with someone? This is the kind of mistrust that poisons a relationship, Collin."

"Maggie, you've misunderstood my meaning. I wondered if perhaps someone saw you coming to this god-forsaken spot alone."

His reply seemed to mollify her for the moment and she mumbled a terse apology.

Colin gently took her hand again, but they only moved a few feet down the path, when Maggie stopped short.

"Wait! There was something Isabella wanted me to look for out here. That's why I came. I don't know what it was, but it seemed important, and she wouldn't name it in front of Leslie."

"Do you think Leslie followed you?"

"No, but...there was someone...I just can't recall who. Maybe I'll remember as we walk back. Let me look around the gazebo first."

"What do you think Isabella wanted you to see?" Collin asked following her back up the steps.

"Collin, look!" Maggie was pointing toward the shelter's ceiling.

The roof was fashioned using tightly placed hardwood boards, thick vines twisted around them. The construct appeared almost primitive, though it lent itself to the wildness of the setting.

Collin looked up and saw an inscription carved into the thick, woody vine at the peak of the roof.

St. Germain Walks among you still

He read it twice before speaking. This was the same name the old woman had mumbled when he delivered Isabella's message. St. Germain, the Count of the vampire legends she talked about in the car.

"What do you supposed this means, Collin?"

"I think this is why Isabella had me fetch the old Voodoo Witch, Mari. There may be something going on here that is beyond our power to deal with."

Maggie looked into his troubled face, feeling like the shadows were beginning to close in around them. She moved closer, placing her hands on his chest. She spoke in a near whisper, fearful they were being watched, like in her dream.

"Collin, I feel like something evil has touched me, and I know it's effecting our relationship. Please believe me darling, I've never stopped loving you. Whatever crazy thing I say, or do, please, don't leave me. Promise me you won't stop loving me."

She sounded desperate for his reassurance and he was desperate to show her how much he cared.

Collin pulled Maggie into a tight embrace, murmuring words of endearment over and over as she melted into his arms.

There was no doubt he felt the change in Maggie's behavior toward him for several weeks, since that damnable dinner at his house when they argued. He also remembered how the dashing Grayson Gerrard had taken her side, interjecting himself into her life as smoothly as a slithering cottonmouth.

Is Gerrard the cause of her discontent with me?

Collin gently disengaged from Maggie's tight arms saying, "Let's get back to the house, darling. Isabella will be worried sick if I don't bring you back soon. And then, I'm taking you out for something to eat young lady!"

Maggie nodded, smiling weakly, but before they left the gazebo she turned and looked back at the carefully inscribed message.

"This is a warning," she said almost to herself.

She gripped Collin's hand tighter as they left the gazebo to the shadows that had begun to gather like hungry, dark creatures from the swamps.

122

Chapter 23

Isabella was not in the solarium but had taken to her bed according to Annette. The maid had a deeply worried look on her face. "I tell you young people, there's something not right around this place." She was speaking in hushed tones, looking around herself as they walked back to the kitchen for the lunch she'd been holding. Isabella had told her to be certain they both ate when they arrived back from the summer house. "Miss Isabella has been taken low these last months. In fact, ever since that Leslie Porter Booth woman arrived here, I've seen a change settle in on her."

Collin and Maggie sat at the heavy oak table in the kitchen, listening intently to the maid while she pulled various dishes from the oven and refrigerator. More than two people could eat, but the assembling of their lunch seemed to calm the woman.

"Annette," Collin said "can you tell us what you think is happening at Butler Plantation? You know, Isabella is family to Maggie and me and we're very concerned with her declining health. Any odd happenings that come to mind?"

"Well, for starters, I don't think that companion of hers is doing her much good! She practically keeps the poor woman locked up in her rooms. Why, Miss Isabella hasn't been out for a good walk in her gardens in nearly two months. And you both know how she loves to motor about in that fancy automobile she bought last year," she said with a quick grin.

"It's very rare nowadays. She's either in that sunroom or lying abed like an invalid."

Maggie hadn't said anything up to that point, but something the troubled woman said, triggered a comment. "Isabella was supposed to drive into Paxton with me this week to make arrangements for that art exhibit she's hosting. You remember Collin, she wants to raise funds for a new clinic to be built closer to the swamp town outside of Paxton."

Collin immediately felt on guard when Maggie mentioned the artist. He wasn't sure why. Grayson Gerrard wasn't the first man to find his beautiful fiancé desirable.

Thinking of Gerrard reminded him of the first time Maggie and he met the extremely handsome, erudite mystery man.

The night I made a fool of myself, Collin thought while cutting into some cold lamb. "Darling, let's go upstairs and check in on Isabella," he blurted out, trying to focus on something other than the inscrutable, Grayson Gerrard.

Thanking Annette for their half-eaten lunch, they returned to the foyer and were half-way up the winding staircase when they heard a scream, followed by a loud, crashing sound.

Collin took the stairs two at a time, with Maggie close behind. They ran straight back to Isabella's bedroom suite. Collin turned the glass doorknob.

"It's locked!"

Maggie used the flat of her hand, banging on the door, yelling out for Isabella, then for Leslie.

Finally, Collin moved in front of her saying, "Stand out of the way, sweetheart!"

He took a few steps backward and slammed his shoulder into the hardwood panel. It moaned under the assault and he repeated the effort twice more, before the door sprang open, its lock ripped aside and dangling from the frame.

The pair rushed in, looking around at a chaotic scene, but despite it being locked, Isabella was not in the room.

The swag canopy on the four-poster bed was in shreds. The comforter trailed off one side, onto the floor. They saw the large walnut armoire lying face-down on the thick Persian rug, where small, dark spots were splashed across the deep pile and onto the wall.

"My God, Collin! What's happened here? Where's Isabella?"

Collin didn't speak but went around the room trying to find a clue to answer that question. In their initial shock, both failed to see the door to the small balcony off of Isabella's bedroom was open to the early evening.

The light breeze of earlier in the day had turned cooler, bringing the damp-chill of the bayou into the room with it.

"Someone's taken Isabella, Maggie. They must have come in through the balcony, but I don't know how they got up there. There must have been a struggle from the looks of the room and the over-turned dresser."

He was studying the scene more thoroughly, trying to understand the situation. He knew the dresser was very heavy and it would have taken a lot of strength to push it over.

It had to be a kidnapping. He believed the dark spots on the carpeting were blood. But whose? And where was the companion, Leslie?

"We have to phone the police, Maggie. I believe someone has taken Isabella, perhaps for ransom."

"But, Collin, who would they ask for the money? She has no heirs. I don't know anything about her will, or who would benefit from her death."

She walked in a daze onto the balcony, her hand gripping the decorative wrought-iron banister surrounding it. She looked down when her hand touched a piece of black cloth. It was snagged on a thick rope of ivy, climbing up the side of the house and fastened firmly onto the iron railing. The cloth was clearly a piece of the dressing gown she saw Isabella wearing earlier.

"Collin, they must have climbed up the side of the house!" she called back excitedly.

Collin joined her on the balcony, looking down at the piece of fabric and the coarse ropes of ivy clinging to the side of the wooden structure. The tenacious plant had not only climbed up the wooden sides but had woven its many tendrils through the intricate ironwork around the structure.

The vines had been growing for as long as they could remember, enveloping many of the sides of the Butler mansion. Maggie always thought the dark green leaves were lovely as they coiled around the white house like a living part of it.

Realizing this was the likely method of entrance for the person taking Isabella, she saw it now, as a sinister presence.

Collin stepped back into the room, meaning to return to the foyer and the phone, when Maggie shouted out to him.

"The blood! The blood spots are gone."

Collin slowly scanned the carpeting. All evidence of any bloodshed had vanished.

"Maggie, we have to find Mari and see if she knows what's going on."

"You won't have to wait long for your answers young man."

Mari's frail, bent figure, stood in the doorway. Collin noticed her steel-gray hair was undone from its tight bun and floated around her small head like a rain cloud.

She was holding something in a gnarled hand. It looked suspiciously like a bundle of bones of varying lengths. Collin hoped they weren't human.

"We don't have any time to waste here. This house has given over all the secrets it owns. Our friend has been taken to the lair of the beast."

"The lair of…" Maggie started to repeat the old woman's comment in a faraway voice.

"You two young people, need to stop your nattering and understand! Dark forces are at work here, at Butler Plantation. You say Isabella had two bites?"

Collin confirmed this and noticed Maggie's hand move automatically to cover her neck. The movement wasn't lost on the Voodoo Witch.

"Drop your hand, girl!" she said in a voice that discouraged argument.

Maggie looked over at Collin, her eyes pleading silently with him. For some reason, Maggie didn't want her own bite to be seen by the old woman.

"Go ahead, darling. She can't help us, unless she has all the facts."

Maggie reluctantly lowered her hand and began unbuttoning the neck of her blouse. She noticed they were all off by one buttonhole and gave Collin a quick, inquiring look.

Mari looked as if she had trouble walking when she came closer to Maggie. Her gait was stiff, her stooped frame making her look like a beetle scurrying across the floor.

She had Maggie sit on the edge of the bed so she could examine her closely. "There are two bites here, not one, as you two likely believed."

Collin rushed over to Maggie's side, bending down to see for himself, a new bite was several inches below the first, easily concealing it from view. It looked like the first when it was newly found, deep, but not deadly, puckered around the bite itself and red with trauma.

"Maggie, when did this happen to you?" Collin asked softly, not wanting to alarm her with his growing fears.

Before she could answer, Mari blurted out, "Doesn't matter! What matters is what we do next. Close your top, dear, we need to search for the lair before the beast has your blood again."

"Her blood, you say?" Collin was as incredulous at hearing Mari's words, as he was with her supposed powers of Voodoo Magic. But there was something deeply frightening swirling around them and she seemed to be their only hope to survive it.

The old woman spoke firmly, while Maggie put her blouse in order. "It will take seven, only seven bites, to turn you from victim into vampire, just like the one who would be your Maker, Jacques St. Germain. We need to hunt him down and quickly, because our dear friend Isabella is in his clutches and will soon be lost to us forever."

Maggie and Collin went pale with fear for Isabella and for themselves. Their safe, predictable world, suddenly ceased to exist, replaced with monsters who drained blood and lived forever. A self-proclaimed Voodoo Witch led them with no means of defense except to trust in her.

Collin gripped Maggie's hand tightly as they followed Mari to the elevator and then through the foyer to the solarium. As Collin went to open the door to the gardens, Annette came out of the side parlor, seeing them as they passed.

"Are you staying for dinner Mr. Collin and Miss Maggie?"

When Collin stepped back, the maid saw the petite Mari, near the opened door.

"Oh, I didn't realize Mrs. Butler had other company."

"And I'm far from company. I've known your mistress since birth practically! Let's go, you two. No time to dawdle here, yammering about dinner plans!"

Annette gave a snort at this dismissive treatment by the strange looking woman.

"Humph! The old Witch!" she muttered to herself as she marched back to the fragrant smelling confines of the kitchen.

Chapter 24

Maggie allowed herself to be guided by Collin as they followed Mari deeper into the gardens. They had grown decidedly wilder he noted, even since his walk through them earlier to find Maggie. It was as if nature was in rebellion, being stirred to spurts of wild growth by some unnatural forces.

Mari kept a quicker pace than Collin expected. He thought back to his impression of her as a black beetle. "A scarab beetle," he whispered under his breath, feeling like he'd just identified a new species of life.

When they came to the more manicured garden area, where the cottage being occupied by Grayson Gerrard stood, Mari put up a hand, signaling them to stop.

"Who's living here, on Isabella's lands?" she demanded.

Collin and Maggie moved to Mari's side. She looked intently at the small guest house. Her face was a mask of suspicion.

Maggie spoke for the first time since they left the big house. "Why, it's the famous artist, Grayson Gerrard. Isabella planned a big gala to show his work in a few months."

Mari stared at the tidy house, as if it would sprout feet and walk away.

"Hmm. I fear the viper has been suckled at her bosom. We need to move on. Try to keep pace you two."

Collin almost laughed at that comment, but then he reflected on the other part of it. *A viper? Suckled? This couldn't get any crazier.*

But there was a definite chill in her words and Collin felt it keenly.

The deeper they walked into the over-grown garden areas, the closer to the surrounding bayou they came. The air thickened with each step, until Collin thought he could taste the mud-bottom land in his mouth.

That's when he realized he'd been panting slightly, because they'd steadily quickened their pace. He and Maggie were nearly running to keep up with the diminutive woman shambling ahead of them.

Her wiry hair seems electrified, perhaps moving her faster, like a streetcar on its tracks. Collin rambled aimlessly in his head, trying to distract himself from his growing fears.

Mari charged forward down the paths, seemingly oblivious to their presence. From behind, Collin thought her back appeared even more stooped, but somehow, this decrepit woman was setting a faster pace for all of them.

Almost as if she could read his thoughts, Mari slowed long enough to smile at Collin's surprised face. Maggie had been struggling to keep up. She didn't want to complain about her own discomforts, since their prime concern was locating Isabella and insuring her safety. But finally, she tugged on Collin's arm.

"Collin, those bites feel like a branding iron made them."

"Mari, wait!" Collin shouted as he undid Maggie's top buttons again.

They were seeping a thin line of watery blood. Mari hurried back to the couple and shoving herself in front of the worried looking Collin, she examined the wounds.

"Ah…this is good."

"Good! What the hell do you mean? My fiancé is bleeding and the bites look inflamed with infection. What's "good" about that?"

Collin was livid with Mari's indifference to Maggie's condition.

"You are a young fool, Fitzhugh! This means we are getting closer to the lair of the beast, where we'll find Isabella. We must bring her back to the house where I can safeguard her and this young girl, else, they are both doomed!"

Maggie said, "She's right, Collin. There will be time later to see to me. We have to get to Isabella."

She turned to the wizened face of the woman saying, "I've been wondering if Isabella is with her companion, Leslie. Perhaps they are both captured."

Mari appeared to consider that. Then she blurted out, "No time for speculation. Soon, we'll know all."

They walked three more minutes and came to the gazebo. Collin saw Maggie look away and realized she was likely embarrassed remembering the way he found her, in a state of sensual arousal. Collin shared the same memory and turned slightly, so she couldn't see his own sudden discomfort.

The old woman broke the silence between them. "The beast has made his place deep in the bayou, among the serpents and green monster lizards. I can feel him and, now, he can feel me."

Collin became immediately alarmed asking, "What do you mean, he can feel you? Does he know we're here, searching for him?"

"Oh, he knows and he feels my power growing as we near him. See?"

With a gesture of a crooked finger, a wind gust began stirring the grasses and low bushes. It grew stronger, moving the dangling moss tendrils like ribbons on a kite.

The wind forced Maggie and Collin to shut their eyes against blowing grit. When they opened them, the old lady was clutching her carpet bag to her bony chest.

"Isabella will need a few things from here when we find her."

Collin knew the bag was back at the big house, tucked into the boot of his auto. By then, he and Maggie were becoming numb to the oddities churning around them. This show of Voodoo magic was no more unexpected than finding the inscription carved into the gazebo.

Maggie noticed more than the discomfort from the bite marks on her neck as they walked on. The touch of Collin's hand began to feel hot and uncomfortable. She jerked her hand away from him, mumbling something about being pulled along like a donkey.

Collin looked taken aback at this odd outburst, but they both kept moving.

After a few minutes of silence between them, he realized they had fallen far behind Mari. He hesitated to yell, instead hoping she'd notice they were no longer in sight.

Maggie walked slower and slower until she finally stopped all together and started to turn around.

"Maggie, what are you doing? We're losing ground and it's getting close to sunset. We need to stay together, darling."

"I'm not going any further, Collin. You can go chasing after the witch's beast. I'm going back home."

Her voice had a flat, mechanical sound to it, as if it was coming from a Victrola player.

She turned her back on him and began moving away, in the direction they had just come. "I'll have Annette send for Isabella's driver and he can take me home," she called over her shoulder in that same dead voice.

She walked faster and covered a lot of ground before Collin finally shook off his bewilderment and ran after her, grabbing her arm and spinning her around. "What's going on with you?" he asked. "We need to find Isabella. She's been taken, Maggie. Don't you understand?"

"I really am too tired to do this right now, Collin," she said, looking blankly into the distance.

Collin studied her face. Her eyes were unfocused and staring. He was about to speak when Mari's voice cut through the air. "What's happened?" she demanded harshly.

She was right behind Collin, nearly stopping his heart with her sudden appearance. He tried to explain that Maggie was having difficulties.

"No time for your nonsense girl! Those bites are letting him work his influence on you now, is what's happening. Here, put this under your tongue and swallow the juices."

Grabbing Maggie's hand, she placed a dark yellow berry in it, but Maggie tossed it away.

"Leave me alone! I'm not interested in your Voodoo. Find Isabella if you must, but I'm not staying." She said this over her shoulder as she moved quickly down the pathway in the direction of the house.

"He's working his charms over her, so he's closer than I thought," Mari said to Collin, looking around into the gathering gloom.

"Can't you do something?" Collin asked, frustration coloring his tone. He watched as Maggie moved further into the distance.

If she was too tired to continue, she certainly recovered quickly, he thought automatically. She was no more than a flickering shadow on the pathway. When he turned back to Mari expectantly, Collin saw the anger at this turn of events flashing across her creased face.

She spoke so softly, Collin strained to hear the words. "So, now I must choose. The young woman, or the old friend. May the bayou strangle the beast in her mud! Come!" she said snatching at Collin's arm to get his attention.

They hurried to catch up with Maggie.

Knowing the gazebo was around the next curve in the long path, Collin hoped she would stop there again, believing it held some kind of attraction for her.

The witch mumbled words in a strange language. A mixture of French and something from the islands, Jamaica or Haiti, he suspected, not knowing the witch's history.

Collin thought he caught a glimpse of his fiancé's slender form in the scant moonlight. She was walking slowly up the steps.

"Maggie!"

She had her back to them, standing in the gloom of the summer house as Collin left the path to follow her.

"Maggie, darling, you're right! We need to get you back home. You aren't yourself."

As if on cue, she turned saying, "You are very correct in that observation."

Leslie Porter Booth had never looked lovelier, smiling mysteriously back at him.

Chapter 25

Mari entered the gazebo directly behind Collin and was the first to react.

Pulling something out of her carpet bag before Collin could move, she flew at Leslie's tall figure, throwing some kind of powder by the fist-full into the beautiful, startled face.

The night was fully upon them now. Collin could barely make out what was happening between the two women. He moved to intervene, thinking the old woman had taken leave of her senses, when an ear shattering scream tore through the swamp-sodden air.

The witch had vanished and Leslie was holding a handful of black cloth obviously ripped from Mari's thin dress.

"Why did she attack you?" Collin was asking, a stunned look on his face as he looked at the shredded cloth.

Leslie's face was twisted with outrage, but she recovered her cool demeanor before Collin actually registered it.

"She must have mistaken me for someone else. I thought she called me Maggie, just before she threw something into my face. Why would she want to hurt Maggie, Collin?"

"She wouldn't, unless she thought…"

"Thought what? She was babbling insanely about vampires and kidnappings. I need to get back to the house to be sure Isabella is safe."

Leslie's beautiful eyes looked frightened and she looked vulnerable to Collin.

Collin reached for her slender arm to stop her and to tell her Isabella was taken. Touching her cool, silky skin sent a thrill through his body like a current of electricity.

Without thinking, he pulled her closer. All thoughts of Maggie flew out of his mind when Leslie's ice-blue eyes stared intensely into his, in a kind of wordless intimacy.

"Leslie, I think I should walk back with you. It's…very dark along the paths now," he said trying desperately to recover some control of himself.

She stood perfectly still, her gaze never leaving his eyes. She moved closer still, standing only a few inches from his face.

Collin's eyes dropped to Leslie's full mouth. Her dark red lipstick looked rich against her pale skin. Her lips were slightly parted and while he watched, the tip of her tongue poked out and licked around her invitingly open mouth.

Before he knew why, or how, Leslie's willowy body was crushed inside his strong arms. He was devouring her mouth and tongue, his hands fondling her breasts under her light top, finding them fuller than her willowy figure would suggest.

Leslie guided his hands to all the places he searched out and helped him find the fastener on her long skirt. He drew in a sharp breath, hearing it slide over her long, shapely legs, to the floor of the gazebo.

He pushed her down onto the rumpled cloth. Freeing himself from the constraint of his own zippered trouser front, he roughly pulled her legs apart, readying himself to take her.

"No! No! You can't Collin!"

For a second, Collin thought it was Leslie, pleading for him to stop. He knew that he couldn't. But when he heard his name repeated, he realized with a shock, it was Maggie.

Collin was kneeling over the prone body of the beautiful woman, panting with his lust. There was no denying his actions, no covering up the truth of his infidelity.

"I gave you my heart!" Maggie was yelling. "I have always trusted you and your love. Now, it's all undone!"

Collin felt confused watching the tears streaming down Maggie's face in the moonlight. *Why is she crying? What have I done that is so wrong?* His thoughts felt trapped in mental quicksand and they slowly sank away from his grip on reality.

Sensing his will was nearly defeated, Leslie put her hand on his hard manhood and stroked it to a passion he couldn't deny. He turned his back on Maggie and thrust himself deeply into the very desirable woman lying open to him. He easily disregarded the sound of the sobbing woman standing witness.

Maggie ran down the steps of the gazebo. Blinded by tears, she stumbled and fell hard against the stone path. She crawled to her feet and began running, ignoring the pain in her leg. The puncture wounds on her neck throbbed terribly.

She reached the garden door to the solarium several minutes later, throwing herself into the room and onto a long couch. She gave herself over to her anguish.

Three walls of windows reflected the dying red embers left unattended in the fireplace. The air was warm, heavy with the musty scent of Isabella's favorite perfume, mixed with the scent of the diminished fire.

Maggie fought back the picture of Collin kneeling over Leslie, ready to possess her. They must be lovers, but for how long? She couldn't guess. Remembering how beautiful their own love-making was only hours before made Collin's betrayal even more painful. His duplicity felt like a knife in her heart.

She sobbed until she could no longer bring a sound to her mouth. She knew her love for Collin would be forever tainted by his brazen infidelity. "It's over," her words hit her like a cold wave and they filled her with a numbing acceptance.

She drifted into a restless sleep, exhausted from the events of the day and evening. In her dream a sleek panther entered the sunroom, as black as midnight, padding quietly toward her sleeping form.

Her eyes flew open as the beast stepped out of her dream.

She watched, unable to move a muscle. As it neared the couch, the creature began to shimmer and blur, until it resolved into the tall, handsome figure of Grayson Gerrard.

Maggie felt nothing witnessing this, not fear, not confusion, only the empty sense of abandoning oneself to an ultimate fate. Grayson held her eyes within his hypnotic gaze. She could no more turn away as they probed her depths, than she could scream for help. Her grasp on reality slipped away like a skater on ice, while she fell into a dream-like state. She could do nothing, but watch.

He knelt down, pressing his full, sensual mouth over hers, until his cold breath became her breath. Every cell in her body responded to this man. Even the light breeze against her skin thrilled her. She was fully aware he was touching her intimately, but any impulse to resist faded before the thought was fully formed.

She gave herself over to the long, hard fingers. She moaned with pleasure and fell into a near-paralyzed state of ecstasy. While she felt her body stiffen with a frozen passion, Grayson deftly opened the buttons of her blouse, letting it slide over the silk chemise beneath. He pulled down the bra to expose part of her breasts and smiled into her wide, unblinking eyes the entire time.

Long canine like fangs showed at the sides of his mouth. Small crystal drops clung to them before dripping on her exposed flesh.

"You are so beautiful, Maggie. Soon, your beauty will be mine, forever," he panted with his desires. His dark head dropped from her sight. She gave a whimper when she felt the sharp pain of those teeth penetrating the soft mound of her breast.

He drank more deeply this time than in his first bites. Maggie froze into her dream state as the pressure of his sucking increased.

There was a tapping sound upon the windowpane, directly across from the unmoving woman and the dark form hovering over her. Grayson raised his head, already knowing he'd find Leslie peering back at him. She was a vampire voyeur and had likely been watching while he enjoyed the young woman's flesh and sucked the warm blood from her body.

Annoyed at this disturbance, he looked down at Maggie. He saw two thin lines of blood slid over her silky skin and onto the cushions beneath her.

He had injected much of his own saliva into her, to mix well with her rich blood. It was only a matter of time before he would make the last bites needed to turn her. Only then, would he have eternity to sate the burning desire that gnawed at him to possess her.

He planned on destroying Leslie, his irritating protégé. She was irksome in her demands for more of his attention and more blood from their victims. He tired of her two hundred years ago but found it convenient to keep her in his thrall.

But then, he found Maggie. That changed everything.

Suddenly, the door flew open and Leslie ran to him. "Master, may I sup with you?" she asked in a little girl's voice, innocent of the malice he knew ate at her dead heart.

"This one is not for you, Leslie. I thought you would have eaten already. Didn't your charms work on Collin back there in the summer house?"

"We were interrupted by the that witch, Mari. She came back just as I was going to have my fill. The witch vanishes like a mist, but she broke my hold over him and I had to leave before he understood my purpose wasn't copulating but feeding."

Leslie gave a snort of derision at Collin's feeble lust.

Her mouth opened slightly as she watched a thin rivulet of blood, snaking its way down the side of Maggie's rising and falling breast.

She moved like a flash of lightning, her fangs a mere breathe away from the beating pulse at the side of Maggie's throat.

Grayson pulled her back by grabbing the crown of golden braids. He yanked her to her feet, bringing her face to within inches of his bared fangs.

"You would dare to disobey me?" he hissed. "You will never touch this girl! Ever! Do you understand?" he asked sharply, the threat no longer implied.

Leslie's blue eyes widened with terror that replaced the lust for blood she felt moments earlier.

Her fangs retracted, her mouth closing in a tight line of resolve.

Grayson Gerrard had hundreds of years to dominate her, taking her from the gutters of London. He transformed her into the beautiful, cool lady who he sometimes called wife, other times, mistress. But always, always, she was his and his alone.

Leslie dropped her eyes from her master's fierce gaze and onto the lovely body of his obsession. In her many centuries of knowing him, Leslie had never seen her Maker react like this to any other mortal woman. She knew Grayson was besotted with his desire for Maggie and would have her at any cost, even if it meant Leslie's own destruction at his hands. But Leslie had plans too and soon Maggie's fiancé, Collin Fitzhugh, would fall to them. Leslie knew she had to protect herself from her Maker's implied threats. She'd use Collin any way she needed, to keep Grayson.

Grayson released the fist-full of braids, letting Leslie stumble back from his reach. She tried to show she still had her own powers, telling him she had taken Isabella's blood to satisfy her hunger. "She won't remember anything, Grayson. I used the chloroform on her, before taking her into the swamp and the Friary's cellars. You know how I enjoy the chambers down there," she said smiling alluringly.

Too late, Leslie realized she'd miscalculated his reaction.

The idea of Leslie bringing Isabella into the hidden sanctuary, without his permission, enraged Grayson even more. He'd been able to occupy the ancient monastery for centuries, undetected. It was his retreat when things became too "hot" with the New Orleans constabulary, or in outlying Parishes such as Paxton.

He found the cloister after arriving in Louisiana a few hundred years ago and it was timeworn even then.

Built on a small, wild island, in the heart of the bayou, it had been used as a kind of religious prison, where errant monks and priests were sent to perform harsh, self-punishment, for grievous sins against Mother Church. The worst offenders, simply were "disappeared" from the eyes of the law and the local people hunting them.

Grayson knew these were among the greatest sinners of the times and enjoyed the reek of their pain, even hundreds of years after they were dust beneath his feet.

Leslie's assumption that she could use this hidden treasure at will was infuriating.

Grayson's hand was a blur of motion as it connected with her smug look. She felt his large handprint on her dead-white cheek and knew it was glowing red.

"Did you not think they would search for Isabella, before you took her to my retreat? It's because of your greed the Voodoo Witch will now prowl the bayous, hunting for my refuge!"

He stalked off a few feet, spinning around. Leslie's hand was covering most of the red mark on her face, but he turned in time to see her fangs drop, knowing she wanted to attack him. They were quickly retracted.

"Is the old woman drained completely or is she still among the mortal?" he snarled, ignoring the threating gesture completely.

She would never be powerful enough to defeat him and they both knew it. But her impulsive nature was undermining his subtle planning.

He resolved, she had to go!

"I left the shriveled old bag plenty of her thin blood, but now she has four bites. Not enough to turn her, but she'll be more "compliant.""

Again, Grayson saw the arrogant self-assuredness flare in Leslie's lovely blue eyes. He had to restrain himself from lashing out again. He didn't want to act on his plans to eradicate her just yet and a conflict now, was unwelcome timing.

"Leave me now. Go fetch the old woman from the Friary Prison and return her to her rooms. I need to finish here."

He tried to sound dispassionate at this reference to Maggie, but he wasn't quite able to hide his inflamed desire when he looked down on her supine body.

Leslie begged to stay just a little longer.

"I'll keep watch against the reappearance of the Voodoo Witch, master. You can enjoy yourself more fully. I'll retrieve Isabella when you're finished."

Maggie was lying in a dazed state, induced by his glamour and the injected saliva from his fangs. One arm hung off the side of the couch, making her vulnerability almost palatable.

Leslie moved off as Grayson watched Maggie's chest gently rise and fall.

She settled herself into the shadows to watch.

Chapter 26

Collin let the Voodoo Witch help him to his feet. He was still in the gazebo. He looked around, confused and wondering why he'd been on the floor. More importantly, why were his trousers open?

He felt like he'd just experienced a young boy's sexual night dream, complete with the pleasantly dull throb of released desire.

His head was beginning to clear. In a flash of unforgiving memory, he saw the beautiful Leslie, lying beneath his thrusting body. He rubbed his eyes, trying to dislodge the truth.

"Pull yourself together, boy. You've been under the influence of a powerful vampire and she's worked her glamour upon you. Not many men could resist that and you, unfortunately, are not among them!"

Collin was shocked to hear what Mari was saying about him. He'd never once been unfaithful to Maggie. She was all he ever wanted. She was the only woman he ever desired or loved.

Mari was shaking her head from side to side. As if reading his thoughts, she spoke more kindly.

"Don't be thinking you are immune to the vampire's manipulation, just because you love your dear Maggie. The she-devil has surely taken stronger men than you and twisted them like string tied to her finger. She will use your carnal knowledge of her now, as a tool to keep your will in check. We're just lucky I interrupted her biting you and making it harder for me to keep you safe."

Moving down the steps, he followed closely while Mari described her fears.

"I have seen my powders won't work to disarm the female. She must be much older than I guessed. This means her Maker will be much older still and even more powerful. I need to think on how to defeat such an enemy.

Because you have been tainted by the she devil, you must be cleansed and it won't be pleasant, boy. It will cause you great pain, but I dare not allow her power to linger upon your body, where she can reel you in like a fish."

Collin didn't question Mari's plans for him. He needed to free himself from any binds upon him.

Shaken by the memory of Maggie seeing him with Leslie, he was frantic to have her understand he wasn't in possession of his will. He wanted desperately to get to her, to explain.

Before they'd gone too far down the path, Mari stopped suddenly, her steely gray head tilted, listening.

Collin was close on her heels, watching as she raised her face and began sniffing the air. She nodded to herself, looking up at him.

"The female passed here already, but she's turned and gone toward the swamps. Why do you suppose she did that?" she asked, looking into a vast darkness beyond the gardens.

Collin knew she wasn't asking for an answer from him. He was still trying to wrap his head around the fact that he'd been untrue to Maggie, with a beautiful vampire.

Mari scurried off the path and into the jumble of brittle old flower beds and long untended shrubs. These grew wild along with of the many varieties of wild flora and vegetation encroaching from the nearby bayous.

Collin was more and more anxious to have her cleanse him before he saw his love again, but she was too engrossed with sniffing and following some unseen trail to notice his agitation. He was going to warn her about getting too near the swamps in the dark when Mari grabbed for his arm. She tugged hard, forcing him to bend down to hear her hushed voice.

"The she-devil has gone into the swamp. I'm sure the trail leads to wherever they are keeping Isabella. There's no time to be lost, boy. We must find her quickly. As weak as she is, Isabella will never live through four more bites." Without waiting for any comment from Collin, Mari moved further into the tangle of undergrowth.

The ground beneath Collin's hesitant feet was beginning to suck at his shoes. "Mari!" he said sharply. "I want to find Isabella as much as you, but I need to be free of the Vampire's imprint on me, as you pointed out. I won't be any help to you if she can bend my will to her own."

"Ah! You are not as ignorant of the dark powers as I supposed, boy. Roll your sleeves back then and open your hands, palms up. Whatever happens, do not move a muscle!"

Doing as Mari directed, Collin watched silently while she rummaged through the carpet bag, sitting on the damp ground near his legs. He saw her pull out a colorful tail feather, perhaps from an exotic parrot and what appeared to be the desiccated body of a rodent, likely a muskrat.

Taking the rodent into her claw-like hand, she came over to Collin's outstretched arms. Holding the rodent over the bare skin. Collin's eyes widened as the desiccated body began to squirm.

Without warning, it let out a high pitched squeal and began to bite at his exposed flesh, over and over, down both arms, until Collin felt faint with the pain. He willed himself into a stone pillar, until the Witch dropped the muskrat back into the carpet bag. Collin staggered slightly and went to his knees.

Moving quickly, Mari picked up the long feather and pulled it slowly down Collin's bleeding arms. The open wounds healed up before his eyes with every feathery touch.

"It is done, boy. You did well. Better than most," she added grudgingly.

"The taint that the she-devil left on you is no more. You had no bite, because I came along. She only had time to do her damage by sharing her dead fluids with you. You are cleansed of her stink!"

Collin felt a renewed energy, as if he'd had a deep, restful sleep. He got to his feet.

"I'm ready to find their lair and our friend. Lead on, Mari."

Chapter 27

Moving deeper into the verdant swamps, Collin realized he was trusting his safety in this danger-filled environment to a witch's nose, as she stopped every few feet to sniff in the sultry air.

He almost laughed out loud at the preposterous thought, but then thought back at a dead muskrat biting at his arms and a feather that healed him and stopped doubting.

The surrounding swamps were anything but quiet, as they moved deeper into them. They stayed to whatever solid ground they could, or walked along, the muddy banks rimming the swamp.

Mari took out her powders again and began throwing them in the air in small fistfuls. She told Collin any of the more dangerous animals would scurry into the underbrush or sink deeper into the swamp waters.

"Have no fear of what is natural to these swamps, boy. I will take care of them. It's what has moved into the Bayou that's to be feared. And I think we have that in our sights."

Collin had been following as closely as possible to the old woman and when she stopped nearly ran into her. He couldn't see anything besides the moss-laden cypress and ancient hardwoods, the never-ending green succulents and wild iris. He could only smell the flowers, among the earthy odors of the swamp. All of life was smothered under a mantle of green-black gloom and his vision was dulled by the heavy weight.

Straining to see what Mari was talking about, she finally grabbed his arm saying, "Island!"

Just in front of them, Collin spotted a round building jutting out of the heavy vegetation on an unexpected island. It was fashioned in a mix of stone, wood and vines, sitting atop massive tree trunks, serving as its platform. The trunks had sprouted more life after being cut down, the new growth interwoven with voracious vines that appeared to be consuming the stone and wood structure.

Mari told Collin the island was surrounded by a natural moat of quicksand, isolated from any approach, except skiff.

"How do you propose we get to it, since we don't have a boat and can't fly," he said in frustration.

"There must be a way through the muck, or it would not be standing here," she said tersely, bending down and grabbing a long limb off the ground.

Mari instructed him to do the same and began prodding the thick mud to her right.

"Keep poking until you hit something solid. There is likely some kind of bridge across and it will lay close by. So we don't need to venture out more than a foot before we'll hit upon it. "

Collin moved off, quickly finding a strong branch. He started jabbing the wet mud that enclosed the island like a shell. He and Mari moved in different directions, slowly circling the small land mass and its perfectly camouflaged structure.

Collin reflected on the unfortunate choice of clothing and shoes he was wearing for such an expedition but forgot the squishy feeling around his toes the second his limb touched something solid.

Mari joined him upon hearing his whistle. She had warned him against shouting to keep their presence undetected.

Standing beside each other, they worked from the spot Collin had found until its end. It seemed solid about three feet across. Mari used her own limb to test the ground in front of Collin's marker and found it was also hard.

"This is it, boy. Follow me closely while I lead our way across. This will be a slow progress, so don't crowd me," she warned.

Collin saw her poking her limb before each step, then she dropped something beside her foot. She kept this up until they were on the firm ground of the island.

"We should leave our sticks here, to mark our path back across," Collin said quietly when he felt he could breathe again.

"Smart boy. Plus, I'll add a little something of my own, seeing how we've barely any light left."

Reaching into the carpetbag that appeared attached to the old woman's hip, Mari pulled out some flat, yellow colored stones, flinging them onto the damp, sandy mud. Collin realized these were what the old woman was dropping along the way too.

Like Hansel and Gretel, he thought, but didn't smile. He was always frightened by that fairytale as a kid. His distracted thoughts were refocused for him as Mari gave his shoulder a tap with a boney finger.

"The she-devil isn't here and neither is her Master, so we can go in and find Isabella and be gone before they return, but we must hurry."

"Who is this Master you keep speaking of?

"No time to talk, boy. You must trust me in this. There is another, much more powerful. Now, let's find a way into this lair."

They were in almost complete darkness when Collin, standing close to her, saw Mari reach into her bag and pull out two more of the flat stones. She mumbled a few words in the odd mix of languages she'd used throughout this venture into the swamp.

Suddenly, the rocks began glowing with a subtle, golden light.

"Take this and don't lose it," Mari said briskly moving to shove one into Collin's hand.

"It won't stay lit for long, but I hope it will be long enough."

They found the vines were thick around the whole of the squat structure. They looked impervious to anything but the sharpest saw.

Mari reached into the carpetbag once more, this time retrieving a small bundle of bones, tied with a leather strip. She ran them down the stout ropes of living vine. Their immediate reaction was to shrivel-up into desiccated string.

"You must not waste any time gawking at things once we're inside. We need to move swiftly and be gone from this evil place once we find Isabella."

"You'll find no argument from me. Lead on."

It was clear to Collin why Mari had warned him not to look about, as they passed through the dark building. The air was permeated with a strong odor of mold and slime, both of which he discovered when he reached out to steady himself against a wall.

Wiping his hand down his trousers, he was more careful about using the light-stone more effectively. Mari moved further ahead and he had to hurry to catch up.

She entered a small cell-like room, barely big enough for the shreds of canvas that looked to have once been ship's sails but were now being used as a cot, hanging like gray moss from the worm-eaten, wooden frame.

Collin had no time to wonder what sort of place they were in before Mari scurried off like a small mouse, to investigate the shadowy depth. He held the glowing stone out in front of himself, trying to illuminate his next foot fall, hoping to avoid the scattered bones, of what he prayed were animals.

Suddenly the amber light fell on something that looked like a trap door, an iron ring glinted dully in the pale light of the stone. "Mari," Collin whispered as loudly as he dared.

As undistinguished as a moving shadow, the old witch was beside him, nearly stopping his heart.

In a hushed voice, he told her about the door. After a few minutes of pulling under her whispered instructions, he was able to carefully lift and then drop it onto the dirt covered floor.

There was an immediate rush of dank air, hitting them both in the face. It carried the distinctive smell of rot and corruption, but it carried one more thing. The sound of a human, moaning. Though low and infrequent, it was clear enough in the dead air around them.

Mari asked Collin for his stone and carefully leaning over the opening, shone the combined light into the cellar below.

All Collin could make out were wooden steps, more rotted than whole from what he could see.

"I'm certain this is where the beasts sleep and where our friend is being kept. Do you think you can go down and find her without my help?"

"What? Where will you be?"

"I need to make certain they can't use this place anymore. I can smell the evil oozing from the very walls that built it. Here."

Before Collin could voice any objections, the Voodoo Witch handed him both stones and vanished into the shadows. Collin stood frozen for a second, forcing himself to move only after he heard another moan from below.

The stairs were as rickety as he feared, but surprisingly, they took his weight. There were only five before he reached the dirt floor below. The iridescent light from the stones bounced off close walls for a short distance. He moved as quickly as possible, listening for another moan.

There, she's just ahead.

His thought gave him a short-lived relief when his light caught the red eyes of extremely large rats running in front of the intrusive light toward a more complete darkness.

Collin tried to repress the shiver that ran down his spine.

He looked around the dirt floor for any kind of weapon he might use if the filthy animals felt cornered and decided to attack. The only thing he found was a half-rotted whip, looking like the fabled cat-o-nine used on prisoners. It still had the long leather strips hanging from a gnawed grip, each carrying a metal barb at the end.

He snatched this up, wrapping his hand firmly around it and striking at the ground as he moved forward. The sound was enough to keep the rodents at bay, skulking in their rat-holes.

Collin heard the groan, much closer now. Holding the stones higher, he saw the opening into another cell. Rushing in, he nearly shouted with relief when his light fell across Isabella Butler.

She was strapped to a medical gurney of sorts, her legs and arms firmly secured. Her eyes were closed, but when the light hit her face, they flew open along with her mouth. She emitted a scream that made Collin's hair rise up on his neck.

"Isabella! It's Collin! You're safe. I'm getting you out of this place!"

"Collin! Oh, thank God it's you! I don't think I can live through any more of her torture. I can't…"

"Save your energy, Isabella. We'll talk when I get you out of here and back to the house. First, these restraints."

Working as fast as he could, he undid the straps, asking the frail woman to try to stand. It was quickly apparent she couldn't walk on her own. He knew she would be very light and lifted her back onto the gurney, sitting her down.

"Isabella, I'm going to wheel this contraption out of here and then I'll lift you on my back to climb the stairs."

She nodded, laying back down and holding on to the sides. Collin rolled her out and down the short tunnel. He had her wrap her arms around his neck while he hefted her up and then climbed the shaky steps.

When they finally made it, Mari was waiting for them at the top. A few seconds for a brief reunion and Mari insisted they leave.

"This is the gateway to hell and we cannot dawdle even a little. I have added some strong Voodoo charms to the place, to keep the beasts from hiding here again. They won't find it so hospitable I promise you!"

They left the dark confines of the building, Collin looking behind for a second as he carried Isabella on his back.

He couldn't shake the feeling that Isabella's prison was a living beast. The vines and vegetation and swamp life had claimed it as one of its own. It was more like an undead thing, breathing in and out with the rest of the dark bayou.

Chapter 28

They hurried down the shadowy lanes until the house emerged above the thinning tree line. "There are only a few electric lights burning on the second floor," Collin whispered to the dark figure beside him.

Collin carried Isabella like a child in his arms. Her slight body was no challenge, but he was tiring after their treacherous trek through the swamps to get back to the house.

He scanned the flat expanse of the structure and then the grounds surrounding it, for any movement. Collin seemed to get a second wind with the end in sight. He looked over at Mari, seeing her more clearly with the moonlight. He noticed the thinness of her arms, the one being exposed after the sleeve was partially ripped away in her skirmish with Leslie.

In a fleeting thought, Collin wondered when, or if, this creature scurrying down the gloomy path beside him, was even human.

The stone columns at the front of the house were casting long shadows across the dark lawns and circular drive. The moon hung almost directly above the bulk of the deathly quiet building.

A dim flicker of light caught Mari's eye, as it struggled against the blackness at the side of the house. It was coming from the Solarium.

"Let me take Isabella from you now. She and I will enter through the front door, while you go through the Solarium. Here, Isabella. Chew this and swallow."

After chewing two red berries, Isabella said she was fit enough to walk on her own.

Collin could see she was stronger and watched for a moment as the two old women made their way up the wide steps, to the front door. He would reenter through that garden door, hoping it was still unobserved. Leslie was somewhere in the area and he wasn't prepared to face her without Mari's help.

Inside the Solarium, the rattle of someone turning the heavy doorknob from outside, roused Maggie out of the strange lethargy that had fallen over her mind and body.

She felt a heavy weight on her and looked down to see Grayson Gerrard's thick, dark hair woven around her fingers. His head lay on an exposed breast. A long, muscular leg pinned her to the couch under him.

Maggie froze. She didn't know how this could have happened, but she knew exactly how it looked.

Collin stood framed in the open doorway. His shadow fell across the floor where it mingled with her discarded blouse and chemise.

"Collin! I swear, I don't know what happened!" Maggie said trying to push the heavy weight of Grayson's body off herself.

Collin passed through the room, silent as if not trusting himself to say a word.

A minute passed and Maggie heard the car roar to life. She strained to listen, until all she heard was the echo of her pulse, beating in her ears.

Grayson brushed Maggie's neck with his lips and was suddenly standing over her, looking down at her naked body. She felt him wake when she did but was too concerned with how Collin had found her to wonder why he didn't speak.

Maggie saw a knowing smile on his sensual mouth.

She jumped to her feet, going around snatching up her scattered clothing. Running from the room to the study, she slammed and locked the door.

Grayson had taken immense pleasure watching her gather up her things, the leering smile never leaving his face.

He stretched his long body, feeling the delicious fullness that came after feeding well. His tongue darted out between his perfect teeth, moving over his full lips, searching for a lost drop of Maggie's rich blood. Grayson's eyes flashed a deep crimson with his contentment.

He was thinking about Collin as he redressed, stepping into in the black trousers and slipping on the loose, red silk shirt. The front was vainly left unbuttoned part-way, showing off his broad, muscular chest.

He couldn't have planned it more conveniently, Collin coming upon them as he did. Lying with Maggie, naked, in a close, exhausted embrace. He sniffed the air.

"Ah, yes."

The pungent perfume of recent love-making, hung tantalizingly in the muzzy air of the room. He took a deeper smell and could taste Maggie's flesh on his tongue. He knew he could have her, but it was too soon to mark her again. He couldn't allow himself to succumb to his desire to possess the young woman and risk killing her in the process.

There was time. That's all he had was time.

Leslie melted from the room, from where he allowed her to watch as he made his next bite on the mesmerized woman, drinking deeply this time. This was something he had fantasied over from the moment he laid eyes upon her at that diner, over a month ago.

Grayson could barely admit to himself he felt more than a mere sexual attraction to the lovely woman. He delighted in her company, enjoyed her intellect and passion for life. She seemed perfect.

"A perfect mate, for an eternity," he whispered.

Thinking on the future jarred his thoughts back to Leslie. Grayson knew she'd have to be destroyed sooner, rather than later. He couldn't allow her to tamper with his plans by indulging her own lusts and exposing them both to discovery.

She complained vehemently that she never got to take any blood from the besotted Collin, because the Voodoo Witch interrupted her in the act. Supposedly, her fangs barely grazed Collin's pulsing artery when the old hag appeared out of nowhere, clutching something in a gnarled hand.

"It must have been blessed bones. The witch barely touched my leg and it was scorched," Leslie related to him earlier. She mockingly said she pushed Collin aside, "while he still grunted like a bear in rut," so she could make her escape.

Grayson knew Leslie had been feeding on Isabella over a period of time now. Only small amounts and only from the same concealed puncture. Until recently that was enough.

He also knew Leslie tired of the thin blood running sluggishly through the old woman. He was certain she was scheming to get alone with Collin, to begin the process of enslaving his will to her own. She could drain him as slowly as she wished then, while he was kept happy with the pleasures of her perfect body.

The plan was working beautifully, she told Grayson, "Until the Voodoo Witch attacked me and I had to flee. And now I'm here, just in time to watch my Maker taking his enjoyment of the lovely Maggie."

Grayson didn't care for Leslie's flippant comment, but once more tamped down the impulse to sink his fangs into her slender neck in a killing bite.

Standing alone in the Solarium, his next move would be to court the woman he would have. He had to let Maggie see he desired more than her body. He wanted her to be his willingly but was prepared to use whatever methods needed to bring her to his side.

Chapter 29

Collin was in shock from seeing his love, his Maggie, lying in the arms of Grayson Gerrard. She had seen him in a similar act of unfaithfulness, but somehow, hers seemed the most hurtful betrayal, especially in light of what he'd learned.

Suddenly, he was blind with jealousy and anger. He made the impetuous decision to drive home, leaving Mari to deal with the insanity that swirled around Butler Plantation. He'd seen enough.

As he drove the long trip back to his house, he struggled with how to explain to Maggie that Leslie was a vampire. How could he explain that he'd been mesmerized by her, or he'd never have given in to her seduction. He felt these facts vindicated him from his own act of infidelity.

The further he drove from the cursed mansion, the calmer he became. He began to reflect on what he'd seen and heard. He felt relieved that Isabella was returned to the house under Mari's care, but was deeply concerned that she now had four bites.

Mari had warned him and Maggie that it took seven bites, before a human was turned into a Vampire, if they didn't succumb to the blood-taking first.

When Collin expressed the fear they could be over-run with vampires, Mari assured him that, "These beasts won't want to share their feeding grounds with others. They will likely kill their hosts after drinking them dry of their life's blood."

That information wasn't very comforting to him at the time.

In the predawn dark of the empty road, Collin began to feel something besides fear. He felt anger with himself. Anger that he fell under Leslie's spell so easily and that Maggie had given herself to Grayson Gerrard in retaliation.

If she loved him I could accept her change of heart, but coming on the heels of my appalling behavior, it was surely her way of punishing me.

His thoughts were his only company and he looked over occasionally at the empty seat his love should have occupied. That's when it struck him. He wasn't seeing the real Maggie! She would never have fallen for Grayson's charms as revenge for his own weakness. Any more than he would have been seduced by Leslie, if she hadn't used some supernatural power over his will.

It was all too clear to him.

"I've been twice a fool!" he said loudly, gripping the wheel tightly and making a wide turn in the empty road. He had to return to Butler Plantation. Maggie needed him more than ever. Her experience with Grayson Gerrard mirrored his own with Leslie.

More urgent still, there was at least one other "beast" as Mari called them, on the prowl. Collin had to find out if his suspicions were valid, but in any case he had to protect Maggie from being bitten again.

Driving recklessly over the rough roads, Collin's mind replayed snippets of comments the Voodoo Witch made while they were on that dreadful island. "The woman will go into hiding, now that she's unmasked. Since you've received no bite, and you've been cleansed of her taint, she has no hold on your will," Mari assured him at the time.

Collin came to the crossroad leading to the Plantation, slowing to turn in the direction of the bayou. It would be another half-hour before he reached Isabella's.

He increased his speed and then his headlights picked up movement coming from the direction of the swamps.

There was no way he was stopping for anything on the desolate roadway, but when the figure of the Voodoo Witch stepped in front of his oncoming vehicle, he slammed on his brakes. The grind of the tires as they fought to grip the lose-packed dirt sounded like a rock-slide in the dense gloom.

"Mari, why aren't you with Isabella? I'm on my way back to the Plantation to see her and Maggie."

"You never should have left, boy! But it's good you're with me now. We have work to do. Drive me back to my cottage. I have things to collect if I'm to defeat the beasts. Also, they'll be one more passenger to carry back with us."

"Passenger?   But what about leaving Isabella unguarded?   And Maggie is there still!"

"No need to concern yourself on their account. Your Maggie is with Isabella in her bedroom. I've left a few items from my bag scattered about the room that will keep them safe until our return."

Collin saw Mari was still gripping the carpetbag close to her boney chest as she climbed into the passenger's seat. He drove on but veered away from the Butler Plantation and toward the swamp town where Mari lived. They drove the twenty minutes in silence, Collin sensing the old woman preferred that to answering the questions roiling in his head.

Without realizing he spoke out loud, "Passenger?"

Mari looked over at him with her beetle-like eyes. "This is a special friend of mine, boy, someone who has dealt with this vampire beast before. He'll be our secret weapon, so to speak."

Collin never thought he'd hear a laugh coming from Mari's withered mouth, but she gave a chuckle, following her comment. Collin took advantage of her improved mood to ask, "How could he know this vampire? He'd have to be as old as the Bayou itself!"

Mari smiled, a flash of small yellow teeth making her look impish in the murky interior of the speeding auto. She crossed her arms, staring off into the blur of night.

When Collin pulled onto the dirt road leading down to the old woman's shack, a flicker of light shown through the window.

"Mari, there's someone inside your house," Collin said as he reached under the front seat for the tire iron stashed there.

"Oh, indeed there is!"

She moved more nimbly than Collin thought possible and was opening her front door almost before he realized she was out of the automobile.

Collin followed quickly and stepped into the crowded room he'd visited earlier, the scent of herbs heavy in the warm air. There was a fire in the small hearth that kept the damp of the bayou from insinuating itself into the cottage.

Standing as erect as a statue in the middle of the room, his head being brushed by the hanging herbs and drying flowers, was a giant of a man, lean as a whippet, his suit hanging off his rail-thin body.

"General! So good of you to come," Mari exclaimed, a slight lilt to her dry wispy voice.

"I am always at your disposal, my dear."

The stranger bent down to take Mari's withered hand, placing a light kiss on the veiny surface. Collin swallowed hard at the thought of performing such an act, but this man seemed truly delighted to see the Voodoo Witch.

"I see you have your young champion in tow, Miss Mari."

Turning his full attention to Collin made him seem even larger than he first appeared. Collin was six feet tall, but this man had several inches on him.

"Good evening, young sir. I am General Benjamin Butler, late of the Union Army, serving President Abe Lincoln during the secession of Louisiana from our fair Union. I led the Federal Troops when we occupied New Orleans in 1862, after the Rebels took their disastrous step, to severe ties. But, my mind tends to wander its own roads. To our current situation!"

He gave Mari a quick commiserating look, "My granddaughter, twice and more removed, Isabella Butler."

He barely took a breath in this long speech.

Collin had been watching the General closely, from the moment he followed Mari into the cottage. There was an odd, ethereal quality to

Butler's physical appearance. His black suit looked as if it was off one of the mannequins at the Civil War Remembrance Gallery, in New Orleans. It dawned on Collin that the Civil War was fought well-over fifty-five years ago and the General looked to be in his early sixties.

He recalled Isabella sharing her family's history, when he was visiting once as a child. She told Collin, General Ben Butler was one of Lincoln's finest generals, at the ripe age of sixty-four.

So why didn't he look like a shriveled old man? He never aged!

Collin tried to fight back the uncomfortable notion that was bubbling up to the surface of his mind. This would have been a preposterous conclusion, until Collin's recent seduction by a vampire and finding a hidden lair for them in the bayou.

Collin made an effort to study the tall, spare figure who should have been long dead, without staring outright. General Butler was as white as a sheet of paper. The eyes that were riveted on Collin were milky blue, as if frozen and reinserted. His wiry, nearly colorless hair was thin, carefully combed over a bald pate. A sparse mustache trailed the sides of a stern mouth, setting off the sharp nose on a blunt, decidedly unattractive face.

"Uh, very good to meet you sir," Collin said a beat too slow.

He noticed Butler's mouth tighten before he turned to speak to Mari, who appeared to be an old friend.

"We need to coordinate our attack, Mari," the General abruptly said, turning his back on Collin and cutting into his anxious thoughts.

"You and your young man, must return to Butler Plantation. My great, great Granddaughter is in a perilous situation. I fear the beast will be leaving his stronghold in the bayou now that you've discovered it. By the way, when you contacted me, I was already aware of St. Germain's return to Paxton Parrish. I also am aware," he added, giving a pointed look at Collin, "that he brought a beautiful woman with him, to add to the enjoyment of his stay. Your good friend, my dear Isabella, has already fallen victim to the woman's hunger for blood. We must act quickly, before there's another attack in her weakened state."

"But, how could you know all this?" Collin blurted out.

The General turned his icy gaze once more on him.

"I too have become a denizen of the bayou. I come back when I am called by the Voodoo Magic that destroyed my mortality but gave me eternal life.

In short, I am a vampire."

Chapter 30

Maggie was sitting at Isabella's bedside. She'd been there nearly three hours. The kidnapping and rescue had left the elderly woman in a state of near collapse. The door to the bedroom suite was locked, the windows closed, their heavy drapes holding back the probing gaze of the moon.

Isabella was restless, moaning dreadfully in her sleep. It was an eerie sound in the gloomy room, tinged with the pain the elderly woman was experiencing from several more bites. Maggie felt lost, unable to relieve her fiend's nightmares.

Mari found the new punctures while helping Isabella into bed. They were deep, though beginning to close by the time she discovered them. Mari said their slow healing indicated much blood had been drained from Isabella's weakened body.

Mari was quick to safe-guard the bedroom against any incursions from the vampires she knew roamed free on the plantation. With little explanation, she gave Maggie bundles of a spicy-smelling incense to burn throughout the long, dark hours ahead. Along with those, she slipped a set of orange beads around both Maggie's neck and Isabella's. "Been blessed twice. Once by the renegade priest I know and by a powerful Voodoo priest from the islands," she'd said by way of explanation.

Before she left the suite of rooms, Mari sprinkled blessed water from the font in a local church, drops spotting the furniture and floors.

Maggie knew Voodoo in Louisiana was a strange mix of African and French influences combined with elements from Spiritualism, Vodun, Catholicism, and Pentecostalism, so the holy water was no surprise to her when a cold drop fell on her arm.

Mari told her she planned to return to her own cottage. "Time for us to bring in some reinforcements, child."

The young woman was watching Isabella closely and felt helpless seeing how she was suffering. "Mari, Isabella is in so much distress. Is there anything you can do to help calm her?"

"She needs more healing than what I have with me now. When I come back, I'll perform my cleansing, but she needs to be stronger than she is now, or it might not go well with her. Keep close to her bed, child and whatever happens, don't open the door or windows. I have them sealed against the vampire beasts getting in here."

Maggie was about to ask how long she'd be gone when Mari began to mumble words in a strange tongue. This was followed by a sharp hiss, like a sputtering firecracker.

Maggie jumped to her feet, scanning the room. A thick gray mist hung where the Voodoo Witch had been standing.

"Don't be afraid my dear."

Hearing Isabella's voice, Maggie sat back down bedside her, taking a frail hand.

"Isabella, you're awake. Did you know Mari was here?"

"I have been awake long enough to see her spinning her Voodoo magic like a spider weaves her web," she chuckled softly.

The effort caused a groan to escape her. When she caught her breath she went on. "She is very powerful, but I fear she is no match for the craven beasts that walk among us."

She started coughing and gasping for breath. The paleness of her skin became blotchy, an unhealthy, inflamed look coloring her face.

Maggie held a glass of dark liquid for her to drink.

"It was prepared by Mari earlier, in case you woke," she explained while the old woman sipped from the delicate crystal glass.

"Isabella, you should know, both Collin and I have been attacked like you. But I don't think Collin was bitten.

Mari told me there is an unnatural power stalking Butler Plantation. She believes there are two hunters and she called them..."

"Vampires! That's what they are and I know the name of one!"

"You believe what Mari said? But surely, these are only folktales. Stories from bayou people, passed down through the generations of such primitive beliefs."

"Maggie, don't be naïve about the reality of the evil that preys on the puny mortals we are."

She closed her eyes for a second, gathering her strength, Maggie thought, as she watched her struggle from the grip of the pain.

"The vampire is Jacques St. Germain, but he has many other names. He's been called, "The man who knows all. Also, the man who never dies like a mortal."

The bayou folktales are not spun from the moss hanging over the heads of the swamp people. They are the accounts told to them by their fathers and grandfathers, and great, great grandfathers, about an immortal being who has lost his humanity, as well as his soul.

This creature marks his victims with these!" she said angrily.

Isabella tugged at the neck on her nightgown, revealing a series of puncture marks scattered around the fleshy folds of her neck.

The latest set of marks, made five. Mari's words came back to Maggie in a rush, hitting her like a punch in the gut. *Seven bites and the victim will be lost.*

The old woman was studying Maggie's reaction. She pulled the nightgown's collar back over the inflamed marks. Taking Maggie's hand into her own, she spoke softly.

 Maggie could feel the fever raging through the thin skin of the frail hand.

"I know he took you Maggie, but you should feel no shame, dear."

Maggie looked down at their twined hands, trying not to let Isabella see the tears welling up in her eyes.

 Isabella went on, "This monster has powers that only a Voodoo Witch, such as Mari, can challenge." She stopped speaking, looking around the shadowy confines of the large bedroom. "My dear, did Mari return to the bayou lair?"

"No, Isabella. She was returning to her cottage, saying she would be back with help."

"Ah. That will be the General no doubt. He's a very old and dear friend of Mari's. He's also a Veteran and my great, great grandfather!" she said with obvious pride.

Maggie was reaching for the glass with Mari's concoction when it dawned on her what Isabella just said. "Isabella, are you saying he's a Veteran of the Civil War? That can't be! He'd have to be…"

"Yes dear. He is very old indeed. You see, when he was here at Butler Plantation, the General fell prey to the beast from the bayou. He had just buried his wife, my great, great grandmother, who having a frail constitution, suffered greatly after the General's public humiliations in politics. The General fell into a deep melancholy they say and wandered into the bayou late one day. His Plantation workers searched for him until it got too dark to venture further, without risk to themselves."

"That's incredible. What happened to him?"

"That night, as the tale unfolds, his workers heard a long series of screams and howls coming from the black heart of the swamp. It was reported these were so terrifying to hear, that after several torturous hours, all the Plantation workers abandoned the place. They loaded two buggies and one wagon and arrived in Paxton before dawn. They went immediately to the local Sheriff's office to report their master's disappearance and what had followed in the night. The Sheriff investigated as best he could, going by short skiff into the swamp armed to the teeth they said."

"Did they find him?"

"The man never returned from the bayou and to this day, the bayou folk say he wanders the swamps with his lantern, still searching for the General."

When Isabella stopped speaking, Maggie had chills running up her spine and goose bumps frizzing the hair on her arms. She had never heard this tale, thinking it must have been written off as another folksy story, originating with the superstitious denizens of the bayou.

In the hush that fell over the room, Maggie could hear activity deep in the house, probably Annette preparing the fireplace in the kitchen. *It must be close to dawn now,* she thought, vaguely aware of a lighter grey tinge in the obsidian night pressing against the curtains of the rooms.

Chapter 31

Collin drove with Mari sitting beside him in the front seat. General Butler sat in back, his face as white as the underbelly of a dead catfish in Collin's rear-view mirror.

With all he'd heard back at the witch's cottage, Collin still didn't quite believe he was driving a Voodoo Witch and a dead man in his car.

The gaunt General had folded his tall frame into the rumble seat, insisting he needed no more room "than a shadow passing over a grave."

A chill ran down Collin's back at the words as he recalled them now and he gripped the wheel tighter.

"When we arrive at the Butler Plantation, son, I'd appreciate it, if you introduced me to any staff as a family friend and a private physician, come to check on Isabella's well-being."

Collin wondered earlier why the General didn't just fly like the crow he oddly resembled, to get to Isabella's side. When the General climbed into the auto, Collin's curious look, must have given away his thoughts.

Mari looked over at him, smiling slyly and said, "The General enjoys the occasional opportunity to be mortal, boy. Nothing more."

They rode in silence until the General's request regarding Annette and Leslie were voiced.

"A few details we'll have to consider," the General said with finality from the back seat.

Collin saw a faint glow falling across the lawns at the rear of the house as he went around the long curve approaching the drive.

Isabella's rooms, he thought.

His stomach clenched for a second, remembering that they were here to find and destroy the vampires responsible for the attacks on Isabella and Maggie. Thinking of Maggie as he pulled under the portico, rattled him even more. *What will happen to us after this is all over?*

Collin got out and went around the front of the car to help Mari. The General climbed out of the rear in one fluid motion, his black suit making a slight slithering noise in the still air.

There was a tinge of light in the dark dome of night sky. They all stood momentarily, gazing upward at the coming dawn. Collin thought the General's expression was even more solemn and determined. Mari's face never changed and was still unreadable to him.

Just as the General predicted, they were met by the maid at the front door when they entered. "Mr. Collin, I am pleased you are back with us. The Mistress is still abed and Miss Maggie is sitting with her."

The haggard look on Annette's face told of a sleepless night.

When they were all inside, Collin introduced the General.

"This is a family friend of Isabella's and a doctor, who's come to check in on her, Annette. We'll be going up now. If you could, we'd appreciate some of your wonderful coffee too. It's been a long night."

While she scurried off to see to his request, Collin closed the heavy front door, and followed Mari and the General onto the elevator.

It was silent as a mausoleum when they walked down the carpeted hallway to Isabella's rooms. Collin knocked softly at first, but getting no response, knocked loudly, calling out his fiancé's name.

"Maggie, its Collin, with Mari. Open the door."

Still no answer. This time Mari stepped forward. Putting an ear to the door, the usual scowl on her face deepened.

"General," she said turning to him as he hovered by her side.

Collin watched wide-eyed, as the wrath thin figure appeared to collapse into himself, until he was no more than a wisp of gray fog. The column of vapor swooped down and entered under the door frame in a single line until it disappeared from view.

Collin sucked in his breath when the door flew open.

Mari and Collin nearly collided rushing into the room.

They saw Isabella lying like a tossed doll on top of her comforter, her black nightgown torn open at the neck. Her face was chalk-white, a milky film covered her dark, staring eyes.

There were several large splotches of deep red all over the bed linen, her night gown looked damp around the open collar.

Collin was dumfounded at the sight of his murdered friend. He knew he would never forget the scene, especially the terror etched upon the elderly woman's face. Her open mouth, silently screaming into the smothering silence.

Tearing himself away from the scene, he searched the rooms for Maggie.

He found her silk scarf draped over the chaise longue in Isabella's sitting room. Scanning the floor, he spotted two pearl buttons from the blouse Maggie was wearing.

He picked these up, returning to the bedroom where the General was standing near the window.

"The Count St. Germain will be waiting for me," the General said looking directly at Mari.

"He is after all, my Maker," he added softly.

Collin and Mari watched as the window rose with a slight squeal of protest.

The General disappeared into a pillar of fog and was lost in an overcast, misty dawn.

Chapter 32

Collin was afraid to ask why the General referred to the vampire he hunted as his "Maker," but it was all too obvious what the answer was. To Collin's reeling mind, it was better not to confirm his suspicions.

"Mari, we must call the police to report Isabella's death and Maggie's disappearance," he said, looking down at the frail figure sprawled across the bed.

She was standing over the cold body of her friend, tears running down her withered cheeks.

"I don't understand how my charms and spells were overcome, how they failed to protect them," she said.

The old woman's voice was subdued and for the first time, Collin heard a note of uncertainty in it. He left her to her grief, deciding to search around the rooms more closely, for something that might explain how Mari's protection had been defeated, leaving Maggie and Isabella exposed to attack.

He returned to the sitting room adjacent to Isabella's bedroom. Moving carefully while he scanned the area, he went to the window. There were long scratches along the wide windowsill. Looking down, he found the outline of paw prints on the dark wooden floor, as if a big cat had walked on the dew covered ground before entering.

Following them with his eyes, he saw they led directly to Isabella's bedroom.

"Mari," he called to her trying not to yell in his excitement.

The old woman entered the room, following Collin's eyes down to the flat prints of a big cat. She was beside him at the window before he took another breath. Placing her hand on the deep grooves, she jerked it back as if she'd touched fire.

"Ah, so now I know. The beast came as a natural creature of the swamps and avoided my charms and spells. He moved as the panther and entered without fear of detection. Once in the rooms, he was able to move around my powders and charms."

"Do you think he murdered Isabella then?" Collin asked, looking back into the bedroom.

"Oh, that was the female! She had already marked Isabella as her prey and her Master would allow her the prize. She came in here with him. Look."

Collin followed Mari's knobby finger where it pointed to a second, smaller set of paw prints, these leading directly to the bedside. Two big cats had invaded the rooms and evaded the Voodoo Witch's magical barriers.

They returned to the bedroom, walking over to the bed. Mari laid a hand on Isabella's arm.

"She's getting stiff. That's a good sign."

Collin gave her a puzzled look.

"I mean, boy that she's truly dead. Not put into a zombie state until the beast can bring her to his side. She will be no slave to the vampire, where she would descend into the darkness forever, preying on human victims until she is destroyed."

Mari moved toward the window, staring intently toward the gardens. Collin followed her there, watching the weak sun mark the boundary between the gardens and the bayou.

The line between good and evil, he thought bleakly.

"Now listen to me, boy," Mari said, turning her rheumy eyes on Collin's pensive face. "We need to go back into the bayou and that old monastery we found. I am certain the vampire and his female will take Maggie back to that corrupt ground for her final initiation."

"What's the General doing? Is he going to help us, or is he joining forces with the other undead?" Collin's voice was filled with fear and exasperation.

"Why, he's going to lead of course! He's still the General. The only difference, is the size of his Army. Just you and me. But he's already gone to search for your Maggie among the cells of those cursed and fallen clergymen. He'll meet us there so we need to leave quickly."

Mari's answer took him by surprise. "But shouldn't we call the Paxton Police first? What do I tell the maid?"

"I'll handle the maid," Mari answered.

After a terse explanation about Isabella's death, Mari told Annette to contact the police station, but to only speak with the Chief. "Tell him Miss Mari asked for him to investigate personally. He'll understand and come quickly."

They left the confused, teary-eyed woman watching through a Solarium window as they crossed the deep green grass onto the garden path and disappeared among the trees and topiary.

They walked for five minutes, when Mari laid a gnarled hand on Collin's arm.

"We first need to stop at the Guest House where the artist is staying. I know you suspect him of seducing Maggie, but I need to prove those suspicions are correct, boy."

"How could you know what I saw?" Collin asked. He was skeptical that the old woman had somehow divined how he found Maggie in Gerrard's arms in the Solarium.

"Don't question the Voodoo, boy, accept the power of my gris-gris to give me clear eyes and sharp ears." She pulled out a small, square shaped pouch that hung around her neck, hidden under the folds of her black dress.

Collin knew enough of the traditional stories to understand this amulet was considered as powerful as any holy relic. He nodded his head showing her he would trust her ways.

They were close to the small cottage Gerrard was occupying. The light of the new dawn barely touched its low roof under the heavy foliage surrounding it. Collin heard the distant rumble of thunder and smelled the subtle change in the air. A storm was brewing, the air, dark with its threat.

A faint glow sprang to life behind the curtains at the front of the small house. Collin and Mari stood still, watching the cottage from the path. They saw the light move to another window at the side of the house. Someone was moving about inside.

Mari touched Collin's elbow, whispering as he bent down to hear her. "We will find the woman in there I expect." She saw Collin's eyes widen and added, "Don't worry. I won't allow her charms to work on you this time. She's out for your blood now and not your manhood." She reached into the depth of a pocket in the ratty black dress and pulled out two of the dark berries Collin had seen Maggie toss away. "Chew these and swallow the juices before you spit them out. Quickly!" she hissed.

Tossing them from his hand into his mouth, Collin crunched down on the bitter fruit and swallowed as directed, spitting the hulk out after. His tongue tingled and a shot of adrenalin raced through his body. It was amazingly bracing and suddenly he felt invincible.

Mari looked satisfied with the results saying, "Time to meet one of the Vampires, boy. And this time, she'll be kissing the ground, not your sour mouth!"

Chapter 33

Maggie struggled to wake herself from a dreadful nightmare. In it, she was in Isabella's bedroom, sitting beside her bed while the elderly woman slept fitfully. The doorknob rattled. She turned to face the locked door and sat immobilized, while a yellowish mist entered through the keyhole in the bedroom door.

It looked like a thin, yellow worm, sinuous and long. She couldn't move a muscle as she watched it settle around the bed and her sleeping friend.

Slowly, it settled over Isabella's face and disappeared down her nostrils. The mist came out of Isabella's partially open mouth and resolved itself into a sleek panther. Ignoring Maggie, the cat padded into the adjoining sitting room. Maggie jerked her head back and forth, trying to dislodge the awful scene from her drugged mind, but the dream continued.

She was back in Isabella's bedroom, powerless to help, or move.

Suddenly, in the dream, Maggie felt a deep chill fill the air around her. It was as if she'd stepped into a meat locker or been set adrift on an iceberg. Shivering uncontrollably, she became aware of a new presence in the room.

Only able to move her eyes, the huge panther she'd seen in the Solarium, stepped out of the shadows.

Maggie's scream was enough to wake herself. She sat bolt upright. Her eyes were wide and filled with dread as she looked around.

She was on a hard, narrow bed, bare of any covering except a lumpy pillow made of rotted burlap and moldy straw filling.

She felt disoriented, seeing the rich décor of Isabella's bedroom, replaced by a Spartan, cell-like room.

There was a single candle stub, struggling to shed its paltry light in a windowless room. Moldy reeds and rodent droppings were scattered over the floor. The air was pungent with decay.

Beside the bed she sat on there was a small stool tucked under a webbed- festooned shelf or desk, constructed of three rough-cut, short planks. Maggie looked down at herself. She was not injured in any obvious way, but her shoes were gone and her blouse was missing several buttons and hung open down to her waist.

She took in a sharp breath of the fetid air when she explored with her fingers and found a new puncture mark on her neck. Maggie didn't know why, but she knew instinctively, this wasn't like the others. This was her fourth bite, but it was made by a different beast. Her mind felt dull, as if she was coming out from under a strong sedative. She began to recall another time she saw the small panther.

It was in the gardens at Butler Plantation. She was in the gazebo, looking into the surrounding trees, when the panther walked out of the lush, green gloom. She remembered its golden eyes staring directly into her own, mesmerizing her as it moved closer.

And now, that same animal had somehow entered Isabella's bedroom. It wasn't a dream. *But how did I get here?*

Maggie was frantic for answers. She needed to escape this place, whatever it was, before that creature returned. She knew without a doubt the lethal cat would be back for her kill.

She got off the low bed, gingerly walking over to the door. Each step brought an unnerving crunch, as she crushed ancient bones, under her bare feet.

 Like the shelf and bed, the door to the room was primitive, looking like the door to an old fashioned root cellar. She shuddered as she stood on the cold stone floor.

Pressing an ear to the heavy door, she couldn't detect any sounds except the thumping of her heart.

Where am I, she thought frantically. She'd lived in Paxton all her life and knew every building around the Parrish, to some degree. This dank place felt like someplace out of a medieval monastery.

"That's it," Maggie said, her voice sounding odd to her ears in the heavy stillness.

She knew this must be a cell, in some kind of monastic dwelling, hidden away from local knowledge, covered in centuries of disuse.

Maggie tried pulling the iron door handle only to find it unyielding. She pushed hard against the door. It gave just enough for her to see a heavy wooden bar lying across it. She was locked in with no visible means of escape.

Her first reaction was to cry and her eyes welled up in tears. She took a calming breath and thought on her situation. After a moment, her tears were replaced by a fierce anger.

"I'll not die like some lamb led to slaughter," she spoke out loud and strangely, the sound of a voice, even though it was her own, helped calm her and harden her resolve.

Standing still, she tried to study the tiny chamber in the poor light from the candle. She walked over to the shelf to see if there was anything she could use to defend herself when her captor returned.

Sweeping aside the ancient dust-filled webs revealed a crude cross lying under a pile of petrified animal droppings. She picked it up, wiping her hands on her linen trousers.

Maggie held the cross close to her face, the weak light from the sputtering candle offered little advantage. It was at least as old as some of the fossils she'd found around other properties, over years of poking through empty houses along the bayou. Artifacts of Spanish, French and English origin, dating back to those country's occupation of Louisiana and specifically, the area that would become Paxton Parrish, after the Civil War.

Do I remember any story about a lost monastery? she wondered. There was only a vague tale she'd heard once from a Cajun woman that came to clean at her house after her mother's death. The woman told her about a special prison, built deep in the bayou for evil priests and monks to live out their days doing penance. Her eyes took on a hidden fire when she recounted how the defrocked priests would perform horrific acts of self-flagellation and walk barefoot over broken glass and hot coals to purge themselves of their sins.

From the sinister feeling that seeped out of the damp walls of her cell, Maggie could well believe the story of horrors and pain that went on in such a place.

She felt as weary as the candle that had all but drowned its tiny flame in wax. In spite of the filth of the coarse pillow, Maggie laid back down on it. The cross was still in her hands and rested on her chest, her breasts rising and falling, making it move with the rhythm of her breathing.

She was so deeply asleep, that when the heavy wooden door scraped open, it didn't rouse her from her dreaming.

This time, she dreamt of a beautiful, man. Tall, muscular and as handsome as Adonis. This time, she dreamt of Grayson Gerrard.

Chapter 34

Collin and Mari left the garden path when the small cottage came into view. Seeing the pale light of dawn did little to comfort him, as it never seemed to brighten the gloom under the trees. Occasional rumbles of thunder sounded and the sky roiled with dark, scudding clouds.

Just when Collin couldn't get any more uncomfortable, hunching down behind a tangle of plants and shrubs, he felt large drops spatter across his head and back. Mari appeared unfazed by their new sleuthing conditions, reaching for his arm.

"The She-beast will be content after draining our friend of her life's blood. She will be particularly amorous too. That's one of the effects of their blood feast. They get as randy as a buck in rut." When she saw Collin's apprehension at falling victim to being seduced again, she quickly added, "The berries I gave you will keep the murdering beast at bay. You won't smell nearly as tasty as you did earlier."

They approached the guest house from the side closest to the wooded area which offered a measure of concealment. Mari moved her amulet out from under her dress, where it lay over her heart.

She began to mumble and he caught an occasional wisp of foreign sounding words. He understood she was chanting her Voodoo enchantments, hoping this time they would work.

The pair crept up to a narrow door, likely leading into the kitchen. Something made a loud rustling sound in a nearby clump of Alligator Weed, its white blossoms full and fragrant. They were bobbed their colored heads as if recently brushed into motion by an errant creature.

Mari hissed between her small yellow teeth, "She's bested me."

Collin barely had time to wonder what the Voodoo Witch meant, when something flew out of the shadows slamming into his back. Sudden, piercing pain shot down from his shoulder, traveling to the base of his spine. Like liquid fire it felt as if his bones were melting and fusing inside his back.

The scream that shattered the night surged like water flowing around a rock, until it came back into itself and continued with the sheer force of nature behind it. Mari pulled the bundle of bones from somewhere under her dress. She lunged at the lustrous body of the female panther that sunk her canines into Collin's shoulder, piercing his collar bone and shoulder blade.

The second scream was the howl of an animal in great distress. The panther's lithe body arched with a shattering spasm. She released her grip on Collin's flesh, her head twitching as violently as her tail. The glossy body of the animal sprawled on the ground, snarling and futilely snapping its jaws.

Mari easily avoided the foaming mouth, her bundled bones maintaining contact with the beast. After a useless continuation of this torturous dance, the cat stopped her efforts to attack. She lay panting on her side, tremors running up and down her smooth form until they subsided and she lay still.

Mari carefully approached, holding the bone bundle in front of herself defensively. The panther's mouth dropped open, the tongue hanging to one side. Mari watched carefully, waiting for the gleam of life to leave the golden eyes before she pronounced her dead.

When she saw the dullness of death claim the beast, she waited another moment to witness the body begin to morph once more and Leslie Porter Booth lay sprawled on her side in its place.

Satisfied the transformation was complete, Mari rushed to help Collin, only semi-conscious, on the ground behind her. "It'll be alright, boy. I'm here now and will help you."

He didn't respond, but as she struggled to help him regain his footing, she felt his body trying to respond to the need to move. Together they limped through the side-door and into a tiny kitchen. The light they had spotted was from a low burning fire in the hearth at the back of the room.

"Here now, you sit on this chair and rest for a moment while I begin what needs to be done."

Again, Collin met her words and instructions in silence, having neither the strength nor ability to verbalize a response.

Mari spoke a few of the jumbled words Collin was becoming used to hearing. Suddenly she was clutching her carpetbag in her boney arms.

Collin didn't blink at the Voodoo magic. He was too consumed with pain and watching his blood running down his arm onto the table to notice as Mari removed a jar from the recesses of the ratty bag.

"This will do for you, boy, so don't you fret. Old Mari will have you right as a gator lying on a sunny patch in the bayou before you know it."

Collin felt woozier and slumped over onto the kitchen table. The last thing he heard was the jar being opened and the loamy smell of bayou mud.

Chapter 35

Collin woke with a start. He'd drifted off into a dream of a large cat gnawing on his shoulder. He tried to move and a shock wave of pain shot through his body. His intake of breath brought Mari over to his side.

"It's all right, boy. Old Mari has done right by you. The bite of the she-beast is well into healing. Can you sit up now?"

That's when Collin realized he was stretched out on a narrow bed, in what he supposed was the bedroom of the guest house. He didn't try to guess how the petite old woman had managed to move him there.

With Mari assisting him again, he sat on the edge of the mattress and surveyed his surroundings. He was feeling almost strong enough to stand and wondered at the Voodoo medicine Mari applied to his wounds. A pungent odor still clung to his shredded shirt, but he was too happy not to be dead, to care.

He began to look around more closely. There was a thick layer of dust on the floor surrounding the bed and cobwebs had interwoven themselves into the bedside lamp and the wall.

There were no personal items on the dresser and the closet door was open, showing empty clothes hangers dangling. The same with the open armoire. No clothing or shoes, not even a simple comb or brush sitting on the dresser.

"If this is where Gerrard was living, where are his clothes? It looks as if no one has been in this place in years," he said to Mari.

"Glad to see you've your wits about you again, boy. We need to return to the cursed monastery on that island. With the she devil dead, there's only her Maker to deal with. The General should be there waiting for us."

"Mari, I need to know. Was that panther that attacked me, Leslie? Was she the vampire that murdered Isabella?"

"Too many questions, boy. I think I liked you better unconscious! You'll have your answers as we move into the swamp toward the island. Let's go."

True to her word, Mari filled Collin in on the identity of the female beast as she called Leslie Porter Booth, confirming her as the killer of their friend, Isabella.

Collin asked if she was the one who marked Maggie, too. Mari looked at him closely.

"No, that would be the Maker and he surely had plans on replacing the She Beast, with Maggie."

She added ominously, "She would then become his paramour through an eternal night."

Collin shivered with that revelation and hurried his steps to catch up with the nimble crone.

He looked up at the sky, noting the sun was beginning its slow crawl toward dusk.

Collin had no sense of time and could only guess how long his healing process had taken. He knew he likely lost a lot of blood from the attack and figured it must have taken most of the day for Mari's medicine to work.

The sun grazed the tops of a stand of old oak when they entered the swamp. He could hear the sweet trilling of the northern parula. He recalled how Maggie adored the tiny migrating bird, saying its gently rising song marked every early spring they spent together as children, and now as lovers.

Would they have other springs together, he wondered?

Collin noticed that Mari was carefully retracing their earlier path to the island deep in the swamp. He knew they'd have to cross the natural moat around the blighted monastery, hoping their earlier passage was still visible.

He saw Mari grab another long stick and prod the murky water surrounding the island. "Here," she hissed into the green air of the bayou.

Collin followed more closely, stepping carefully onto the unseen path Mari was finding. Five tense minutes passed as she poked the thick waters and he followed blindly. He nearly laughed out loud, thinking of the old nursery rhyme, of the three blind mice.

They stood for a few seconds on the banks in front of the crumbling stone and wood building and worked at removing clinging vines and slimy green tendrils of some kind of swamp grass off themselves. Mari gave her long skirt a tight wringing out and nodded to him to follow.

Studying the abandoned prison in the dying light filtered through a thick umbrella of tree limbs, Collin could almost see the evil oozing out from between the cracks in the walls.

They were covered in the massive vines that insinuated themselves into any available opening. Drifting air currents carried strange, tangy odors. The smell of rot was everywhere.

Collin listened to the wind as it moved through the empty shell of the monastery, like a hunting cat. He wondered why he hadn't noticed all this as intensely on his first visit.

He was snapped out of his daydreaming when Mari tugged on his sleeve. "Time to meet the General and see to the business of vampire killing."

Collin didn't miss the gleam in the old woman's small, black eyes. They moved through the door-less front of the building, slowly making their way back toward the interior where they discovered Isabella the night before.

Mari raised a hand, but in the darkness of the passageway Collin barely caught the movement. He reached into his pocket for the lighter he always carried and brought up a small flame.

Mari spun around. "No light, boy! You'll alert every spirit that walks here, with our intrusion on their sleep. These are not kindly dead and they can smell your innocence like a gator can a duckling."

Collin snapped the cover over the lighter dousing the tiny flame. He missed it immediately, feeling the damp, chilled air seeping into his pores.

He strained his ears, listening for any human voices, hoping one would be Maggie's.

He moved behind the dark, squat form of the Voodoo Witch, catching glimpses of the rooms they passed through, whenever a sliver of moonlight insinuated itself through a missing roof tile, or hole, in the thick walls.

He recognized one as the likely communal dining hall, chairs and tables rotted away like lepers huddled together on the stone floor. Carefully shuffling his feet to push anything out of his way, Collin nearly collided again with Mari in a sudden stop. He instinctively bent down to her. In a muted voice she told him something was in the room with them.

"Stay perfectly still, while I sort this out," she wheezed the words into his ear.

Collin nodded, forgetting the gesture was lost in the darkness.

A shift in the clammy air around his body alerted him Mari had moved, without actually seeing her in motion.

When a guttural moan came out of the inky shadows to his left, he turned immediately to the sound and waited.

His whole being tensed, poised to run. Collin wasn't sure if he should move away from that awful sound or toward it to help the old Voodoo woman. He never would have considered himself a coward, but neither did he feel himself some kind of hero of the paranormal.

Making his decision spontaneously, Collin moved left, stopping every few feet, listening. A whispery sound reached his ears and he was puzzling out what it was when something hard flew at his ankles and before he could react began encircling his legs like iron hoops round a barrel.

Snake!

Collin fell as the heavy snake climbed his body. A sharp cry escaped his tightly closed mouth, sounding shrill as it bounced off stone walls. His head slammed against the rough surface of the flagstone floor, but he was able to use his hands to buffer the fall.

Collin expected the large snake slithering around his chest to begin to tighten its grip, constricting his breathing until he passed out. After that, there'd be nothing but a slow, agonizing death for him.

With his arms and hands still free of the creature, Collin was able to access the pocket where he stashed his lighter. Allowing the snake to make its slow progress up his torso, Collin reached into his pants, his fingers searching around for the lighter.

With the lighter precariously held by two fingers, Collin began to move it out of the pocket until he could secure it with his other hand.

There was a sudden metal click, followed by a sharp, yellow flame. Collin held the puny fire near the moist, white skin of a giant python. It was a rare albino of the species, but one Collin had heard stories about all his life living on the bayou.

The giant snake twitched like the recoil on a bull whip. Collin was quick to apply the small flame to another part of the thick underbelly as it continued to uncoil. There was a loud thump as the heavy creature fell off Collin's pinned legs and onto the hard stone floor. Collin kept touching the flame to the snake's long body, making it retreat into the shadows where it had hidden.

Collin kept the lighter open using it to try to penetrate the near pitch-black of the room, ignoring Mari's warning. He backed away from the shadowy direction the white strangler had taken. Breathing in large gulps of air it dawned on him that he'd lost track of Mari.

Using the slender flame from the lighter, he strained to see and realized he'd moved out of the communal eating area, into a different part of the monastery. He didn't dare call out to the old woman, but he didn't like the idea of moving further into the building without her.

Gritting his teeth against a gnawing fear in his gut, he quietly lowered the cover over his lighter. *Can't disturb the ghosts,* he thought grimly as he began feeling his way along a cold, stone wall. He had to find Maggie and rescue her before it was too late, if it wasn't already. He wondered if the General and Mari had joined forces yet.

A tight smile crossed his face at the preposterous thought of a Voodoo Queen and a reformed vampire general. "Good Lord!" he mumbled under his breath, the slim-covered wall under his hand.

Chapter 36

Maggie began to wake. She lay with her eyes shut, letting herself drift off for a moment longer. The sound of her name filtered through the gauze of sleep, until her mind snapped awake and she knew exactly where she was.

She bolted upright.

The unyielding surface of the rough bed had left her feeling sore all over. The heavy odor of mold and decay clung to her clothes and filled her every breath.

She looked around herself. The guttering candle had been replaced with a new one, lighting the cell more completely, except for the farthest corners. She stayed on the bed a moment longer, becoming aware of something she clutched in her hand.

"The cross I found," she whispered in a rush of words, knowing instinctively it was important to her.

Getting up stiffly, she moved to the door. She had little hope of forcing it open, but she had to do something to save herself. That thought jarred a hazy recollection of seeing Grayson Gerrard in the cell before she fell into her deep sleep. Was he only part of her dreamscape? The handsome, alluring Grayson, the man she'd given herself to, in a rush of passion and abandonment. It still baffled her because her love belonged to Collin. It always did.

She felt herself flush at the memory of his touch and mouth on her body.

Was he really with me here? Was I only dreaming he came to me?

A jumble of thoughts were running wild in her head. She was desperate to understand what was happening to her.

Someone locked her away in a filthy cell, smelling of age and rot. She had to escape before whoever abducted her returned. Again, Grayson's handsome face, with his seductive mouth and deeply unsettling eyes came unbidden to her memory. She shivered at the thought of his strong hands caressing her, his teeth brushing at the hollow of her throat.

No, I can't give in to him. Not ever again, she told herself. But she knew she'd have little defense against an overpowering desire to have him take her again.

That vivid picture of lying with Grayson jarred yet another face to appear in her mind.

Collin! Collin, help me. Please find me. Please find me. This repeated in her head like a mantra, willing it true. Maggie's eyes filled with tears thinking about her fiancé, the man she genuinely loved. She couldn't believe she had succumbed to Grayson's charms and highly charged sexuality. Not when Collin was the only man she ever wanted to give herself to. No matter how many lovers she'd taken over the years, she had always returned to him, her only love.

She had been so lost in her emotional rambling, she hardly realized she was standing in front of the wooden door. She was almost too afraid to see if it was still bolted against her escape. Placing her shoulder to it and pushing, she was shocked to hear a loud scrapping sound, as it grated against the stone floor. By leaning against it with all her strength, she was able to widen the opening enough for her to slip through.

Standing away from the candles low glow, Maggie found herself in a shadowy passage, looking both ways into total darkness.

Trying to give herself courage, she whispered low, "I can do this."

Slipping back into the cell, Maggie snatched the candle and quickly scooted through the narrow opening she'd made.

Shielding the flame from the drafts stirring the fetid air, she was able to see enough to move without tripping over some of the debris scattered over the floor.

Her feet were going numb with cold. Each step brought its own fear of stepping on something alive and dangerous. The bayou had its share of venomous snakes and it wasn't unheard of for Alligators to move into abandoned shacks in the bayou, hunting for the large rodents called nutria.

Maggie crossed another hallway, deciding to keep going straight until she could find a door leading outside. After that, she'd be facing the bayou at night, but she feared that less than whoever held her captive.

There was a vague light insinuating itself through a chink in the masonry. Maggie realized she must be nearing some sort of opening, perhaps a courtyard.

I just need to get outside, she thought, her nerves fraying with every step.

Her candle was sputtering, the hot wax already burned her hand, but she didn't dare let the flame drown in the soupy wax. She tipped it constantly, to keep it alive.

There was some kind of furniture in the room she entered next as she headed in the direction of the slender light. Some of the more sturdy chairs were scattered around long plank tables. These were covered in dust and debris several inches thick.

Dining room? she wondered.

Maggie decided to try making a torch for herself before she lost the flickering flame altogether. Crouching down and holding the candle away from herself, she was able to illuminate a larger area. She spotted something that made the breath choke up in her throat.

Hanging at eye level near the table was a human skull. Slowly moving her arm in a line, several other heads sprang out of the darkness. They were hung every few feet, like decorations on the walls.

Maggie gradually rose to her feet. This was a house of horrors. She snatched at a piece of wood, likely a chair leg, off the floor nearby. Holding the candle under the worm-infested wood, she waited for it to begin to smoke, blowing on it to encourage a small fire to ignite.

The enhanced scene was even more ghastly with the added light. Maggie moved quickly toward the outside wall and located a door. It was frozen with age, but with persistent pushing, it gave enough for her to squeeze through.

The moon glowed from directly above a thin canopy of trees, their veils of Spanish moss hanging languid in the chilled air.

Maggie took gulps of the night air, tasting the bayou on her tongue. She held up her make-shift torch, lighting her surroundings. She was shocked to see she was standing on a tiled patio. It was swept clean of any litter, unlike the building.

Maggie moved around the more civilized looking grounds.

There was a beautifully designed fountain erected in the middle of a mosaic floor tiling, depicting beautiful nymphs in provocative sexual poses with human lovers. Upon closer inspection, Maggie realized the lovers were all the same man. She studied his face more closely because it had a familiarity about it.

"Oh dear God! It's Grayson!"

""Indeed it is my dear, Maggie."

Chapter 37

Collin managed to wend his way back to a main passageway. Just as he was about to turn left at the juncture, his hair was ruffled. He knew this was supernatural activity.

"Whoever you are, I am only passing through here. Sorry to have disturbed your... peace."

There was a barking laugh and the General stepped within the small circle of Collin's light. "Very considerate of you, sir. I see you've been separated from Miss Mari," he added looking around.

It took Collin a minute to gather his nerves before he could speak. "General Butler, sir, I would appreciate a little warning next time you decide to make an appearance!"

The General gave another barking laugh and said, "Come on then, boy. It's time to rally the troops."

He began to move in the opposite direction Collin had chosen. There was a faint glow emanating from his wraith-thin body and Collin easily followed.

They reached a door leading out to a courtyard. Collin was relieved to see patches of moonlight penetrating the web of trees and vegetation that invaded the monastery over centuries.

He scanned the area, much of the yard heavily shadowed. Still behind the General, he stepped through a half-open door.

In the center of the courtyard, a large stone fountain stood like a sentinel, guarding the unseen inmates of the night. The base of the fountain was covered in hideous carvings, depicting naked men and women being tortured while others were fornicating in provocative positions. He was about to turn away from the gruesome display when something caught his eye.

One figure was repeated over and over on the relief. A tall male, his mouth open and long incisors clear on a god-like face. He was naked too and his hair flowed around his shoulders. Though the mystery figure was only seen from the side, his patrician features were clear and burned into Collin's memory. "Dear God! It's Grayson Gerrard!" he said too loudly. The name reverberating off every surface it touched.

"Shush your voice, soldier. The enemy is near," General Butler hissed in Collin's face.

Collin began to sputter the name, but clamped his mouth shut when the General loomed over him, a dark look on his ghostly face.

"We need to find the Voodoo Witch to gather ourselves for the attack. Follow me and no noise."

The General headed toward a stone building the size of a storage shed. It turned out to be a huge, brick oven, likely used to bake loaves of bread for the Monastery's population.

Collin wondered how many wayward priests and monks were sent here to spend their days in pain and solitude. As if he'd read his thoughts, the General leaned down to Collin saying, "At least three-hundred souls passed through this place over the same amount of years. All despicable men and the occasional fallen nun. They used the females horribly as you can imagine."

Collin thought a gleam came into the General's lifeless eyes when he mentioned the fate of the condemned women.

As they got closer to the oven, Collin saw a small door to the left of the oven's enormous mouth, likely used to clean out the ash from the massive baking.

The General passed through the door like a breeze would pass through the leaves of a tree.

Collin was suddenly alone.

He moved quickly to the door, finding it eaten away to a vertical slab of sawdust. It appeared to be held together by a coating of blackish-green sludge, likely fats off the meats they cooked here as well. He raised a foot and slammed it hard against the frail surface. The door disintegrated. Its absence revealed a small space with no ventilation save a funnel-like depression in the stone. The ash would accumulate here and eventually be swept into a metal container beneath the lip.

Collin would have been impressed with the efficiency of the system if he weren't getting claustrophobic. The tiny space must have been as hot as the furnace and the poor souls tending this task must have suffered greatly with the heat while breathing in the fine ash.

"Life sentences were likely short," he mumbled as he backed out.

A dead end!

Thinking along those lines, Collin wondered where the General was. Feeling frustrated he crossed the courtyard, reentering the U-shaped building.

This was clearly where the prisoners slept in the bizarre prison. The passageway on both sides was faced by small cells, most of their doors rotted into pitted lumps. Narrow plank beds, roughly cobbled shelves on each wall and stone floors, littered with the detritus of ages, leeched their smells into the air as he passed them.

This was the dormitory no doubt, of little interest to Collin who never expected Maggie would be held in this section. He was about to leave when he thought he heard a faint voice coming from further down the long hallway.

He froze, straining to listen.

Mari. Her old voice creaked and wheezed and he heard it enough of late to be sure it was the Voodoo Witch. Since he was moving away from the open door and the pale moonlight, he took out his lighter again. Its small flame was almost swallowed in the inky darkness. He moved carefully, going deeper into the building.

He came to a place in the maze-like passages, where it jogged around, completing the U-shape. He stopped to listen, trying to block out the sound of his pulsing blood, which was roaring like a seashell held to his ear.

He heard Mari speaking again. She clearly sounded agitated, perhaps even angry. She was close by, but from the muffled words must have been inside a room.

Collin was relieved when he came to a section of the building where the tiled roof had sunken under the weight of tree limbs and other debris. It was hanging in a few places where ropey vines had attached themselves to the tiles and ceiling beams. Under the cold moonlight, it looked like a crib mobile for a giant's baby.

Mari's voice rose like an air raid siren. Collin could hear the odd hodge-podge of languages. The old woman seemed to be calling someone, *or something*, Collin thought with a slight chill down his spine.

He hurried his steps until he saw a closed door at the end of the corridor. He could smell the heady spices he remembered from Mari's cottage, as a whiff of scented smoke escaped from under the shut door.

Collin knocked hard.

"Mari, let me in. It's Collin."

There was immediate silence on the other side of the door, as if Mari pretended not to be there.

Another knock only this time harder.

Mari flung the door wide. It was the same kind of Spartan room as all the others he'd seen. Only this one was occupied and the occupant didn't like being disturbed.

Chapter 38

"So, you've finally made your way here, boy!"

Mari stood in the doorway of another cell, a small light coming into the room from the hallway.

"As you can see, I'm at work and can't attend to you. Stand by her feet and stay out of the way of whatever you see come into this room."

Mari barely took a breath in her tirade. Collin didn't need her warning in any case. His full attention was riveted on the woman lying on the narrow bed. The woman he knew he loved with all his being.

Her name came out of his mouth like a drawn-out sigh, "Maggie."

The old Voodoo Witch laid a bony hand on his arm. Giving him a small shove. His eyes were fastened onto Maggie's lovely face, but he shuffled his feet until he was in the room. Mari closed the door behind him.

His knees rubbed-up against the hard planks that made the bed when the windowless cell was thrown into utter darkness. Collin stood like a statue. Knowing Maggie was within touching distance, made his control nearly impossible.

Suddenly, the room was bathed in a soft glow. Sitting on a shelf near the bed, a stout candle shadowed its dancing flame against the damp wall. Beside it, a small bowl of incense began to smolder. Both gave off a spicy aroma that had a strangely calming effect on Collin's strained nerves.

He looked back at Mari, watching the concentration return to the old woman's face. Collin saw her eyes roll back in her head until only their yellowish-whites showed. She began chanting in the alien tongue.

Collin returned his gaze to Maggie, expectant and hopeful.

In the better light he began to study her body. She still wore her linen trousers and silk blouse, but that was ripped open down to the waist. He saw where several buttons were missing, unconsciously slipping his hand into his pocket where he had saved them.

Her silk chemise was spattered with dark spots. Collin didn't want to admit what they were, but he had to look closer.

He leaned in and saw two more sets of bite marks. One just above her breast and the other on the side of her slender throat. Both were recent from the look of trauma to the skin around them.

He was about to touch her face when Mari's claw-like hand clamped over his wrist in a surprisingly strong grip.

"Don't be a fool, boy. The General will be here any second and he'll do for her then."

Collin was going to object, when the candle's flame shuddered, casting crazy shadows on the walls and ceiling of the cell, shadows that weren't theirs.

A sharp, whistling sound filled the small room. Collin instinctively covered his ears. Suddenly, the bowl of incense shattered and a thick column of smoke rose up from the scattered pieces.

Out of this turmoil stepped General Butler.

He looked as if he'd just come from the battlefield. His black suit was in shreds and long streaks of blood marred his face. His head was blown open, matting his hair with dark clumps of matter.

Collin blinked at what seemed an apparition from a mad house.

"General. I see you've engaged the beast," Mari's voice grated out each word.

Collin detected the slightest tremor in her voice.

Is she afraid? Collin thought, immediately alarmed.

"He is more formidable than he was in his younger years, Miss Mari. As you might recall, he was able to pluck me from my death bed while I was surrounded by armed guards at the doors, with two inside my rooms. And yet, he prevailed and returned to claim me. It was only your own Voodoo powers that kept me from entering his darkness forever."

Mari looked at his ravished body. Her face, a web of wrinkles, hiding the emotions Collin clearly heard in her faltering words.

"But…I could not save you from a blighted life as…a Vampire, General."

"I am not in his clutches, or under his control, dear lady! And that is all that matters! Now, we must proceed with the ceremony before we lose this girl to him."

Collin wanted to speak, but a sharp look from Mari who must have anticipated his questions and he swallowed his words. While his attention had been drawn away from Maggie, her eyes fluttered open. When they all looked back at her, she was trying to push herself up on her elbow.

Before he could reach her side, the General stepped in front of him and swiftly gathered Maggie's slender body into his arms. She looked into his lifeless eyes and let out an ear shattering scream.

Mari joined the General, effectively blocking Collin from touching the screeching woman. She slumped back against his tattered suit coat, fainting with fear.

Collin roughly pushed Mari aside and reached for his fiancé, trying to pull her from the General's tight embrace.

"I must take her to the fountain, man! Can't you see? She is close to passing from this life into the life of everlasting damnation?"

Mari came to Collin's side as he held Maggie's arm and threw something in his face. He immediately began to gasp for breath.

"No!" he croaked between hacking coughs.

He doubled over and when he straightened again, the General and Maggie had vanished.

Chapter 39

"You need to calm yourself, boy! You've no idea of what we are facing here. Your interference nearly cost your woman her life."

Collin sat on the side of the empty bed. He could feel the warmth of Maggie's body on the wood slates beneath his hands. He finally stopped hacking his guts out and was recovered enough to ask, "What fountain is the General talking about?"

"Ah! So you do listen! The fountain you passed in the courtyard of this cursed place. The waters are blessed. I have made the fountain flow again with the help of the General and he will take Maggie there to cleanse the new bites you likely saw."

"I could have done that. Why are you keeping her away from me?" he demanded angrily.

"It's for your own protection, boy. She is just as likely to try to bite you as she is to kiss you, in her state. I understand you have questions about General Butler, so I'll tell you some of his history with the beast, while you settle yourself. And we wait."

Collin sat still. Mari was so short they were almost at eye level.

"The General was badly wounded during the taking of New Orleans in 1862. In all the confusion, he got separated from his troops when they advanced on the docks, on the outskirts of the city. He was looking for a way back to his lines when something came flying out of the shadows, taking him to the ground.

He thought it was a deranged Confederate soldier, when he began to bite the General on his arms, eventually lunging at his throat. The attacker's incisor caught on the collar bone, tearing it loose from the General's body.

His men heard his screams and came running. The beast vanished back into the shadows.

The men brought him to my cottage, it being the closest shelter for their mortally wounded General. They discovered I was a healer and asked that I make him comfortable before he died. I did better than that, much better.

I prepared a juju to place around his neck. My magic would guard him from what I knew was "the man that never dies," the Count St. Germain. I had the soldiers carry him back to his quarters by buckboard wagon, instructing them to post guards around the house and inside his rooms. In the darkest hour, he came for him."

Collin had been following her story closely, but something was nagging at him while he listened.

He blurted out, "Wait a minute! You said "you had his soldiers carry the General back to headquarters. But, that means, you were alive during the Civil War!"

Mari threw a pinch of whatever he inhaled earlier and he coughed for a minute, but when he stopped, he was calm.

"Listen to old Mari, boy. I am a Voodoo Priestess and have powers you can only imagine on the Day of the Dead. I am here to protect you and your woman from the beast that feeds on human blood and would own your souls. I am not the one to fear! This man, this artist that my friend Isabella trusted and brought into her home, he has walked these grounds long before Isabella drew her first breath. He has seen wars and famines, plagues and purges. He has drunk the life from Queens and paupers carrying bedpans for the gentry. He knows most every language spoken or written. He's translated Egyptian hieroglyphs, unearthing vast treasures, making him wealthy beyond comprehension."

Collin gasped. *Just how old is he? How old is Mari?*

"This man is a beast," Mari continued, her voice rising with her obvious hatred for the vampire she called a beast. "He craves human blood and will be satisfied only when his victim is drained to the last drop. His body will glow with a twisted health that only his kind possess. You'll know he's well-fed when a deep red transforms his black eyes. Grayson

Gerrard is the vampire who made General Butler one of the Undead! I saved him before he claimed him as his slave. The General belongs to the shadows, but found some peace there, until I had to call upon his pledge to aid my magic."

Collin hadn't twitched a muscle while Mari described what he believed was only a character drawn from a writer's vivid imaginings. But Grayson Gerrard was a vampire, hundreds and hundreds of years old. Grayson Gerrard had made love to Maggie and he saw with his own eyes, how she had wrapped herself around his muscled body. Did this mean his Maggie would be turned into a body servant to this monster? Would she become a beast herself, hunting innocent victims to drink from them until she was drunk with their life blood?

Collin sprang to his feet, nearly knocking the old woman over in his haste.

"I'm going to Maggie! Don't try to stop me, Mari. I can help and I will."

Collin rushed out of the room into the dark hallway. He could hear the Voodoo Witch praying to whatever gods she knew, but within a few minutes her voice was lost in the swirls of shadows closing like doors around him.

He had his small lighter out again and snapped it open. He was alarmed to see the flame wavering and knew the fluid must be getting low. With the small halo of light, he found his way back to the entrance to the courtyard.

Outside again, he was thankful to see the moonlight bathing parts of the yard and most of the surrounding building. Looking around him, the monastery seemed even more sinister. He snapped the lighter shut.

The fountain appeared as a darker form among the black shadows.

Collin heard the splashing of water, and crept toward it, keeping to the clutches of thick shadows and small piles of rotting debris.

He stopped, crouching so he wouldn't stand out from the other shades of black while he listened. He didn't want to go charging in and run into something he couldn't handle. *That could be just about anything from this damned place,* he thought grimly.

There were no voices or sounds, other than the rise and fall of the newly flowing water. He hoped the General had washed Maggie off by then, or whatever ceremony the vampire general needed to perform.

He was about to get up when Mari's voice creaked into his ear. "Stay down, boy. The General has stirred more than the waters, I've been told."

Collin nearly jumped out of his skin when Mari appeared out of nowhere. He felt her rustling with her dress pocket. Before he could object, or question her, she grabbed his hand and slipped some kind of beaded bracelet over his wrist.

"Old Mari won't let you face the Dark Forces without juju, boy. The General has lost his battle with his Maker, the Count St. Germain."

Collin stiffened beside her at this news. "What? Does this mean Gerrard has Maggie?"

"Be still now and listen. The General was able to hide the girl beneath the Fountain of the Damned before he challenged his Maker for the last time.

He discovered a secret room there during his long years of wandering this place with the beast. St. Germain knows nothing of the room and your woman is safe there, until we can bring her out."

Collin was both relieved and deeply afraid. If General Butler couldn't fight the vampire St. Germain, how could he? Only him and the old woman squatting in the shadows beside him stood between the ancient vampire and the woman he loved.

Losing to the beast would condemn Maggie's soul and like the defrocked priests, she would live an eternity of evil and blood.

Collin looked over at the Voodoo Witch. The bracelet she'd slipped over his wrist began to heat and give off a subdued glow. Rather than burning him, it shot warm currents into his muscles.

He knew logically it was impossible, but he believed the juju gave him a supernatural strength. He found the witch watching him carefully. "I'm ready," he said, looking into her black eyes.

Chapter 40

"You need to calm yourself, boy! You've no idea of what we are facing here. Your interference nearly cost your woman her life."

Collin sat on the side of the empty bed. He could feel the warmth of Maggie's body on the wood slates beneath his hands. He finally stopped hacking his guts out and was recovered enough to ask, "What fountain is the General talking about?"

"Ah! So you do listen! The fountain you passed in the courtyard of this cursed place. The waters are blessed. I have made the fountain flow again with the help of the General and he will take Maggie there to cleanse the new bites you likely saw."

"I could have done that. Why are you keeping her away from me?" he demanded angrily.

"It's for your own protection, boy. She is just as likely to try to bite you as she is to kiss you, in her state. I understand you have questions about General Butler, so I'll tell you some of his history with the beast, while you settle yourself. And we wait."

Collin sat still. Mari was so short they were almost at eye level.

"The General was badly wounded during the taking of New Orleans in 1862. In all the confusion, he got separated from his troops when they advanced on the docks, on the outskirts of the city. He was looking for a way back to his lines when something came flying out of the shadows, taking him to the ground.

He thought it was a deranged Confederate soldier, when he began to bite the General on his arms, eventually lunging at his throat. The attacker's incisor caught on the collar bone, tearing it loose from the General's body.

His men heard his screams and came running. The beast vanished back into the shadows.

The men brought him to my cottage, it being the closest shelter for their mortally wounded General. They discovered I was a healer and asked that I make him comfortable before he died. I did better than that, much better.

I prepared a juju to place around his neck. My magic would guard him from what I knew was "the man that never dies," the Count St. Germain. I had the soldiers carry him back to his quarters by buckboard wagon, instructing them to post guards around the house and inside his rooms. In the darkest hour, he came for him."

Collin had been following her story closely, but something was nagging at him while he listened.

He blurted out, "Wait a minute! You said "you had his soldiers carry the General back to headquarters. But, that means, you were alive during the Civil War!"

Mari threw a pinch of whatever he inhaled earlier and he coughed for a minute, but when he stopped, he was calm.

"Listen to old Mari, boy. I am a Voodoo Priestess and have powers you can only imagine on the Day of the Dead. I am here to protect you and your woman from the beast that feeds on human blood and would own your souls. I am not the one to fear! This man, this artist that my friend Isabella trusted and brought into her home, he has walked these grounds long before Isabella drew her first breath. He has seen wars and famines, plagues and purges. He has drunk the life from Queens and paupers carrying bedpans for the gentry. He knows most every language spoken or written. He's translated Egyptian hieroglyphs, unearthing vast treasures, making him wealthy beyond comprehension."

Collin gasped. *Just how old is he? How old is Mari?*

"This man is a beast," Mari continued, her voice rising with her obvious hatred for the vampire she called a beast. "He craves human blood and will be satisfied only when his victim is drained to the last drop. His body will glow with a twisted health that only his kind possess. You'll know he's well-fed when a deep red transforms his black eyes. Grayson

Gerrard is the vampire who made General Butler one of the Undead! I saved him before he claimed him as his slave. The General belongs to the shadows, but found some peace there, until I had to call upon his pledge to aid my magic."

Collin hadn't twitched a muscle while Mari described what he believed was only a character drawn from a writer's vivid imaginings. But Grayson Gerrard was a vampire, hundreds and hundreds of years old. Grayson Gerrard had made love to Maggie and he saw with his own eyes, how she had wrapped herself around his muscled body. Did this mean his Maggie would be turned into a body servant to this monster? Would she become a beast herself, hunting innocent victims to drink from them until she was drunk with their life blood?

Collin sprang to his feet, nearly knocking the old woman over in his haste.

"I'm going to Maggie! Don't try to stop me, Mari. I can help and I will."

Collin rushed out of the room into the dark hallway. He could hear the Voodoo Witch praying to whatever gods she knew, but within a few minutes her voice was lost in the swirls of shadows closing like doors around him.

He had his small lighter out again and snapped it open. He was alarmed to see the flame wavering and knew the fluid must be getting low. With the small halo of light, he found his way back to the entrance to the courtyard.

Outside again, he was thankful to see the moonlight bathing parts of the yard and most of the surrounding building. Looking around him, the monastery seemed even more sinister. He snapped the lighter shut.

The fountain appeared as a darker form among the black shadows.

Collin heard the splashing of water, and crept toward it, keeping to the clutches of thick shadows and small piles of rotting debris.

He stopped, crouching so he wouldn't stand out from the other shades of black while he listened. He didn't want to go charging in and run into something he couldn't handle. *That could be just about anything from this damned place,* he thought grimly.

There were no voices or sounds, other than the rise and fall of the newly flowing water. He hoped the General had washed Maggie off by then, or whatever ceremony the vampire general needed to perform.

He was about to get up when Mari's voice creaked into his ear. "Stay down, boy. The General has stirred more than the waters, I've been told."

Collin nearly jumped out of his skin when Mari appeared out of nowhere. He felt her rustling with her dress pocket. Before he could object, or question her, she grabbed his hand and slipped some kind of beaded bracelet over his wrist.

"Old Mari won't let you face the Dark Forces without juju, boy. The General has lost his battle with his Maker, the Count St. Germain."

Collin stiffened beside her at this news. "What? Does this mean Gerrard has Maggie?"

"Be still now and listen. The General was able to hide the girl beneath the Fountain of the Damned before he challenged his Maker for the last time.

He discovered a secret room there during his long years of wandering this place with the beast. St. Germain knows nothing of the room and your woman is safe there, until we can bring her out."

Collin was both relieved and deeply afraid. If General Butler couldn't fight the vampire St. Germain, how could he? Only him and the old woman squatting in the shadows beside him stood between the ancient vampire and the woman he loved.

Losing to the beast would condemn Maggie's soul and like the defrocked priests, she would live an eternity of evil and blood.

Collin looked over at the Voodoo Witch. The bracelet she'd slipped over his wrist began to heat and give off a subdued glow. Rather than burning him, it shot warm currents into his muscles.

He knew logically it was impossible, but he believed the juju gave him a supernatural strength. He found the witch watching him carefully. "I'm ready," he said, looking into her black eyes.

Chapter 41

The General was reduced to a rotting corpse, skeletal arms and legs jutting out from shreds of black cloth. A silver dagger protruded from the chest cavity. What was left of his skull was mostly yellowed bone, empty eye sockets and broken teeth.

"You don't appear as magnificent after this battle as you have in past ones, my dear General." Grayson Gerrard's voice was honeyed, without a trace of rancor as he studied the remains of the General.

This was a man he turned during some terrifically dark years for the country. In fact, in the chaos of Civil War, the vampire and his woman fed well upon the stricken inhabitants of Paxton Parrish.

Collin and Mari watched from their hiding place, as he yanked the skull from the ravished body of the General and continued speaking to it, making him an audience of one.

"You should have remained loyal to me. Your vainglorious character has destroyed you, not my dagger. Though, it was skillfully applied as need be."

Gerrard's small bark of laughter buzzed in Collin's ears. Collin turned to his skulking partner, looking for some guidance on their next move. She remained silent.

Listening to the vampire, Collin noticed how Gerrard had dropped all pretenses at being a modern man, slipping back into his true persona, from centuries past. His way of speaking was too formal and sounded as if he should be standing in a drawing room in Parisian high society, not a decrepit Monastery.

His dark, wavy hair fell to his shoulders, worn brushed back from a high forehead, highlighting strong, perfect features.

He wore a loosely fitting silk shirt, button-less and hanging open to display a broad chest. The thighs of his long legs bulged with muscles in a pair of tight dark trousers, tucked into high riding boots, buffed to a dull-black luster. There was a sheathed knife on his right leg.

Studying this transformation, Collin thought the vampire could have stepped out of a painting from the Renaissance, hanging at the Metropolitan Art Museum. To Collin's mind, Grayson Gerrard no longer existed. He knew this handsome man's true identity. The Vampire, St. Germain.

"What now?" Collin hissed in the old woman's ear, tired of her silence.

His whisper carried to the highly sensitive hearing of the beast. He spun around, fully facing their direction, in the same motion, flinging the General's skull onto the ground.

The sound of the bones disintegrating upon impact held an eerie power over Collin's courage. If he wasn't there to rescue his love, he knew without a doubt he'd be tearing through the swamps like the devil was chasing him.

Collin and Mari were crouched, shoulder to thigh, her boney elbow jabbing into his side. He was watching the tall vampire a few yards off, when a tremor ran through the frail body beside him. He heard the breath leave her body in a rush of warm air.

He couldn't move a muscle, frozen into a solid block of fear.

He slid his eyes away from the tall figure by the fountain, long enough to see the Voodoo Priestess vanish.

He blinked into the darkness she left behind.

While St. Germain slowly scanned the courtyard, a dark cloud crossed the face of the moon. The already pale light dimmed and Collin almost missed the ripple of movement in the deepened shadows, where the island rose out of the swamp.

He lowered himself onto his belly, hidden completely behind a mound of rotted and encroaching vegetation. From this vantage, he watched as ethereal forms began to rise from the miasma of bayou surrounding the island. They surfaced without so much as a splash of the sluggish water, gliding toward the fountain at an unhurried pace. Shocked, Collin realized the brownish-colored creatures were once human.

They all wore some kind of monkish robes, tied at the waist with thick rope. Heavy cowls covered their heads, keeping their faces in deep shadow.

They drew near to the vampire forming a semi-circle around his tall, domineering figure. Their heads all bowed as if in the presence of a holy man.

For his part, St. Germain appeared disinterested in the approaching shades.

The dead priests and monks. He's called them, Collin thought, watching several more ghostly clerics enter the courtyard to join the others. Collin felt like his heart had stopped pumping blood, becoming like petrified wood in his chest. With Mari gone from his side, he suddenly felt vulnerable and unsure. His thoughts raced, trying to figure some escape route, but he knew the futility of such thinking. He could never leave without first finding Maggie. His only potential weapon was his flimsy lighter, low on fluid.

Pulling himself back to a crouch, feet under himself, ready to sprint, Collin decided his best defense was an offense.

He moved his hand to reach for the lighter in his pocket when a streak of moonlight caught on the beaded bracelet Mari put on his wrist before vanishing.

He touched it and tiny sparks flew out of his fingertips. Before he could react to this phenomenon, the deep silence shattered when the vampire shouted in a venomous tone, "It's time to end this, Collin. But first…"

He held out the head of Mari, the Voodoo Priestess.

A great chorus of howling rose up from the dusty throats of the fallen churchmen.

The Cyprus trees shuddered with the force of their combined voices, the Spanish moss swaying violently from side-to-side, adding a sound like a thousand bristles scrubbing the stone courtyard.

Collin flew into a silent fury at the sight of the old woman's head dangling from Germain's hand. Rather than react blindly to this provocation, Collin turned to face the back of the monastery. Knowing his voice would reverberate around the U-shape sides of the stucco building, he called out. "A coward's deed, St. Germain! Did you have one of your fallen priests do the job for you?"

"Ah. You have discovered my identity. You are not as empty-headed as a pumpkin after all," St. Germain responded.

Collin turned back in time to see the gleam of the vampire's white teeth in the pale moonlight. He looked up, realizing the moon was fully overhead, the gray clouds swept away from its yellow face.

He knew he'd immediately be seen, but Collin stood, angry and defiant.

Sparks shot out from his fingers as he touched the bracelet, but this time he felt that same surge of energy run up his arms as well. *Mari has armed me,* he thought.

With a warrior's roar, Collin ran at the tall figure and his band of evil swamp shades.

Chapter 42

Collin took courage from the juju bracelet Mari tied around his wrist before she vanished, only to be killed by St. Germain. He saw the fiery sparks shooting from his fingertips and felt a surge of supernatural strength pump up his body like Samson come alive!

He ran straight at the powerfully built vampire. St. Germain's handsome features twisted in an arrogant sneer at such foolhardiness. Dropping the witch's head, it rolled away, her steely-gray frizz matted with gore as it came to rest beside the General's shattered skull.

Collin closed on the imposing figure, but feinted left when he saw the blur of the vampire's right arm lash out at him. He felt like all his senses were heightened to unknown levels of awareness under the influence of the juju's witchcraft.

St. Germain smiled at the move saying, "Very nimble, my friend."

Collin let the juju bracelet slip down his wrist, gripping it in his right hand and making a tight fist.

He ducked under the taller man's left arm as it shot out to grab him around the waist to bring his neck to within striking distance of the long fangs shiny like blue-white daggers in a morbid grin.

Collin sprang up, his bunched fist connecting with the square jaw.

A flurry of fiery sparks flew from his knuckles, falling among the vampire's thick, shoulder length hair. The smell of burning flesh accompanied the singed odor of smoldering locks, momentarily distracting St. Germain.

Collin took advantage of the vampire's efforts to snuff out a small nest of orange flame rooted in his black hair and spreading to his silk shirt.St. Germain screamed out a curse while using his hands to slap at the fire.

Collin knew the old stories of how vampires could be destroyed by fire. He was getting ready to try to ignite another when his adversary vanished in a whirl of black smoke.

The vampire's abrupt disappearance triggered a surge of activity among the dark spirits he called from the depths of the bayou. The horde of phantoms began shrieking and crying out in eerie voices, making Collin's hair stand on end. The maddened spirits surged forward like one enraged being.

Collin stood rooted in place near the fountain, staring at the hooded mass moving slowly toward him. The murmur of the falling waters was drowned under the crescendo of their crazed shrieking.

Collin felt a swell of confidence in the face of this mass hysteria when the juju bracelet heated his hand. It felt like he held a lightning bolt.

He raised his arm as if in greeting. Hot sparks sprayed outward, like so many falling stars into the darkness of the courtyard.

The loose line of robed figures slowly moved closer. Then, the sight of sparks shooting from Collin's hand stopped them. They swayed in place as if waiting for a sign to move again. An eerie sound hummed in the air around the mob of spirits.

Thinking he may be safe from the screaming banshees, Collin backed up toward the side of the fountain.

He knew the General had been taking Maggie to the healing waters and that there was some kind of secret room within the imposing structure. He had to find it before she was lost to him forever.

He kept shuffling backward, watching the agitated spirits, when a robed figure broke from the line, charging him. It brandished a double-edged sword over its head, a glint of red eyes peering from the shadowing hood. A scream from the depths of Hades tore the heavy air as it hurtled toward Collin.

Suddenly, a rush of heat from the amulet turned Collin's hand into a burning torch. A thunderclap tore through the courtyard when a jagged bolt of fire hit the phantom squarely in the chest and it evaporated like water on a hot skillet.

Without pausing, Collin aimed yellow bolts of fire at the screeching line of the damned spirits.

Confused for a moment, he stood panting, looking around the moon-splashed piazza of the ancient monastery. All he saw were the dark outlines of the gently swaying cypress, their burden of gray moss absorbing the pale moonlight, looking eerily like Mari's wild head of hair.

"Mari," he whispered, in a gasp.

Her death caused a mix of sadness and rage to sweep over him, as his adrenaline-pumped body began to relax from its fighting stance.

Collin stepped over to the side of the fountain where the Voodoo Witch's head rolled beside the General's smashed skull. He needed to confirm what his eyes had seen.

Blinking rapidly, he saw both were gone.

Turning in a slow circle, studying the flagstones of the courtyard, he tried to understand the disappearance of the decapitated heads.

He moved to the base of the fountain, beginning to feel around its rough surface, for some kind of clue to a secret room, when he his arm felt a sharp pinch.

Looking down, he found Mari's piercing black eyes glinting back at him in the ghostly light of the moon.

"Mari! I saw your head!" he nearly shouted.

"Calm yourself, boy. It will take more than the vampire's evil eye to top old Mari's juju. St. Germain is an old enemy. I've hunted him over many years and this here was only a bit of a dust up."

Collin felt both relieved and terrified at the sight of the Voodoo Witch. She was apparently able to fake her own death and resurrection, but his relief far outweighed his fear of her powers.

"Is the General with you, Mari?" he asked hopefully.

"That honorable man has finally found his peace and is free of the curse St. Germain laid upon him. But we'll talk later, boy. Young Maggie is nearly his and if the beast turns her, I'll need to destroy her as well."

Collin barely felt the gnarled hand of the old woman guiding him to the other side of the fountain. All he could focus on was the possibility of having to kill his only love to save her from the undead life of a vampire.

Chapter 43

Mari checked to be sure Collin's juju bracelet was still secure on his wrist. Pulling his arm down so she could whisper close to his ear, she told him her plan.

They would enter a hidden room where she knew Maggie was being held by St. Germain. Collin was reminded that Maggie would be under the influence of the handsome vampire.

"He's likely bitten her again and it would mean only one more bite and she'll be turned. We need to get to her now, or lose her to the darkness," the old one wheezed.

Collin felt her sour breath tickle his neck, raising goosebumps on his skin. He still hadn't completely accepted that he was talking with a woman whose head he'd seen dangling from the vampire's hand. Everything had become inexplicable to him and Collin was a man who needed explanations.

Mari's shrunken body leaned away from him. She moved as silently as a puff of wind toward the back of the fountain.

"It's here," she hissed, pointing to a portion of moss-covered stone supporting the bowl of the large fountain.

Collin crouched low, running his hand over the slimy stone base, until his fingers brushed over a depression in the hard surface. He slipped his fingers deep into the spongy moss, gripped the lip of the handle he found and pulled.

Surprisingly, there was no sound as a narrow door pulled away from the fountain's base, noiselessly opening to the night air.

Collin was about to rush inside when Mari's strong fingers snagged his belt at the back of his filthy trousers.

"I need to lead the way, boy. He's likely set traps while he waits for us."

"But he thinks you're dead, Mari."

"Oh, that head was just one of my little diversions you could say. He'll have discovered his mistake by now. Keep close to me and whatever happens down there, remember your juju will protect you and the girl. Now, follow without another word."

Collin had more than a word he wished he could speak. He wanted to know how they could defeat a centuries old vampire who had already avoided Mari's powers for most of that time. Did she possess new Voodoo magic that could finally put an end to St. Germaine's blood lust?

He moved quickly behind the hunched figure. He found he had to bend his six foot body to enter a low-ceilinged chamber where the ceiling was domed and he could stand naturally.

A faint streak of moonlight followed them inside, where it struggled to overcome the inky darkness. Collin reached into his pocket for his lighter. The click of opening it sounded like a rifle shot as it was magnified and bounced off the solid granite walls of the secret room.

Mari was at his side in an instant.

"Not your light, boy," she warned in a hushed voice.

Suddenly, Collin saw the same, small glow coming from Mari's wrinkled hand he'd seen on his first visit to the island.

Their surroundings were brought into stark relief, exposing trickles of water streaming down thick stone, covered in a slimy blackish-green slime.

Collin felt he'd been swallowed alive by the bayou.

He saw his companion's squat figure move ahead, but Mari was now holding something pale and long in her left hand.

Bones, he thought, remembering the Voodoo Witch's use of this macabre weapon.

She moved ahead, the magic she'd called up clenched tightly in her gnarled fist.

Collin was told this fountain was used to cleanse the fallen clerics and monks being punished on the dreadful island. But he suspected the hidden room was used for something else. Torture of the condemned men and the few women passing through this hell was most likely common and brutal. The jailors were likely as demented as their prisoners.

He gave himself a mental shake to refocus on his own mission, vaguely wondering why this place kept insinuating its evil into his thoughts.

Mari was dragging the bone over the surface of the circular walls, making a soft scratching sound, like tiny mice feet on the rough stone. Without warning, the bone shot a bright bolt of light directly into a recessed area carved into the thickest part of the wall. It was little more than a narrow cleft in the granite base, but large enough for the single coffin installed there.

"Here!"

Mari's shout stopped Collin, freezing him mid-crouch.

Her arm was held straight out, with the long bone pointing at the outlined crèche and the beautiful woman lying on top of the stone sarcophagus.

"Maggie!" Collin said in a rush. He was stopped from running to her side when Mari's arm shot out like a guard rail.

"Don't be a fool, boy. This is the beast's first trap. He will be out feeding now no doubt, not wanting to drain the girl completely and ruining his plans for her. Old Mari needs to study this trick before we can take her out of here."

Collin wasn't convinced and was chaffing under her restrictions.

In the light from Mari's hand and brighter light coming from the bone in her other hand, the burial niche was well-defined.

The coffin Maggie was lying upon was a dark, gray stone. It was covered with intricate carvings of devilish creatures with split tongues and long tails, cavorting with what appeared to be beautiful girls. Collin noted all the women were marked on their necks and over their hearts.

"Mari, you must do something before he returns," he whispered frantically.

Without speaking, the Voodoo witch reached her free hand into a pocket, somewhere in her shapeless dress. When she withdrew it, Collin saw her holding what appeared to be a clump of human hair, absurdly tied with a black ribbon.

"Mari, is that…"

"Hair? Yes, boy. The General brought it to me when all this evil began to rise from the bayou like the stink of wild cat urine.

It's from St. Germain. The devil himself. Took from him by the General's sword when he was fighting for his life, with the beast those many years ago. It was tied in a neat tail and came away from his head in a swift arc of the General's blade. Now I'll use it to let us enter this room holding your Maggie."

The old woman took the hair and wrapped it around the bone. There was a crackle like the snapping of freed electricity through the air.

Collin moved with Mari and they entered the burial chamber, silent except for the sizzle of current running ahead of them. When they came to Maggie's side, Mari made a quick count of bites she'd already received, while Collin had to restrain himself from scooping her into his arms.

"There are six and I smell the putrid milk of death flowing through her already. See that crusted, white stuff?"

Collin leaned closer to Maggie. Except for the gentle rise and fall of her chest, she was completely still. She was naked except for her silk panties. He saw that a whitish fluid, trailed down the soft mound of her full breast.

"She's nearly turned, boy. No time left to fret over her. We have to move her now and hope the beast doesn't return before we get out."

Collin took off his badly ripped shirt, slipping Maggie's arms into the sleeves. His brawny chest and shoulders flexed slightly when he reached down to lift her unconscious body.

"We're going home, my love," he whispered, kissing the chilled flesh around her ear.

Mari kept waving the bone with its bunting of thick black hair, back and forth, like a divining rod.

Chapter 44

They made it back to the secret doorway leading out of the fountain base, with Mari's juju bone creating a shield from attack during their retreat.

The unconscious Maggie began to stir, murmuring against Collin's bare chest, squirming in his arms. He tightened his grip around her, moving faster to keep up with the old woman as she crossed the moon-swept flagstones of the courtyard.

There was no sign of any swamp spirits rising up from the muck. Collin began to feel more confident that they would escape the evil place unobserved.

As he followed close behind Mari, he realized she was heading toward the hidden path through the bayou's brown waters. He didn't relish the notion of trekking through the dangerous sludge of the swamp, but his biggest fear was rousing the condemned spirits of the fallen priests and monks that confronted him earlier.

He shifted Maggie slightly, so he could be sure he still wore the juju bracelet that saved his skin earlier. It was wrapped loosely around his right wrist. He felt more secure even though his feet made sucking sounds when he stepped onto the muddy ground surrounding the island.

Mari looked back over her shoulder at him.

"Listen carefully to me, boy. This here part of our trip is going to get a touch more difficult with the girl along. You need to keep her from touching the water with any part of her body. If as much as her finger stirs the waters, it'll raise the dead, scattered below like clam shells waiting to be pried open.

That lot you dispatched with your juju were just some the beast called to divert your attention. Below the waters of the Bayou lie his personal guard, sworn to his service."

"Are they vampires too?" Collin asked, looking down at the cloudy brown water.

"Nay, not blood leeches like the beast, but twisted souls, happy in his service as they were doing their sinful deeds in life. Come, no time for tongue wagging. Keep your woman raised out of the water, lest you stir the spirits beneath with her scent as one he has chosen."

Setting his feet as securely as he could on the hidden stone path beneath the water, Collin's knees shoved the top-floating debris to the side, as he carefully placed his next step on the slippery rock beneath.

He knew this path would give out soon and he'd be treading through the weedy muck until they reached the Butler Plantation and the gardens where they first entered the swamp.

Mari never appeared to hesitate in her own crossing, occasionally looking back at him and the restless young woman wrapped tightly in his arms.

After several long minutes plodding through knee-deep water, Collin realized Mari no longer walked on the hidden stone path. The thick waters had already climbed to her waist, her dress billowing around her like a black jelly fish. He knew it wouldn't get any deeper during their crossing but couldn't help feeling alarmed when Mari began to slip and had to right herself by grabbing a low hanging Cyprus branch. Somehow, she managed to do this without uttering a sound.

The piercing sound like a blunted horn blast tore through the damp air. All natural rustling and chittering of the swamp stilled.

"Conch horn! The beast knows we have Maggie!" Mari shouted back to Collin.

"He won't know we've discovered this pathway, so just keep walking, boy, and don't stop till we're out of the swamp. His minions can't leave its foul waters!"

Collin heard another blast and cut a quick look in the direction of the old monastery.

A light shone through the secret fountain doorway, backlighting what looked like a giant of a man, even at a distance. St. Germain. The dashing figure stood with his long legs apart, his white silk shirt open to his waist. Collin couldn't make out his features, but he saw him comb his fingers through his shoulder length hair, shining blue-black in the moonlight.

The vampire seemed to be unhurried in his movements, but slowly raised a hand and the sound of the horn blasted the darkness once more.

Collin had an urge to cover his ears from the sharp sound. It stretched into the long, unbroken scream he knew could only come from the belly of a monster. His feet automatically moved over the slick rock path while he struggled to raise Maggie higher. With his next step he was suddenly off the pathway, his feet sinking into the muck of rotted vegetation.

His jostling of her body dislodged Maggie's arm where it was pinned under his own. Collin felt it slipping toward the water, stirred into low, brown waves, washing over his knees.

Mari reached the swamp's edge, coming out onto the footpath near the plantation's gardens. She turned back to watch Collin's progress and saw Maggie's arm dangling within inches of the murky water.

She rushed back into the swamp, her dress heavy with muddy water and pulling her lower into the vile muck. Collin lifted the semi-conscious Maggie higher, but this quick movement caused the water to splash upward, soaking her forearm.

A slight stirring of the waters surrounding them drew Collin's attention.

He looked down in time to see a skeletal arm shoot out of the murky water to his left. This was followed by the head and torso of a hooded creature wearing the familiar monk robes.

The rank odor of death and corruption washed over Collin where he stood.

The spectral being moved silently through the sluggish water toward him.

Collin struggled to pull his mud-caked shoes a few feet more, stirring up a swirl of muck around his legs.

The brown clad phantom mimicked his movements, keeping pace from five feet away. It was not hurried, or trying to rush at Collin, but slowly glided like a shadow through the water, never making so much as a single ripple.

Mari was mired down by the weight of her sodden dress. In a gesture of frustration, her knobby fingers plucked open the buttons of the garment and ripped it over her head, where it bunched up and sank beneath the brown water.

Her upper body was bleached corpse-white, little flesh covered the ropey muscle of her arms. She wore a loosely fitted undergarment, now plastered like a second skin to her flat chest.

Collin heard Mari's garbled language. A few words floated across the water as he cautiously moved a few more steps toward land.

At the last word, the Voodoo witch disappeared under the murky surface. Before Collin could react, she was standing beside him. Tiny waves washed against his thighs, as Mari grabbed his arm, pulling herself up.

"There are at least ten of the beast's chosen Death Bringers down below and more answering the call of human flesh."

"But I kept Maggie from touching the water. How…?"

"When the water washed over you both, it carried the scent of their vampire master. They will never allow us to pass, so we must make our stand here and now."

Collin's face reflected the doubt and fear roiling around in his head and gut.

"What can I do with Maggie? I can't very well fight and carry her."

"Leave that to me."

A few more mumbled words in the guttural tongue and Maggie was ripped from his tight grip and hung in the damp air above them. His shirt hung down like a limp flag.

"Why can't you send her back to the house?" Collin asked, frustration tinging his voice.

"If I do that, you and I will never survive. She is a deterrent to a full scale charge by the Death Bringers. They won't chance her being lost to the waters and they understand I can drop her like a stone if I want."

"In other words, she's our hostage!" Collin stated.

"Only as long as need be. Now hold that bracelet tight in your hand. I see the first one has been joined by a brother," she said softly.

Mari stood at Collin's back, barely coming up to his shoulder.

Collin moved the juju bracelet into his hand, wrapping his fingers tightly around it, feeling it beginning to heat up. He shook his fist and spikey shards of yellow current buzzed through the air like maddened fireflies.

Mari watched the first arrival. She didn't have to warn Collin this was a fight to the death. Their only weapons were the Voodoo charms and the hope that floating Maggie's body above them, would stop any all-out assault.

The first spirit moved within easy striking distance for Collin.

The ghostly monk glided over the brown muck like a water spider. The bottom portion of his face, was a patch of black space under the deep shadow of the cowl. Collin clearly saw the blood-red glow of his eyes.

Collin threw his arm back in an arc, using his perfect soft-ball pitch. Suddenly, the blackness clinging to the Cyprus trees lit up with a spectacular shower of jagged yellow bolts. Scorching the spectral body and turning the Death Bringer into a green vapor, fusing with the drifting swamp gas.

Behind the thick mist, three more hooded creatures sprang up. They passed through jutting tree limbs, mired in the thick bayou mud and tiny islands of dirt, covered in wildflowers like floating gardens.

Collin shot a look at Maggie, still suspended above. He was alarmed to see she had somehow drifted several feet back, in the direction of the monastery.

He didn't have time to puzzle out why Mari would move her, because the three Death Bringers had closed on him in a semi-circle.

He turned his attention back to the immediate threat, but not before he saw the Voodoo witch waving the long, yellowed bone in one bony hand, while holding what appeared to be a glass shard in the other. Before he looked away, he saw a searing red light, as straight as an arrow, shoot from the sparkling fragment.

The Death Bringers never uttered a sound as great holes burned through their ethereal bodies.

Chapter 45

"Mari!"

Collin clambered over to the old woman's side.

"Get Maggie down and let's get out of here before more Death Bringers show."

The Voodoo witch was still holding the long bone in front of her and without facing him pointed upward with it.

Maggie was gone.

"What? Where?" he gasped.

"Listen to me carefully, boy. The beast has called to the serum he injected into Maggie's body. It answers to him like a dog to his master. Your woman has returned to St. Germain and he will be preparing her for his final bite. After that happens, she is lost to us and will have to be destroyed like St. Germain."

Collin was too stunned to speak, but began moving back toward the secret path through the swamp. There were no other Death Bringers to fight and nothing but the sound of his ragged breathing as he lifted his mud-heavy shoes for the hasty return trip to the island monastery.

Collin began to speak to Mari, but she held her hand up to stop him.

She pointed to the outline of the algae-smeared cloister, standing starkly against the moonlit sky. A room at the top of a lookout tower was shedding a feeble glow into the inky night.

Collin recalled the tower was attached to the refectory by a small companion way. They hadn't searched up there since the vampire had taken Maggie to the secret room below the fountain.

Mari hurried along the hidden stones and the two of them set foot on the monastery grounds a few minutes later.

"He must believe his devils have done us in ,while we tried to cross the swamp, else he wouldn't be so bold to show that light up there," Mari said in hushed tones.

Collin listened for any sounds that might prove his Maggie was still alive and still human. A cry, a word. Nothing, but the bayou whispering its riddles.

"We need to climb stairs that will be crumbling into dust, but I will go along first to try to mend them enough to hold your weight, boy. Do not rush ahead of old Mari, or I can't protect you from the beast and his trickery."

Collin had no intention of moving without the Voodoo witch's protection. He was no good to Maggie if he was dead and there was no doubt in his mind that was the fate the vampire planned for him. They quickly crossed the flagstone courtyard, making their way undercover of the shadow of the high stucco walls.

The Guard Tower loomed above, a dark finger pointing to infinity.

Collin swallowed hard as the old woman slipped her hand into the iron loop hanging on the wooden door and pulled. The silence surrounding them went undisturbed.

They stepped into the entryway, a spiral staircase filling the narrow space. Collin had to stoop in order to clear the door lintel, his broad shoulders brushing the fuzz growing over the rock walls of the tower.

He noticed Mari somehow retrieved her dingy black dress from the water. It hung like a wet rag thrown over a chair back, making her seem smaller and more fragile.

Collin was quickly dissuaded of the notion that the old woman as weak. Her veiny hand stretched over the curved wooden banister and she began mumbling in her foreign tongue. He saw no discernable difference in the crumbling wood of the steps, but when Mari began to climb, he took confidence from her and quickly followed upward.

Only a pale light coming from the room above guided their feet over the worm-eaten and warped stair slats. They reached half-way up the twisting staircase, when they heard a long scream followed by uncontrollable sobs.

They both froze, the dust motes they raised in their passage floating down to the floor far below.

"He's begun," Mari whispered, her voice tinged with despair.

Collin made to shove past her on the narrow stairs, but Mari barred his way.

"Nay, boy. There's no helping your woman by barging in. We must find a way to draw him away from her."

In the smothering confines of the staircase, Collin watched as Mari carefully shuffled around in one of the hidden pockets of her sodden dress. When she withdrew her hand, a small white bird lay in the nest of her fingers. Its snowy colored feathers had a dewy shine to them, as it nestled down like a newly hatched chick. Beady, pink eyes, stared up at Mari's wrinkled face, as it turned its head from side to side in jerky motions.

"Yes. You will do nicely," Mari whispered close to the bird's head.

The bird stepped out of her grasp and onto the spiral banister. With a shudder, it opened its wings to their full width.

Collin blinked several times, watching as the bird transformed and grew to the size of an enormous eagle before his eyes.

The white feathers puffed out, while the bird pecked gently at them, preening itself, before closing the wide wings upon a body more dragon, than bird like.

"That will do," Mari crooned to the massive creature. "We have work here for you."

The old woman's face took on a kind of inner glow, emphasizing the deep creases in her skin. Collin watched her closely for a sign of what was to follow.

Mari leaned close to the waiting bird and spoke again in the jumble of languages Collin was familiar with by then. The bird cocked its huge, sleek head, seeming to nod with understanding of her orders. Holding its perch on the railing, it spread its wings to their full span and flapped them twice before leaping from the banister.

The wind it raised at it circled around the confined space ruffled through Collin's hair, chilling his bare chest with the damp air swirling in its wake. The tips of his massive wings swept the dank, round walls of the tower, breaking lose the grime and dust of hundreds of years.

Collin knew it was Voodoo that called the creature flying upward in tight spirals. He watched as it folded its massive wings tightly to its body, diving into the room at the top.

The pale light coming from above them was momentarily blotted out. The two stood in pitch blackness for a few heartbeats, on the rickety staircase. Collin felt a shudder of the wooden staircase and knew Mari was climbing again. Gripping the crust-covered railing, he groped up the next few steps.

A deep-throated screech from the monstrous bird tore through the tower, amplified by the stone walls until it sounded like a tortured soul from Hades to Collin's ears.

Collin saw the old woman at the top of the stairs as he hurried up to a small landing outside the room. Mari took his arm to pull him down to her, her dry lips brushing his ear. "The bird will have snatched up your Maggie and is taking her back to Isabella's. I ordered it to bring her back to the solarium. But I can't be certain the beast hasn't defeated the bird. If he isn't in this tower, he may have interfered with my magic."

Collin's feeling of frustration doubled. He wanted to see Maggie for himself and now she'd been whisked off like a piece of carrion by the great bird.

His face betrayed his anger at this plan, but Mari seemed not to notice. They heard another screech, only this time muted by distance and finally swallowed by the night.

The old woman retrieved the long bone from wherever she had stashed it and checking his juju bracelet once more, they crept toward the dim light of the silent room.

Chapter 46

It was empty. Collin and the Voodoo witch stood inside a room barely more than an alcove in the tower. Likely a guard post, with rough cut windows every few feet around the walls. It jutted like a boil from the side of the tower, large enough for two men to act as sentries for the monastery.

A bell had likely been housed there to signal the residents below. The wide niche where it hung was long abandoned to nesting birds from the swamps, entering through gaps in the rotted rafters.

"Where is he? How could he get past us on the stairs?" Collin was turning in slow circles, addressing his questions to the vacant room.

Mari moved closer to the opening overlooking the grounds below, turning to Collin to answer.

"St. Germain is 'the man who never dies.' Do you think he can't exit a room as easily as we entered? Come, boy, we need to get back to the plantation and the solarium where hopefully, my white shadow bird stands watch over Maggie."

As they left the tower, movement near the fountain caught Collin's eye.

"Mari, I think we have company over by the fountain."

The witch nodded, already noting the figures melding back into the shadows beneath the stone dish.

"It'll be a few of the beast's Death Bringers. He's trying to keep us from returning to the mansion before he has turned Maggie. We need to deal with this lot quickly, boy, else all is lost."

She signaled for Collin to move off to the left, while she was absorbed into the blackness around them.

Collin's eyes had long since adjusted to the night. Every glimmer of moonlight was heightened by his sensitivity to the dark. The blur of movement he first noted, took shape and he saw two Death Bringers standing close to the fountain.

They wore the robes and cowls he had seen rising up from the swamp waters, but these two held scythes in their hands.

Like two Grim Reapers, Collin thought, a shiver running down his spine. The lack of his shirt, somehow, made him feel more vulnerable.

He touched his wrist, finding the bracelet had grown extremely hot. He marveled that it never burned him. *Who needs a shirt if I have this,* he reasoned, trying to steel his nerves as he approached the fountain.

Collin raised his arm as he got closer to where the two hung back under the great stone basin. He pretended not to notice them. When he saw them raise their weapons, he sent a dozen ragged bolts of yellow current, arcing directly into the ghostly forms.

They each lit up and their long scythes began to flame like candles while the hot current ran through them. He wasn't sure how ghosts could burn but moved quickly to send more of the deadly heat crackling into the spectral beings.

Great cries of torment rose from their dry throats. The bayou answered these screams with a cacophony of night screeches and howls, splashes, and slithering, into the murky waters.

The silence that followed was so profound Collin had a moment of panic, thinking he'd gone deaf with the uproar.

He turned, trying to locate his companion, but as usual, the old woman seemed to have vanished into the night. *She's infuriating,* Collin thought while anxiously beginning to move toward the covered walkway leading to the Refractory. As he made for the rough door into the common mess room, he felt a deep chill surround his body.

He was unable to move or retract his left hand from the iron door ring. He could barely make out his extended arm in the darkness but saw a glowing white frost creep up from the fingers to his elbow and onto his shoulder. To move meant the risk of snapping his arm clean off at the shoulder where the unnatural hoarfrost stopped.

He carefully crossed his free right arm over the numb left forearm, letting his juju bracelet come into contact with the blueish skin. He had no idea if that was the right move, but it was all he could think to do.

There was a sizzling sound as the heat from the amulet touched his blue-white flesh. He didn't dare scream out and give himself away until he was free. He moved the bracelet up and down the arm until he nearly fainted with the pain but was able to pull his arm free after two passes with the charm.

Slumping to his knees for a moment and avoiding any further contact with the cursed door, Collin stood, cradling his injured arm against his chest. He shuddered as the ice-cold skin of his arm came into contact with his bare skin.

He whispered Mari's name, desperate to call her to his side before he was caught in another of the traps laid by the beast.

That thought triggered a mental picture of the vampire, St. Germain, known to him and others as Grayson Gerrard. His charismatic presence and impossibly handsome looks had always nettled Collin whenever he was in his company. And now he had his love, his Maggie.

This line of thinking seemed to energize him and he moved back to the inviting door. He needed to find the Voodoo witch before he could face the vampire back at Isabella's. She knew him and his powers and Collin was barely holding his own against his mere minions. He'd never survive a confrontation with the beast by himself.

With a tight grimace of determination, Collin began peppering the thick wood with sharp bolts of yellow current. The door exploded inward ,forming scattered piles of debris, releasing an acrid odor into the clammy air.

Collin rushed through the opening, pausing for only a second, before he heard Mari's wheezy voice in the stillness. He followed her husky voice until he reached the row of monk's cells where they'd discovered Maggie earlier.

Is she back here, he wondered hopefully. He saw a flickering light. *A candle.*

Moving carefully so as not to scrap his shoes on the stone, Collin laid his hand on the partially closed door.

Before he could enter, he heard Mari speak. "Come, boy. I've taken care of this one."

He pulled the door open and was immediately rushed by a Death Bringer slamming into his mid-section. It was incredibly solid for a spirit, but Collin didn't have time to puzzle that out. He spotted Mari lying like a corpse on the plank bed as his head slammed against the stone floor with such force he saw blotches of white light.

He was sprawled between the small room and the hallway when he saw the phantom was armed with a scythe. Collin rolled, springing to his feet, using his strong legs and back to propel him upward. The wicked cutter struck the stone where his head laid a moment earlier, raising sparks like fiery dust motes off the floor.

Collin held out his arm, the bracelet hot on his wrist. He willed it to shoot its deadly jagged bolts, but it merely hung off his arm. While it didn't send the sharp current into the shade, something in its nearness to Mari seemed to rouse her.

A raspy sound came with a deep breath as the old woman struggled to clear her head. She looked over at Collin just as the scythe was once again raised for a killing chop. She shouted out, making the malevolent being spin in her direction. It was met with the long bone that materialized in her scrawny hands.

Touching it to the Death Bringer, it immediately fell into a pile of gray ash, picked up and blown with a sweep of Mari's gnarly hand.

"What kept you, boy? I could have been buried deep in the bayou by now."

Collin gave her arm a gentle tug as he helped her stand. She didn't resist when he steered her out of the cell and then out into the night. The silence was complete and yet Collin felt hundreds of eyes watching them.

"Mari, I heard your voice, and followed it until I found you, but you were under some kind of spell when I arrived. It couldn't have been your voice that led me here. Who was it?"

"Good thinking, boy. You're fast learning the tricks the beast can employ. The Death Bringer mimicked my voice, right down to my chants, though I doubt he had any sense of what they meant. They're ignorant creatures, the Death Bringers. All they really know is how to follow their master's orders."

They exited the building, Collin following Mari closely, not wanting another separation along the way.

"Hurry, we need to get back to the Solarium where I'm certain we'll find St. Germain is holding your woman. He'll be waiting for us to show up and we won't disappoint him. They'll be a few alterations in how he finds us, however."

Mari gave a soft, almost maniacal laugh, pointing the way back to the submerged stone pathway through the swamp with the long, yellowed bone. Following the grisly pointer, Collin was reluctant to re-enter the thick waters, but more fearful of losing sight of the old woman.

Maggie was in grave danger from the vampire. If they couldn't reach her before he inflicted his last of the seven bites on her body, she would also be destroyed by the Voodoo witch.

Collin kept Maggie's lovely face before him while they trudged back into the verdant Bayou. An alien environment and one he'd never understood. *It's like another planet in here,* he mused, lifting one foot, then the other out of the sucking, mud bottom.

Chapter 47

Several lights shed their warm glow onto the grounds and portico of the grand house. It gave Collin a jolt seeing the stately mansion looking so welcoming and full of life, when he knew its mistress to be murdered.

This fiend must pay for his crimes, he thought, remembering his old friend Isabella's loving nature toward him and Maggie. When he saw her last, she was stretched out on her bloodied bed, her face contorted in unimaginable pain and terror.

All these thoughts tumbled around in his head, while he moved stealthily from shadow to shadow behind the Voodoo witch.

Collin knew they were headed toward the solarium but had not figured out how they would enter without St. Germain knowing it. Mari told him she was certain the vampire would be holding Maggie in a room situated in a remote spot from the rest of the huge house.

"He'll take his time to inflict that seventh bite. It's likely he'll keep Maggie under his influence for his enjoyment.   Then he'll turn her and she'll be lost to this world," Mari explained as they approached the side of the sprawling house.

"The beast fears nothing in this human world. Least of all, you and me," she snarled out the last words.

"He'll regret that arrogance, I promise you."

Collin wouldn't allow himself to think about what St. Germain was doing to Maggie. The picture of her lying beneath him was still too vivid in his mind.

He struggled to stay focused on the path they were taking, as he followed Mari.

He was told they were headed to the Solarium, but the old woman made a sharp turn when they reached the side of the house. She was moving instead toward the kitchen at the back.

He didn't question her, figuring she had her reasons, but this route would add several minutes to their rescue plan.

Does Maggie have those minutes, he wondered with growing alarm.

A single, unshaded light hung over the back door leading into the kitchen.

"Annette won't be down here for another two hours," Collin whispered to his companion.

Though Mari had never been a dinner guest at the Butler manse, she had often visited with her good friend under the cover of darkness. She was well aware of the functioning of the antebellum household but kept her silence at being instructed now.

"When we get inside boy, you must find a secret door built into the pantry. That passageway leads directly to the solarium. I will be near. Now go."

Before he could object to her abandoning him once again, Mari melted back into the dense shadows cast by the house. Collin stepped up the small cement stoop and tried the kitchen door. It turned easily. The expected screech of old wood was gratefully brief as he slipped through.

The shadowy room was fragrant, years of cooking smells clinging to every surface, along with the rich, woodsy scent of an old fire in the large hearth. Collin reasoned the maid would be down with the dawn, even though her Mistress was dead. *Old habits don't die as easily as people,* he thought, searching the room for the pantry.

He remembered when he had lunch with Maggie in the kitchen, noticing a door opposite the fireplace. The maid had gone in and out of there several times bringing out supplies for the evening meal.

Collin moved around tables and chairs crossing the large, tiled room. Opening the door, he grabbed his lighter, flicking for the small flame and began searching the surprisingly large pantry. He moved a few items of dry goods, feeling around the wall behind and was about to give up when his hand knocked over a tin onto the hardwood floor.

The sound reverberated like a gun shot, its sharp echo making him cringe where he stood frozen, waiting for a response. A minute passed and all was still, except for the thrumming of his pulse in his ears.

Resuming his search, he moved his tiny light to the corner of a lower shelf. Reaching in, his fingers connected with a lever. It had been cleverly folded in until it was nearly smooth with the wall.

Pulling this toward himself, Collin watched as a hidden door swung into a narrow passageway, leading away from the kitchen. Deciding to keep his lighter working a bit longer, Collin began moving along a sinuous route he was told would lead to the solarium.

That thought made him move as quickly as the dank, twisting passage would allow. He knew his lighter would be out of fluid any minute but hoped it would last until he found the way. He stopped once to orient himself as best he could, imagining how this trailed through the downstairs rooms. He figured it had more than one turn-off and didn't want to end up in the wrong part of the house.

While he stood encased in the tomb-like silence, something ran across his feet. He jumped back a little and heard a squeal as his foot connected with the rodent. Collin hated rats and prayed these were merely mice, heading toward the kitchen.

Collin wondered if the vampire's extraordinary hearing had already detected his movements within the walls. Maybe the pack of rodents would mask his own movements. He moved on, careful to search the floor ahead with his foot to clear his way of any furry interlopers.

The yellow flame began to tremble as the passage made a sharp turn into what appeared to be a dead-end. Collin tried again to visualize the layout of the huge mansion. Recalling a parlor and some kind of storage closet just before the room he sought, he guessed this was the closet.

He held the dying flame close to the wall, locating a carved-out hand grip. Pulling this toward himself, the tiny fire sputtered out, leaving only the oily smell of a spent lighter behind.

Collin found himself in the long, carpeted hallway, running from the foyer, to the cozy sunroom at the back of the house. It was only a matter of several feet that separated him from Maggie and the vampire.

The bracelet on his wrist was oddly cold, with none of the expected heat encircling his wrist. Colin knew little of Voodoo and wondered if the juju had worn off the talisman given to him by the old woman.

Mari's wrinkled face popped into his head as he hugged the walls and moved down the hall. His shoes were soundless over the plush floor covering.

Where the hell is she? he thought, wishing the Voodoo witch would do her usual popping up act.

More afraid than he could admit to himself, Collin caught sight of the intermittent glow of the relit-fireplace in the Solarium. It was casting jumping shadows on the Persian carpet a few feet from where he stood against the wall. He touched the bracelet to see if it was hot yet and came away with only a chill feeling of dread in the pit of his stomach. He had no weapons, so he'd have to improvise until Mari showed herself.

Collin stood in the shadow of the wall directly across from the invitingly open door. He had a clear view into the solarium, lit by the jittery flames in the hearth.

The vampire wrapped his strong hands around Maggie's upper arms, bringing her face closer to his. Maggie's beautiful face was as pale as alabaster, making her appear more statue than living human. She still had on his torn shirt, but it barely covered her as it slid down her slack arms.

Collin held his breath as the beast released one of Maggie's arms for a moment, to brush aside the lustrous black hair from her slightly arched neck. His movements were unhurried and looked almost loving to Collin, watching the intimate gesture from the hallway shadows like a sick voyeur.

St. Germain glowed in his own masculine beauty. His perfect body exuded a strength that was undeniable and intimidating. This was no match for Collin's resolve to rescue his love the curse of eternal life with the Dark Lord she would serve.

Collin entered the room with a howling charge, throwing his height and weight at the vampire's side, dislodging his hold on Maggie.

His scream of blood-lust was rewarded as the beast fell hard to the floor. Collin was still roaring his outrage, when the vampire surged under him, pushing him aside like dandruff off his shoulder and disappeared through the open window.

Maggie stared straight ahead into empty space.

Collin jumped back to his feet, grabbing her around the shoulders and bringing her close in a tight embrace. Her body felt stiff and unresponsive. He was calling her name over and over, trying to pry her loose from the hypnotic spell.

Still holding Maggie it dawned on Collin how simple it had been for him to send St. Germain scurrying into the night. *How did I do that without my juju working?*

He held Maggie at arm's length to study her more closely. He had to determine if she'd already received the seventh bite, marking her as dead to him forever. He gently slid his tattered shirt, letting it drop to her waist. Her breasts were as white as her face. She was unresponsive to his gentle touch. He studied her closely and counting the wounds on her neck. *Still only six bites.* Relieved, he sighed deeply as he struggled to put the shirt back on her, before sweeping the transfixed girl into his arms.

A thought stirred in him and he hurried back to the elevator.

"Time to find the old woman," he said to the silent female lying stiffly against his chest. Her breath on his bare chest was as cold as her skin, stirring an unknown emotion inside of Collin.

He felt afraid of this beautiful woman in his arms.

Chapter 48

All of Collin's questions remained unanswered as he took the squealing elevator to the second floor. Maggie hadn't stirred in his arms. He wasn't even certain she breathed.

Collin placed her in one of the guest bedrooms of the silent house. Her body was still icy to the touch, as he covered her with a heavy quilt, tucking it carefully around her shoulders. No spark of recognition shone in the dark blue pools of her eyes. The hypnotic hold the vampire had over her was strong and Collin feared he would never break through to her.

"I have to leave you, love, but only for a little while."

Slipping the juju bracelet off his wrist, he placed it on her chest. The gentle movement of her breathing gave Collin some comfort as he watched the amulet rise and fall.

"I can't say this will help you if he comes back, but it might. Mari might be somewhere up here and I need to find her. I'll be back, Maggie. I love you, darling."

He placed a kiss on her forehead, immediately shrinking away from her. That brief touch of his mouth brought to mind the stone walls he had touched at the cursed monastery.

He shut the door firmly after one last look back, knowing the bracelet was no deterrent to St. Germain's plans to have Maggie for himself. As he walked over the deep plush carpeting of the upstairs hallway, Collin poked his head into every doorway. He desperately hoped he'd stumble across Mari somewhere among the shadowy rooms.

He reached the last of the many guest rooms, when it dawned on him that he was unconsciously dodging the wing occupied by the Mistress of the house, the now deceased, Isabella.

Thinking it cowardly, trying to avoid searching her rooms, Collin quickly jogged to that side of the hallway before he could change his mind.

He checked the first room, an office for Isabella and moved on to the comfortable sitting room and bath area. That left the bedroom. A vision of his friend lying like a torn doll in a black nightgown sprang vividly to his memory.

Moving toward the closed door, Collin was reaching the glass knob when he heard the strange dialect Mari spoke when working her Voodoo charms. But there was something very different about this magic casting. There was a hint of desperation in the old woman's voice and it sounded strained, as if not her own.

Collin pulled his hand from the knob, afraid he might have already given himself away. The flow of the thick language was uninterrupted and went on a moment longer.

Collin leaned closer to the heavy door. There was a high cackling laugh. *Someone else is in there,* he thought, jerking his head back from the door.

He was unsure how to proceed. He didn't want to leave Maggie for much longer, but he needed to know who was with Mari. His fear stirred some old folk tales up from his earliest childhood memories. Voodoo was used to raise the dead. He now knew Mari and Isabella were old friends, though that wasn't general knowledge.

Wondering if Mari would use her powers to restore her dear friend, seemed preposterous to him. It was time for answers. Collin twisted the doorknob and burst into the semi-darkness of Isabella's bedroom.

He only saw a woman dressed in black stooped low over an unmoving form on the bed. Running toward the scene, Collin shouted out as he grabbed the thin arm.

"Mari, no! Don't bring her back!" When he spun her around, Collin let out a long gasp. Standing before him was the revived body of their friend, Isabella Butler.

Her face still bore the ravages of terror, just as her neck was still torn open in several spots. The front of her nightdress was crusted with her spilt blood, the coppery odor coming off her still strong. Collin froze, holding Isabella's arm a breath longer, but then he threw it away from himself as if he'd mistakenly handled a cottonmouth from the swamp.

There was another sharp cackle from the bed. He shot a quick glance at the occupant, seeing Mari's deeply lined face grinning back at him.

"No need to concern yourself, boy. She hasn't been able to hit on the right combination of words yet. I am only here long enough to see what she's capable of and now I know." Without another word, Mari came off the bed with more alacrity than he thought possible. She interjected her small body between the shocked Collin and the resurrected Isabella. "I know you aren't my old friend, Isabella," she wheezed softly into the dead-white face.

Glancing over at Collin, she shook her head sadly. "There must have been one last bite that I somehow missed when I found her. It was given by the beast's woman, Leslie Porter Booth, no doubt, like all of the others. My friend was drained of her life's blood over a few months, so changes in her health would go unmarked by those closest to her. She was a vain woman when it came to her independence, Miss Isabella was! And now you stand here, wearing her tortured flesh, as if born to it. Well, I'll have none of that I tell you!"

Collin was transfixed by Mari's harangue and barely registered her hands shoot out, throwing an ochre colored powder directly in the face of the newly made zombie, Isabella. There was an immediate reaction by the possessed woman, her hands flying up to her face, trying to scrub at the thick coat of dark red. At one point, she turned her back on the Voodoo witch and the immobile young man, muttering dark phrases that took shape, flying around the room like crazed ravens.

Collin tried to cover his ears but found he was unable to move a finger.

Mari swatted at the phantom birds viciously with her ever-present long bone. Whenever the bone connected with a dark shape, horrific screams that might have come from a madhouse shredded the air.

Silence abruptly descended on the room when the possessed Isabella stopped her curses and stood rigidly by the side of the empty, blood-spattered bed. Slowly, she began to turn toward the waiting pair, her face in deep shadow until she turned completely in their direction.

Collin took an involuntary step backward and Mari's voice nearly faltered.

"Annette!"

Chapter 49

The maid glared from one to the other, finally settling on the Voodoo witch. "You never guessed I was one of the superior beings, did you old woman? You thought me a simple house churl no doubt. While I have lived as such many centuries ago, I have also enjoyed the luxuries of a king's bed and a Sultan's Harem. Oh, you look skeptical of my past lives being lived in such a beautiful body that men would desire me above all else. But I can assure you, I had the pickings of lusty women spread out for me across all of Europe, for longer than either of you could possible imagine"

Mari spoke at last. "Am I correct in thinking you have hunted the beast for yourself over many lifetimes? Lost him to the Count, didn't you, in one of your more unattractive bodies I expect."

"Ah! You are clever to have guessed at my scheme to find him. Yes. The beautiful body and soul of the man known as Grayson Gerrard will belong to me and me alone."

"I don't expect he'll desire you much in your current state," Collin said, a sneer in his voice.

"And you are the most annoying fiancé. My Grayson so desires your woman he began making my other puppet jealous. You both remember the lovely Leslie no doubt?   She inflicted most of Isabella's bites on the tiresome old biddy as a consolation from me for the loss of her Grayson to a mere human. Naturally, I took the heaviest flow of blood from your dear friend." Her last word dripped with sarcasm, showing her complete disdain for Isabella.

"When did you take Annette? Was it in our time, or in another?" Mari asked, seeming genuinely curious.

Collin guessed she was stroking the vampire's vulnerable vanity. He noticed the Voodoo witch had pushed a hand deep inside her copious pockets, keeping any attention off her movements by talking.

The vampire had only revealed the maid's head and face to them, jutting from Isabella's body like a head on a spike. Now she shed Isabella's fragile body onto the bed, like another skin, while she answered. He watched how it reverted to its death mask and sunken form. He felt relieved his friend was no longer being used so miserably.

"Annette was a former landlady of mine in London. I hated her for her house rules. Among them, not allowing young men into my rooms. So unsophisticated and backwards of her. I needed a quick disguise, however, after I joined a close friend in some casual blood orgies. You might know him as "Jack"? Covered Whitehall in red, we did!"

Her laugh was like a physical punch to Collin's gut. It sickened him even more than the sight of Isabella's used up body.

"Where is your pretty young man, Grayson, or should I say St. Germain?" Mari asked politely.

Collin watched for her hand to reemerge holding some kind of juju to use on the vampire until they could dispatch her with fire.

That thought made him think of his empty lighter. There was usually enough in the way of oily fumes for one more strike to take and flame. He reached into his own pocket and covered the lighter with his hand.

"Aren't you a tad jealous of his falling in love with this boy's woman? The way I see it, he's ready to make her his, permanently. That would put you in a rather odd position," Mari said, with fake sympathy.

The vampire was completely transformed at this point into Annette. The woman she had been manipulating to her ends for several hundred years.

Though her current body was plain looking and frumpy, the vampire made gestures like a woman who was used to her beauty being the topic of conversation. Her hand smoothed her coarse hair away from the fine lines on the sixty-year-old face. Her eyelids fluttered coquettishly at Collin.

"My Grayson shall be totally committed to me and pleasuring me, in whatever form I happen to take. So, enough talk from you both. I'm feeling a bit peckish from all this tiresome chatter." Before he could muster a response, the vampire sprang at Collin. In a blur of movement her arms went around his naked torso, locking him in an iron-like embrace. She cooed into his ear, "I'll begin with you, my dear. Just enough to keep you quiet and lying here for my next snack. I love young blood!"

Her mouth clamped down hard on Collin's neck. He tried to kick out at her, but within a few seconds of her sucking on his neck, he collapsed into her incredibly strong arms. Annette effortlessly lifted his six-foot frame into both arms, depositing him onto the bed, bedside Isabella's corpse.

She looked back to snatch up the tiny old woman, thinking to drain her until she expired. "Where are you hiding, you stupid woman? Why not feed me? You'll be gone before long, forgotten, dust and bones. You might as well give some nourishment to me. If you show yourself now, I won't have to take your darling Maggie for a little while more. I will need her lovely body soon, but if I feed on your scrawny flesh, she can live in her own skin until Collin here says his goodbyes. Now, isn't that kind of me? I do have a heart after all, just not one that's beating?"

Her laughter became a howl of rage as she turned over furniture, swiped at heavy drapes and tore through closets. She screamed dark curses, again filling the chilled air with phantasms, their voices penetrating the unmoving Collin's mind like shards of glass ripping along every nerve ending.

Finally, frustrated beyond control, the vampire, went over to where Collin lay, stretched out and vulnerable. His naked chest was heaving with his own frustration as he struggled to overcome the effect of the serum she injected into his system when she took his blood.

"Oh, my dear boy, you look positively delicious," she panted over his broad chest. She raked her fingernails over his arm until small pools of blood came to the surface of his torn skin. Bending over his arm, she began to lap at the blood seeping out. Lifting her frizzed head for a moment she said, "Think how delightful this will be when I possess the beautiful Maggie's lush body. Think about her soft skin rubbing you all over. I have been thinking about it for quite some time now. When the old woman is found, I think I'll roast her before dining."

Her laughter was quickly muffled as she sucked and lapped at new scratches on the helpless man.

Chapter 50

Collin came to with Mari holding his hand and gently stroking his tousled dark hair. He shivered when he realized he was propped up against Isabella's large bed. He began struggling to get up. "Don't fret yourself so. Old Mari has taken care of things here and placed Isabella in the family crypt."

Collin's eyes slowly came into focus. He remembered. "I've been bitten by Annette!" he blurted.

"Yes, but my magic was very potent and finished the nasty creature off."

"But my juju didn't work and I gave the bracelet to Maggie. Mari, she said she was going after Maggie! I need…"

"You need to sit a moment longer, so I can explain what's happened."

Collin felt wild-eyed but forced himself to settle down.

"Your juju is no longer contained in that leather bracelet I put on you. Listen to old Mari now. You can't know the secret ways of the ancient Voodoo practices, but when I tied the gris-gris on your arm, I also made you into a "Trojan Horse." Do you recall that tale?"

Mari's laugh sound like a horse's snort. She explained her ingenious method of destroying the vampire, enjoying every detail she related.

"After she bit you, I had to disappear so she would turn her hungry eyes back to your young blood. Your blood was the "Trojan Horse" and held a secret inside every drop! The juju filled your rich blood with the magic of the purest silver. A deadly brew for any vampire."

Without thinking, Collin began rubbing his arms. The muscles burned, as if he'd been lifting heavy weights. It was a good feeling and he swung his legs off the bed and got to his feet with a renewed strength.

Mari smiled and took his offered hand to scramble to her feet. Though her dress was only slightly damp, Collin could still smell the pungent odor of the bayou. *I must really stink to high heaven! he thought.*

They went directly to the guest room where Maggie was stashed for safe keeping. Collin noticed her eyes were finally closed. She looked to be sleeping peacefully until they approached the bed. As they leaned over her, Maggie's gentle breathing became labored and her eyes suddenly snapped open.

"Collin! It really is you!"

She began to sit up, but with a gentle push Collin kept her from moving. "Darling, I carried you into one of the guest bedrooms at Isabella's. You're safe now, my love."

Mari came close to the bed, her voice full of concern.

"We need to move out of here, boy. No time for lingering looks. But tell me, girl, has St. Germain been with you

"Here, in this room?"

"Who's St. Germain?"

"Ah," Collin interjected.

"You and I know him as Grayson Gerrard, Maggie," he answered her.

This time Maggie did bolt upright and in doing so dislodged the bracelet Collin laid on her chest. "What was that?" she asked, looking more confused.

Mari gave Collin a little shove and stepped closer to the girl.

"You have been bitten several times by a vampire, girl, and he wants one more bite at you to make you his in his dark world. Now, get up and we'll leave this place until I can figure where the beast is hiding."

They helped Maggie to her feet where she swayed for a moment before signaling she was strong enough to walk. Up until then, Collin had used his hands to help pull her out of the bed, but when he wrapped an arm around her shoulder, Maggie screamed and jerked out of his grasp as if she'd touched an open flame.

"Oh, my. It's the pure silver character I laid upon your blood I fear. Best let me handle her myself," Mari said, taking Maggie's elbow to help her shuffle slowly from the room.

"But Mari, I thought your spell on my blood, or whatever it was, would only affect vampires."

"It will give a jolt of unpleasantness to any who are as close as this girl to turning," Mari answered, nearly pulling the girl along the hallway. "Our time here at Isabella's is over. You two young people must go to ground, as if the devil himself was hunting you. He is!"

With Maggie struggling to keep up with the old woman's pace, Collin kept a sharp watch around the hallway as they entered the elevator.

The whine of the mechanism during their descent sounded to Collin like it could raise the dead, a thought that made him instinctively reach for Maggie's hand. She let him take it, but he saw a look of pain pass over her face and withdrew his fingers.

"It'll be alright, darling. Mari will have us both right as rain before long," he said, trying to sound convincing.

He gave her a forced smile and moved toward the front of the elevator, expecting to hold open the door and mesh grate for the women. Instead, when they reached the foyer there was a brief hesitation followed by a deep rumble beneath their feet. They were suddenly being thrown around the small elevator car of the still-moving machine.

"This can't be happening!" Collin called out incredulously.

"This elevator can't go to the cellars!"

The compartment came to a halt with a hard shudder when it hit bottom.

Collin was at the grate, pulling it back so they could get out. All of them seemed badly shaken by the unexpected ride and abrupt stop.

They were met with stark silence as they huddled together in a Stygian blackness. Somewhere, a soft drip etched itself into the fabric of the dark cellar. Collin thought it as damp and foul smelling as the bayou mud still caked on his shoes and clothing. A puff of clammy air stirred the hair on his neck, raising goose bumps on his naked torso.

Mari brought a small light to her right hand, still holding Maggie's with the other.

Maggie looked down at the shriveled palm. A round stone glowed with a small yellow flame. She made no comment.

"We have been waylaid, I fear," Mari said, her voice sounding strained to Collin's ears.

Maggie finally spoke, her gaze darting around, trying to penetrate the pitch black of the cellar. "I think he's down here, waiting for us. For me!"

Collin stepped closer, trying to calm her fears, but knowing she had to be right. *Why else are we down here?* He turned away so she wouldn't see his own fear rising like a gas bubble in his gut.

Mari gave Maggie's hand a quick tug.

"No more of that kind of talk, missy. Old Mari is sworn to protect you and this boy here. The beast brought us down here to torment us before he carries out his plans for Maggie. I have my own plans and you young folk need to trust me for it to work. First, I need to rid you of the silver curse I put on your blood so's you can keep this girl close."

"But I'll need another of your juju bracelets, right?"

"I'll be leaving you better defended than a trinket like that." She mumbled a string of foreign words, putting a brown spotted hand on Collin's arm, saying, "There. You're free of my charm."

She handed over the long, yellowed bone Collin had seen used effectively against the vampire's minions and Leslie. He took it gratefully, hoping he wouldn't need to use it.

"You, girl, must wear this around your neck and don't remove it, no matter what words that beast uses to persuade you." She slipped a heavy-looking necklace over Maggie's head. When it flattened out around her neck, Collin realized what he took for beads were actually teeth. They may have been from an alligator, but somehow Collin knew they were from an animal unknown to any, but the Voodoo witch.

"Now, you are both ready. I will leave you to find your way to the staircase and your escape from this place."

"But the darkness...we need your light," Maggie said hurriedly.

Mari reached into another deep pocket, bringing out a stone the size of a quarter. "This will do for you and it won't draw too many eyes." Handing the rock to Maggie, Mari moved toward the deepest part of the cellars. Within seconds, her small form was absorbed by the hungry darkness.

Chapter 51

With Mari somewhere in the cellars, hunting down the vampire, St. Germain, Collin and Maggie were left to fend for themselves in the dank confines below Butler Mansion. They only moved a few feet when Maggie grasped Collin's arm in a tight grip. In the tiny glow radiating from her hand, he saw her beautiful face fill with something other than fear.

"Collin, no matter what happened before to either of us, I need you to know I have always loved you and nothing will change that no matter how I change."

Collin was touched by Maggie's words and with his free arm drew her in close to him. Their kiss was gentle and when they pulled apart, Maggie's eyes glittered with unshed tears of relief.

After a moment and a whispered conversation on the layout of the basement area, they began moving toward the only room they remembered exploring when visiting Isabella as children. The wine cellar.

Constantly busy with the many soirees hosted at Butler Plantation, it was an invitation for adventure to the two as youngsters and they were often found wandering through its seemingly endless rows of bottles. Now, the small light cradled in Maggie's hand turned out to be more reliable than they dared to hope. Moving slowly along the hard-packed dirt floor, they found the door carefully marked *Wine Stores*, with a heavy padlock joining the handles.

The area dedicated to preserving the expensive selection was huge, with an anti-room beyond the padlocked doors and another locked door before reaching the wines.

When they were small, all this was exciting to see. Now, they needed to use this room to orient their search for the staircase they knew would lead to the first floor and freedom.

"We'll come out in the kitchen and Butler's Pantry once we find the stairs," Collin was saying in a hushed voice.

"They should be close by," he added, with more confidence then he felt. Though they hadn't seen or heard anything threatening, they both admitted that they felt eyes watching their movements. Maggie held his free hand tightly, staying close to his side. He gently moved her toward some huddled shapes that turned out to be old chairs and a sofa.

Maggie held her light higher to study the pile. They both froze. The soft plop of the gentle drip they heard earlier morphed, growing in volume until it became the roar of a wave, crashing against a seawall at high tide.

"My God, Collin! It sounds like…"

Before she could finish, a mighty rush of water raced toward them from out of the darkness. Colin lunged for the settee in the cast-off pile. Flinging Maggie face-down on the narrow seat, he wrapped his body around hers just as the black wave hit.

The sturdy couch floated free of the bunch, with Collin and Maggie holding on to the improvised life raft. The force of the wave pushed them further down the long corridor of the cellars. They rode in complete darkness, the light from the fire stone gripped close to Maggie's chest.

After a minute of the wave's sweeping energy, they were smashed against a wall and stopped. They lay stunned and shivering. The flood had carried them deeper into the cellars and further from the staircase to freedom.

Collin shifted off her, helping Maggie stand. She opened her hand, relieved to see the small flame pop into life when she uncurled her fingers.

Collin's spoke in a hushed voice, leaning close to her ear. "Do you remember Isabella telling us a family legend about how General Butler had another level built below the cellars of the Butler mansion? It was supposedly used for slave running. Isabella told us it was built over an underground river, remember?"

Maggie watched Collin's serious face, closely. It had taken on a ghostly quality, hanging over a void where his lower body stood close to her.

"Do you think that's where we've ended-up? In some kind of subterranean hideout? "

"Makes sense. The beast will do anything not to lose you, Maggie. That wave proves he can use some powerful forces to prevent our escape. And he knows this old mansion from long before Isabella was born in it."

"But how…"

"No time to explain, darling. We've got to find the way out."

The soggy couch had come to rest against thick walls, carved out of natural rock. Maggie held the long bone Mari had given Collin, while he held the fire stone, moving it around, trying to study the area.

He crouched down trying to see where the water was draining, figuring it might lead to the outside.

"Maggie, hold the bone straight out, like I saw Mari doing, it may create some sort of protective barrier for us. I'll keep the stone until we locate the exit from this hellish place."

Collin gripped her elbow and they started out, small rivulets of water splashing around their feet as they moved. He felt a definite incline to the ground as they followed the receding water. After several minutes trying to penetrate the blackness around them, foot by foot, Collin began searching the stone walls for sconces and possible torches.

Maggie spotted something in one of his quick passes over the rock face.

Collin used the long bone to push a torch through the bracket holding it in place and after several frustrating attempts he lit the dry bundle of material with the fire stone. Shoving the stone into his pocket, he smiled at Maggie for the first time since they started their nightmare journey.

The area was instantly lit up and less threatening as he moved the torch in a slow circle. Collin insisted Maggie take the torch so he would be free to use the bone if needed.

They set off, looking around themselves in amazement. It became clear quickly they had entered another world.

The world above and this one below the heavens. This one, closer to hell.

Chapter 52

Mari had been patient long enough. She let the wave wash over her, tumbling within its suffocating grip until she felt as battered as a beaten rug. *He's up to some of his fancy tricks,* she thought grimly, wringing water from her dress skirts. *I can't let him know he didn't succeed in drowning me like a rat in a floundering ship. I'll leave a little something to show I am lost in his black waters.*

Mari reached under her dress, pulling her gris-gris free of the sodden chemise.

"Hate to part with this," she muttered.

Sighing, she slipped the thin leather string the amulet hung from over her head. Her own fire stone bounced its small glow about with her tugging. Its light fell across a pendent with a moon-like stone surrounded by tiny bird bones and all mounted in a pure silver setting.

"The beast can't touch you my darling, but he'll think me dead as I'd never part with you," she muttered, placing the charm on the sodden ground. Mari knew the vampire would detect its powers and investigate. She was sure he'd believe her drowned in the dark avalanche of waters he freed upon the tunnel.

Mari followed the two young people, relying on the light from the fire stone they used and the smallest sounds they made as they moved. She'd been doing this since they parted. They didn't need to know they were her bait, used to lure St. Germain out of his crypt, wherever that was in the endless underground.

That boy is fairly clever, for a dandy, the old woman thought. She'd grown fond of the young man and was glad he'd managed to save himself and the girl.

Mari couldn't let them know that destroying the vampire was paramount, even to saving them. It was a difficult choice, but she really had no options. Letting the vampire live meant unleashing his vengeance upon the people of the bayou. He would harvest the innocent like a human scythe and create others like him to serve his passions and needs.

Mari had watched this happen many years ago when the beast took the General from this world of the natural. Fortunately, his humanity was not completely lost to him, but Maggie was much closer to that fate. If she was turned by the vampire, St. Germain, Mari was prepared to destroy the monster she would become.

Moving along the wet corridors of the tunnel system, Mari heard the soft footsteps of the couple just ahead. She knew they were trying to move in silence, but unlike her, they didn't have the skills. Her own feet were shoeless, those being lost in the flooding of the cave. This proved uncomfortable to her bunions, but helpful to her stealth.

They stopped just a few yards away, but as she was hidden in the shroud of blackness she was certain they hadn't a clue she walked behind. When a torch flared into life, Mari quickly moved out of the fingers of light probing the shadows where she hid.

Very clever boy, she thought with real pride in Collin's resourcefulness.

Listening closely to their hushed voices, Mari made out a few words.

"We'll need to follow…tunnel…yes…until …outside."

The broken conversation was enough to know they were going forward.

Mari watched as they moved off.

After a good ten minutes of careful walking and groping through the snaking tunnel, the pair stopped. Mari followed their gaze as they looked upward. The torch revealed a gruesome collection of skeletons, hanging in long lines of cages suspended from the rock ceiling. Many appeared ancient, mostly reduced to fine dust with only a few arm or leg bones showing through. Others, still retained their features, though they looked shriveled.

Mari knew this must be the beast's feeding grounds.

The old woman heard the gasps and intake of breath as Collin and Maggie moved hurriedly through the grisly collection above them. It was a few minutes before they finished running the grim gauntlet.

There were likely hundreds of victims here, taken by the vampires over the centuries. Mari felt her resolve to destroy him harden inside her. To her mind, he was not surviving this night, no matter what, or who, would be sacrificed.

The Voodoo witch clearly heard Collin tell Maggie he heard something. She moved closer. "I think we're being followed," he said, lowering his voice.

Mari knew it was not her silent footsteps he'd detected. *Will he show himself?* Anticipation building, she dropped to the tunnel floor, wrapping her black dress like a cocoon around her body. She would look exactly like part of the rock face at a glance. She felt herself meld into the stone wall while she waited.

Her heart hammered in her thin chest at the prospect of the vampire's approach. A tingling sensation began running up her arm where it was in contact with the wall.

He found my amulet and the silver isn't enough to prevent his handling it! I can feel the stone dying in his cold hand. I must get it back before I lose its power to his darkness.

It wasn't long before the tall, stately figure passed out of the dank gloom and into the stray beams of light from the torch. He stopped, studying the scene ahead. His dark hair was now held back in a thin strip of leather, better defining his handsome profile.

To his mind, the two lovers had moved on, oblivious of the fact that they were being hunted and the hunter was closing in.

The old woman watched as St. Germain removed something from his pocket. Maggie's silk chemise.

In an uncharacteristic gesture of tenderness, the vampire held it to his patrician nose and took a great whiff. She heard him sigh deeply. The old woman knew his longing for the beautiful girl would not go unanswered for long.

The vampire suddenly spun on his heels, peering back into the depths of the darkness behind. Mari could feel the cold stare of his slate-gray eyes as they scoured the area for an enemy. *He senses me near. The amulet must have heated when it came close to me.* Mari scarcely breathed, slowing her heart until it barely fluttered. She knew this would make her vulnerable, but there was no choice if she was to remain undiscovered.

Her vision began to blur as faintness crept into her consciousness.

The vampire abruptly turned back when he heard voices.

Mari came to herself, feeling the vampire's attention drawn away from where she was hiding and slipping into unconsciousness.

From their voices, she was guessing the couple had discovered the old cart tracks running from their position in the tunnel, to the opening that emptied into a ten-foot drop into the bayou.

The old woman knew this was where the General had been carrying out his secret smuggling missions after the Civil War. He moved munitions, arms and mercenaries through this underground system, selling all of it to other men, no better than war lords after the American conflict.

The tall figure began moving away from her hiding place, allowing Mari to raise her heart rate and breathe normally.

A close call. If the beast had discovered her she would be no use to the young people she'd promised Isabell she'd protect. Finally able to get back on her feet, she cursed the stiffness creeping into her old joints as the chilled air invaded her frail body.

She stepped away from the wall and took up her position behind the undead beast she vowed to kill once and for all.

Chapter 53

Maggie and Collin stood next to a rickety wooden cart, its iron wheels badly rusted but still in place on the narrow-gage tracks.

Collin examined it to see how rotted the cart was. "It's not too bad, Maggie. I think we should get in and ride down the incline ahead. It doesn't appear too steep from what I can tell."

Maggie was exhausted. Being able to sit and ride out of the chilly tunnel system sounded wonderful. "That would be great, Collin. I'm so tired."

Collin reached out to her, placing an arm around her shoulders. The long bone in his other hand hit the ground with a dull thud.

There was an immediate response in the ground surrounding them. Collin tightened his grip as the bone began to vibrate violently in his hand. They both felt a tremor under their feet. The cart moved an inch, then another.

"Maggie, throw away the torch and get in! Now!" he yelled.

With his help, Maggie was able to scramble over the lip of the cart. Collin caught his trousers on a ragged edge when he jumped in after her. A quick tug freed him and he grabbed for a wooden side, still gripping the bone.

The trembling continued, becoming more violent. The earth under the cart bucked like a wild mustang. The area around them was lit by the torch lying a few feet away. They were moving forward and Collin could see the dim curve of the horizon, further down the track.

Without any warning, the cart groaned into life, beginning to trundle down the crusted line of track. It gained momentum the further it moved along the gradual slope of the tunnel floor.

"Hold on tight, Maggie! This may get bumpy as we pick up speed. I'm certain this is our way out!"

Collin was almost giddy with the notion of escaping the cellars and their dreadful secrets. He was beginning to feel less threatened as their speed increased. His relief was fleeting, however, as they began to move faster and faster, indicating he'd underestimated the extent of the incline. He kept his fears to himself, scooting over to position himself directly in front of Maggie.

While her eyes were squeezed shut, he took a last look into the murky tunnel they were leaving.

His eye caught a momentary distortion caused by movement in the shadows, black on black, but shuffled, like a deck of cards. Suddenly, as the cart shook madly, going into a sharp bend in the tracks, they heard a high-pitched screech.

The cart hurtling down the line like a rock shot from a sling suddenly screamed under them as it struggled to a dead stop. Collin was thrown forward and then backward, as he tried to shield Maggie with his body. He felt his ribs and arms being slammed into the sides of the cart and was afraid his back would be snapped when they came to a jolting halt.

He could see how close they'd come to freedom. There was a vague light on the track, further ahead. He reasoned it was the opening from the tunnel, the escape they'd been searching for.

Maggie's voice brought him back to their current situation and he looked down at her face.

"He's found us, Collin. I can feel him nearby."

Collin felt something warm trickling down the side of his forehead, onto his cheek. His fingers came away wet and he probed the wound, making sure it wasn't more serious than a deep cut.

Maggie seemed to focus on him more clearly. Her own fear blotting out the circumstances.

"Collin, you're bleeding!"

As if her words conjured the vampire, he appeared at the back of the cart.

"I can actually *smell* your blood Collin, but then, I suppose you already know that about my talents."

Collin was momentarily stunned at St. Germain's unexpected appearance, but the vampire's soft laughter infuriated him. He grabbed Maggie's arm, making her move behind him. The wobbly cart groaned with the shifting movements. Maggie crouched in a corner, her arms wrapped tightly around herself. When he looked back at her, Collin saw her eyes were wide, but he wasn't certain it was fear he saw there.

He turned to watch the vampire for his next move.

Never taking his eyes off St. Germain, Collin called back to Maggie.

"Maggie, remember how much we care for each other. Don't let him confuse you. He's using some kind of glamor like Mari told me, trying to keep you under his control. You have to fight him!"

"You are a pathetic creature," St. Germain said, inching closer.

"Her very blood answers to me now."

Turning the full power of his dark gray eyes upon Maggie, he said, "Come to me now, beauty." He moved to the other side of the cart in a blur of motion, suddenly looking down at Maggie's upturned face.

"Collin, my God! Help me!" Maggie pleaded, even as she began to stand.

Collin looked down, furiously searching the bottom of the cart. He finally reached down, grabbing the long bone. It was lodged against a corner, but with one angry pull, Collin was armed.

Praying silently that it still held the Voodoo magic that Mari had demonstrated, he thrust the bone at the extended hand being offered to Maggie by St. Germain.

The second it connected there was a sizzling sound followed by a sharp yelp of pain. A surprised look crossed the vampire's face. With an uncanny gesture of control, he used the uninjured right hand to cover the blackened skin.

Collin smelled the unmistakable odor of burnt flesh, feeling his stomach lurch at the sickening stench. He felt no pity for the beast and quickly followed the first jab with another at St. Germain's perfect face, connecting with a high cheekbone and upper lip.

"Enough!" roared the vampire, taking hold of the bone and ignoring the pain of scorching skin yanked it out of Collin's grip. He threw the weapon back into the oblivion of the shadows, panting like a bull ready to charge.

Collin looked over at Maggie only to find her standing and offering her hand to St. Germain.

"Maggie, no!" Collin screamed as the beast took hold of her hand and elbow and floated her out of the cart. Collin had no time to react. The vampire moved like a streak of lightning, wrapping his arms tightly around Maggie. He stood only long enough to sneer at the stricken look on Collin's face.

"You have proven more foolhardy than coward, but you have lost never-the-less." St. Germain and his captive vanished back into the inky depths of the tunnel stirring the shadows like a dark wind.

Collin leapt from the cart, but knew it was useless to try to follow. He needed the Voodoo witch, but for now he'd have to retrieve the long bone. He had seen it hurt the vampire and looked forward to using it on him again.

He could still see somewhat, with the ambient light coming from the tunnel exit.

We were so close, he thought as he felt around on the ground with his shoe. He nearly lost his footing when he connected with something and it spoke.

"No sense kicking in this black porridge, boy. I have the bone."

"Mari!" Collin almost shouted in his relief at finding her.

"Hush now. We don't need to stir up anything unwanted just yet. You did well with the bone as I saw...and smelled." She chuckled.

"He's taken Maggie and we need to find them before..."

"Calm yourself. Maggie is well protected from the last bite. She still wears the necklace I gave her before he arrived."

"You saw him? How long have you been watching? Why didn't you help us against him?"

"I have been following you for quite some time but wanted to remain unknown to St. Germain until I had more help."

The old woman raised an arm without turning and a familiar form emerged from the shadows.

Chapter 54

Collin lurched to grab the long bone from Mari's hand.

"It's her! Annette!" he yelled.

"Not the possessed woman you helped me destroy, but a better behaved version indeed."

The woman in question stepped close to Mari, her dead eyes staring into some unknown distance. Collin studied her closely for any hint of the vampire he knew she'd become. Her skin hung loosely from her face and upper arms, like melted candle wax that had hardened. She still wore the dress and apron of the maid she once was.

Collin knew she had coordinated the attacks on his poor friend, Isabella. "What's she doing here?" he demanded holding the bone in front of himself.

"It's all well, she's under my control now. The same silver poison I put into you, now animates her, and ties her to me alone.

As if proving that point, the Zombie woman shifted her eyes over to Mari speaking with a dry voice. "You have called me from my sleep, Mistress, and I have answered"

Mari stepped in front of the creature she had destroyed only to be brought back in her zombie form. "So you have. You will show the boy and me to St. Germain's lair in this pit of death. He has kept his secrets long enough."

Even in her newly dead state, Collin saw a flare of recognition in Annette's eyes when she heard the name of the vampire.

She began to wring her hands together, clearly anxious at the order.

"Mari, she seems afraid to help us. Surely he can't hurt her in her current form."

"He can snatch her spirit away from her if I lose my grip over her. I can't let that happen."

Without another word she pointed the zombie forward and she followed. Collin was close behind.

Mari had retrieved the dropped torch when she picked up the long bone. They walked in the comforting circle of its light. Colin held it high after giving the bone back to the old woman.

"In case I need to prod her a little," she whispered to him while they followed the once live woman in the frumpy housedress.

Collin noticed there was no hesitation about what directions to take. He and Mari needed to hurry their own progress to keep up with the jerky, shuffling pace of the zombie.

Just watching her movements gave Collin an unsettled feeling. She *should be dead,* he thought, trying to move faster. Mari looked over at him and gave a quick nod as if she'd read his thoughts.

They were moving deeper into the tunnel system away from the tracks. It was a relief to Collin when he realized they wouldn't pass under the hanging cages, with the vampire's countless victims.

They came to an obviously well-used passage in the underground network of roads. There were signs of recent activity, with footprints scuffing the dirt and dust, leading to a heavy wooden door.

The zombie stood to the side, allowing the following pair to approach the door.

Collin was excited to see a possible exit out of the hellish cellars, but when he reached for the iron loop on the door, Mari put her hand on his arm.

"She goes first, boy. If anything is amiss, she can be our bird in the mine so-to-speak."

The resurrected maid didn't object to being used in this manner and pulled the heavy door open, after a stern look from Mari.

The creature, shuffled her feet until she crossed over the threshold and stood on a dirt path leading upward.

"A secret road out of the tunnels," Collin said with rising excitement.

With the door open wide, they both felt a damp breeze swirling around them. Mari's nose twitched on her wizened face before she tugged Collin's arm.

"Smell the bayou? She's letting us know we're close. Let's move."

"What about Annette?"

Mari thought for a second, "She'll return to her resting place in one of the crypts of the Butler cemetery. Dead is dead for her, at last."

The zombie walked away from the pair, quickly becoming one with the shadows.

Collin stayed close to the Voodoo witch. The pungent vegetation and soggy earth filled his head with bad memories. He dreaded crossing back over to the Monastery.

Once again, Mari guessed at his thoughts saying, "There's no need for us to return to the damnable Friary, boy. So, put your mind at ease."

"But where else would St. Germain take her?"

She answered without slowing, "Back to the Butler Guest House, I expect. It appears to me he has a special connection there and if I'm right, this Plantation has been his home since he set foot in America with his Maker, Annette. Vampires are dark creatures, but creatures of habit too. They prefer to stay in familiar hunting grounds, being careful not to over-hunt their territory. When they get too near that danger point, they leave off picking the healthiest and begin culling out the sickest, weakest humans. I suppose you can say they practice good farming techniques."

Her laugh was almost as chilling as the pictures she conjured in his mind with her macabre comment.

Colin ditched the torch when they exited the tunnels. There was enough hazy moonlight to follow a trail blurred by vegetation. "Mari," he called softly to the small, hurrying figure. Mari, I spotted a path to the Guest House."

She spun around looking in the direction he pointed. "Good on you, boy. We can split up when we get to the house. You find Maggie and get her away from here. You'll need to get to your automobile and drive as fast as that contraption will move. Go directly to the Church of St. Anthony of Padua. You'll be met by Father Patrice, the local padre there. You understand?"

"I understand, but I don't know why I have to go to the priest. And what about you? Won't you need my help?"

Mari looked at him as if seeing him for the first time.

"I'm touched you care about old Mari's wellbeing, boy, but I'll be fine. As for the priest, he will know what to do to exorcise the vampire's hold on your woman. No more time for talk, it may be too late already."

Chapter 55

St. Germaine stopped pacing in front of the bed. It's red satin comforter lay half on the floor by his feet. Maggie huddled against the headboard. Her wide eyes never left his handsome face. His sensual mouth looked so inviting to her, as he watched her pulling the filthy white shirt around her near naked body.

Though clearly showing her terror, he unmistakably saw something else in her beautiful face, something he hadn't expected. Determination. He spoke softly, coloring his words with charm and desire. "Maggie, can't you see how much you already mean to me? We are meant to be together darling, for all time. I can save your beauty into eternity, keep the ravages of the passing years from marring your perfection. Your body would never know pain or mortal corruption."

He stared intensely in her dark blue eyes, putting a subtle command into his next words. "You need only to slip off the necklace my sweet."

Her hand went up to Collin's shirt collar instinctively, pulling it tighter around her throat. Though badly torn, the shirt had concealed the juju necklace Mari put on her back in the tunnels.

The vampire had only discovered it when he deposited Maggie onto the bed and ripped open the shirt in enflamed anticipation of his feast.

His fangs had already descended as he knelt over her, his gray eyes alight with need and hunger. He threw his dark head back, ready to plunge the incisors into Maggie's supple skin, above her heart. They dripped with the poison that would transform her at last, into his Immortal Companion.

The necklace looked out of place around her slender neck. St. Germain paused, using extreme self-control to study it closely.

When he saw the fine bones strung around some kind of dried berry, he knew.

He scooted back on his heels, putting a safe distance between himself and what he identified as a powerful Voodoo charm.

From that moment, he had begged, harangued and threatened the beautiful girl to remove it. He knew he couldn't touch it himself. He would immediately suffer the consequences of the spell placed upon it.

The beast chose a different tactic. "Maggie, I know you mourn the loss of your dear friend, *our* dear friend, Isabella. Her death was only slightly premature, I can assure you. Her age and frailty were factors in her speedy demise. That and my jealous protégé, Leslie and the maid, Annette."

His smooth face reflected sincerity when he continued, still looking deeply into Maggie's terrified eyes. "I can promise you my darling, I had no idea they were complicit in her death, until it was too late. I would never have allowed her to suffer. Just as I know you wouldn't cause me to suffer. That's why you must remove the necklace my love."

Maggie nearly spat out her response to this weak plea for understanding. "I know all about you. You are a twisted monster! We found the cages where you've been keeping your victims, Grayson...or whatever you call yourself in this century. You use innocent people as food! You have no compassion for human suffering, or regard for human life! I should have seen it. I should have recognized your charm and attention were only a subterfuge, until you could take control of me. You tried to destroy my love for Collin and his for me, using that creature, Leslie. She was no better than a whore and you created her! Is that what you'd have me turn into? Is that your planned fate for me?"

The intensity of Maggie's outrage came as a surprise to St. Germain. He was sure he had seen the sexual need growing within her. But Maggie displayed an iron will. He couldn't wait until she submitted, for submit she would. His own desire had not dimmed in light of her resistance, rather it became more inflamed.

He moved toward the edge of the bed, inching his way closer to the girl. While he shifted his place, he slipped Maggie's chemise out of his pocket, turning slightly away from her, so she wouldn't notice as he carefully wrapped it around the palm of his hand.

"Maggie, won't you let me bring you the pleasure your body is craving? I can feel your hunger for my hands on your body, until I bring you screaming..."

He lunged at her neck, grabbing the necklace, crushing the fragile bones and scattering the dried berries. Using her own clothing to snatch at the charm, it had come away from her throat in one hard pull.

Maggie froze, still huddled close to the carved headboard for support. Her hand had been flung aside when the vampire gripped the amulet and tore it off.

She smelled the sickening odor of burnt flesh and realized St. Germain had touched the necklace at least partly. She couldn't help but marvel at his ability to block what had to be horrific pain.

The whole time he was removing the necklace his eyes never left her own. The moment the juju was ripped off her, Maggie felt herself falling into the depths of his stormy gray eyes. She knew this feeling all too well. He had used his mesmerizing powers to seduce her before and now, she felt herself slipping away from the very core of who she was.

She felt no terror, all she could feel was the beginning of a wet heat, building in her body. It would never be quenched without this man, this god, taking her until her body screamed for rest. *Would that be eternal rest*, she wondered as the vampire's hands quickly stripped away the last vestiges of Collin.

Maggie heard the ripping of Collin's shirt as St. Germain tore at it savagely. The same way he would tear at her.

Chapter 56

Collin watched Mari's petite form melding with the shadows around the plantation guest house. He felt uncomfortable with them splitting up but was anxious to recue Maggie. Mari needed to create a diversion for him to get in unnoticed. Mari's Voodoo powers were all that stood between him and the vampire. For that matter, the old woman was his only hope of saving Maggie,

He glanced up into the night sky. The moon was still shrouded in a thin veil of clouds. It barely provided enough watery light for him to avoid tripping over moss covered statuary and low fences, sprinkled around the large gardens.

Mari explained she would be entering by the front door, confronting the vampire and "holding his attention" as she put it. Collin was to go to the back bedroom, where the old woman was certain he'd find Maggie. He'd go through the bedroom window and carry her out the same way.

"You'll have to run with her in your arms, but you seem plenty fit for that," she assured him. You must get to your automobile and then on to the Church. You'll be expected by my friend, Father Patrice," Mari added.

Collin found it strange that the Voodoo witch had a friend who was a practicing cleric, but everything about the woman was strange.

Approaching the back of the small house, he was careful to keep to the patches of darkness cast down by the hulking stands of tall Cyprus trees.

The air was chilly, carrying the moisture from the nearby swamps. Collin found yet again being shirtless was proving an uncomfortable disadvantage as he crouched between scratchy shrubs and small trees.

He listened intently for the sound of a crashing door or the screeching of a flock of White Shadow Birds. Mari always had some kind of Voodoo mischief to unleash on an adversary.

Surprisingly, the only sounds rattling around in the night rode the night winds from the bayou. The night birds and hunters were still out and on the prowl. Collin looked about himself, wondering if the old woman had decided on a different plan. Maybe she found something new in her hidden carpetbag to throw in the vampire's face.

He stopped moving when he had the back bedroom window in view. A gauzy curtain hung across the window. It wasn't rustling in the wind. It was shut. Collin prayed it wasn't locked too. Breaking it would surely get quick attention from St. Germain.

What the hell am I thinking? Am I really able to confront this monster? As if in answer to those nettling doubts, Collin heard a series of shrill cries from overhead.

Looking up, he saw huge shapes, moving like scudding clouds across the face of the pale moon. "She *did* call her White Spirit Birds!" " Collin muttered to himself in amazement. He wasn't as comforted as he might have been, seeing the massive birds circle the cottage. St Germain had easily altered Mari's orders to the Spirt Bird she conjured when they were in the tower.

Instead of bringing Maggie to the solarium, it brought her here, deep in the gardens. He couldn't help but marvel, watching the flock of at least fifteen, great birds. Their wide wings blotted out the thin moonlight, as together they began to bank, turning toward the guest house and circling in close formation.

The raucous calls of the flock, were followed by the shattering sound of wood being split.

With the signal he was waiting for, Collin tore his attention from the birds ringing the house from above. He realized Mari had gone inside to confront the man she called the beast.

It was time for him to move.

He rushed from the safety of the shadows, crouching low beneath the bedroom window. He tried to control his breathing , half afraid his panting would be heard by the vampire inside.

Mari was speaking. Her usually wheezy voice was clearer and stronger in volume. Her words cut through the night air and the cries of the birds circling above.

Collin pressed his ear to the cold pane. He heard Mari say, "You have no doubt wondered, who hunted the hunter, Jacques. And now you know."

St. Germain's deep voice, as smooth and rich as a Cajun coffee, answered. "Mari, you have indeed caused me to wonder. It has been too many years to count, but you wear each one like the shed skins of a water snake.

I see the once ethereal beauty you possessed has been sucked out of you by trying to live a mortal life, leaving you a shriveled, dwarf of a creature. So sad. If you had come to me, you would still be the remarkable beauty that I so desired."

Collin was trying to conceive of a time the old woman had ever been a ravishing, desirable beauty, when he heard Mari's sinister laugh ringing through the small house. "How naïve of you to think I could ever want eternal life with you, especially after you murdered my family."

Mari barely whispered the last words. Collin strained to hear, "All I've ever wanted of you, is your destruction."

Collin took this as a cue, believing Mari might escalate her actions on that threat. It was time he moved too. Pushing on the window frame, he prayed to find it unlocked. He was relieved as it rose stiffly, but quietly and he could scramble through. He paused as his eyes adjusted to the low light from a single candle, then moved toward a figure huddled close to the headboard.

 Maggie's head was bowed, her glossy black hair reflecting back the soft glow of the flame. Her long legs where pulled close to her body, the soft curve protectively covering her near nakedness. *She might be tied to the bed post,* he thought alarmed. He had no knife to cut her free if that was true.

Collin realized the voices outside the room had stopped, but he heard the distinct sound of the White Spirit Birds directly overhead. He rushed over to the bedside and finding her unbound threw a cover over her and scooped the barely aware girl into his arms.

His foot slid a little on some kind of hard beads or stones, under his shoe. Looking down at the semi-conscious Maggie, he saw her naked breast.

The juju necklace, he thought frantically, seeing it was gone.

He was stepping carefully over the windowsill when Maggie stirred in his arms. He crouched low to clear the top of the window. With a foot firmly set on the ground he swung his other leg over the sill and was outside.

He glanced down at the dark head slumped against his bare chest. She raised her face up to him. "Collin, I knew you would come," Maggie whispered languidly.

He had no response as he still fought back the fear that he was too late to save the woman he loved.

Chapter 57

Mari watched St. Germain closely. She sensed the moment Collin took the girl and fled into the gardens. She watched the vampire's face and figured he also felt the change in the small house.

She smiled to herself as she quietly thought about his look. *The beating heart of your intended victim is no longer music to your overly sensitive hearing. Her body's sweet fragrance is gone from your sexual awareness.*

Mari knew the beast had the smell of his prey deeply imprinted on his libido. His desire for her was permanent unless he was destroyed. St. Germain spun around. His dark gray eyes narrowed as they fastened on the closed bedroom door.

He began to move when there was an explosion of wood and tile from the roof. It poured down on him in an avalanche of debris, covering him in a fine dust and pelting him with heavy roofing.

Mari knew this was no real deterrent to the vampire's powers of survival, but it bought a few minutes for Collin to make good his escape with Maggie.

The birds tore into the roof of the cottage as if were made of straw, diving at it with beak and talon at the ready. As the opening enlarged, a lone bird dove through it to confront the vampire. St. Germain's imposing figure was the perfect target. The White Spirit Bird entered with high screeching, ready for battle. The vampire shed the wood tiles and ceiling laths like mere droplets of water. The initial fragments of rubble slipped off his head and shoulders adding to the heaps around his booted feet.

St. Germain looked over at the Voodoo witch for a second, his eyes flashing with anger. "I see you still have some annoying habits, Mari. Using your Spirit Birds was always one of your favorite tactics as I recall."

He moved toward her while speaking, clearly focusing his attention on the small figure.

The White Spirit Bird stepped directly in his path, hissing and tearing at the hard floor, his sharp talons flexing on splayed, scaly feet. The vampire stopped for a moment looking over this new threat.

The bird danced in front of Mari, keeping her body covered with its own, so no part of her was vulnerable to the vampire.

St. Germain sneered at the bird's faithful protection as he worked his way closer.

"I wouldn't get too close, Jacques. I keep my birds hungry to inspire them. You'd make a tidy snack."

The vampire spoke softly, stopping just out of striking distance of the sharp beak.

"Mari, you surprise me with this antiquated, vulgar beast of yours. You and I both know I can bring the flock down with my bare hands, and yet you put one directly in my path. It makes me wonder if you are trying to distract me."

His face blurred with the speed of his flight to the bedroom. The door was flung wide. She knew the vampire would never be contained now that he knew Maggie had been whisked away from under his very nose.

St. Germain's handsome face became a dark mask of seething rage.

Mari had to get away before he turned that ferocious hate upon her. She needed to stay alive to finish the job. She had to destroy the beast. Her history with this creature flashed inside her, jolting every fiber of her being with loathing.

This would be her revenge on the creature that murdered her parents in the islands. Her grandmother escaped with her, a girl of eleven, to the safety of a home in the torpid land of the bayous.

But the beast would find her again and again, no matter where she tried to hide. He sensed some kind of innocence in her that he was driven to own.

The Voodoo her grandmother taught her, was her only salvation from falling into his arms totally and losing her soul. She would do that, she thought cynically, on her own.

He was beautifully handsome. He came to the hothouse of the bayous in the guise of a ship owner, transporting goods from Spain to the communities sprouting up like the wild orchids of the bayou, all around Louisiana.

Watching him now evoked an image of his warm smile, white teeth flashing from his deeply tanned face. She recalled how he stood at the railing of his vessel looking down at the innocent faces of the villagers as they came out to welcome the big ship to their waters.

She shuddered inwardly, remembering how he found her not long after his arrival. He entered the room she shared with her grandmother who was fast asleep beside her. He moved like a shark beneath the waters, smoothly and silently.

 Mari would learn later the beast used a charm to induce such a deep slumber in her guardian.

She recalled how he glided over to her side and with a gesture, pulled the sheet away from her nubile body.

He knelt beside her and gave her the first bite of seven she would receive over many years of his tormenting her.

Her eyes were old and rheumy now, but she saw the flash of incisors drop from the vampire's perfect mouth. Before she could take another breath, St. Germain sank his teeth into the side of the guarding Spirit Bird's snowy neck. She heard a sharp snap as the bird's neck broke and then saw his head ripped from his body. It fluttered around a few more seconds, its red blood pumped out, turning its body crimson.

Mari groaned, but immediately five more of her White Spirit Birds dropped through the opening. They flew at St. Germain in a flurry of wings, beaks and sharp talons digging into his flesh.

She knew they could never kill her enemy. He was of the undead. He was the man who never dies. She used the chaos of the attack to run from the house into the night. The birds would all be dead in a few minutes and then replaced by the remaining ones until he tore them all apart. They were of the spirit world and she conjured them to do battle and was grateful for their sacrifice.

She moved like a small tornado down the paths of the extensive gardens.

Her plan was to meet with Collin at the church where her friend and fellow vampire hunter, waited with blessed waters and a large silver cross.

Chapter 58

After he bundled Maggie into his vehicle, Collin ran around to the driver's side, snapped on the headlamps, and pressed his foot to the gas pedal. The screech of his tires as they fought for purchase on loose gravel triggered a memory of the large white birds he saw circling the guest house.

He wasn't able to think about the Voodoo witch, or her safety. He needed to concentrate on getting to the safety of the Church of St. Anthony de Padua. Her priest friend would be expecting them, though Collin didn't know how in God's name he could know they were coming. For that matter, he couldn't imagine how this Father Patrice could really help him protect Maggie and rid her of the vampire's hold on her.

His hands gripped the wheel, willing the large automobile to go faster still. The dark countryside flashed by under the haze of moonlight. Only an occasional light probed the bayou's complete hold on the night.

Maggie sat close to his side, her head bouncing gently on his shoulder over the rough roads. Collin slipped his right arm from under her so he could wrap it around her shoulders, holding her close. Maggie shifted in his grip and called out a name he'd never heard before.

"Jacques," she sighed, tossing her head slightly from side to side.

"Darling, it's me, Collin. I'm with you now and won't let anything harm you. I promise." His grip tightened until Maggie stopped her restless movements and relaxed into a deeper sleep on his chest. The warmth of her breathe and velvety cheek on his naked skin, was enough to ignite a flame of desire for her. He was holding her so tightly that she made small sounds of discomfort whenever his fingers dug into the smooth skin of her arm. He was barely aware he might be hurting her.

He lowered his head to Maggie's silky black bob, inhaling the scent of her fragrance and the natural scent of her body. He skidded the lumbering auto to the side of the dark road.

As he began to climb over her limp form, his body hot with desire, a screech tore through the night directly above them. He turned to look out his front window.

A White Spirit Bird floated down in front of the idling vehicle. It folded its wide wings, making no other sound as its pink eyes watched Collin intently.

Collin was certain he heard Mari's voice come out of the open beak. "Don't give in to this, boy. He has tainted your Maggie with these ugly desires and would hold you fast there until he can gain his freedom from my birds."

Collin shook his head as if he needed to dislodge water from his ears. He slumped back into his seat, gripping the wheel with moist hands. "What was I doing? Got to get her to the church!" The pale bird rose up and in an instant he was again alone, along the empty road.

To safeguard against succumbing to the lust that almost ruined the plan to save Maggie, he placed an old picnic blanket around her and propped her lolling head against the side window.

Once more he gunned the motor and returned to the roadway.

He reasoned they must be getting closer to the church as his sexual frustration began to slowly subside. His only thoughts now were to rid Maggie of the vampire's hold.

Collin reached the city streets. Following Mari's directions, he finally saw the cross atop the old Church of St. Anthony de Padua. Mari said Father Patrice would be waiting for them. He pulled in front of the plain, double wooden doors at the front, and a slightly built man stepped into his headlights.

Collin turned off his engine, quickly stepping out of the auto. He opened the passenger side door and carefully re-wrapped the blanket around Maggie's body.

Without a word passing between them, the priest helped lift the dead weight of the woman into Collin's arms.

Collin followed the priest through the foyer and into the modest church. Its dark wooden pews gleamed softly in the candles set around the altar, lovingly polished over centuries.

The priest bowed quickly before the altar and motioned for Collin to come through to the Sacristy. The room was small and stuffed with vestments and accoutrements for the sacred Masses held here daily.

Father Patrice spoke first. "She must be cleansed of the beast's curse upon her body and spirit, my son. In order to accomplish this, we will submerge her in the Blessed Waters that run beneath this holy place."

Collin was listening to the priest, but more fastened on his looks than on his words. Father Patrice was thin to the point of gauntness. The flesh around his pinched face was a sickly white, emphasizing a blueish tint to his full lips. Suddenly, Collin knew and the question burst from his mouth before he could re-think asking it. "Are you like General Butler? Are you one of his victims that escaped his control?"

"It is as you describe, my son. I no longer serve the people of this tiny parish, but I live, or rather, exist, in the secret catacombs beneath the church.

We must act quickly, else your lovely lady will suffer a similar fate, or worse. She will be taken by the vampire and serve his carnal needs for all eternity."

Collin watched the undead priest as he pushed aside a heavy table covered with books and ancient looking ledgers of church business. When this was moved out of the way, he rolled back the carpet revealing a trap door.

"We must go now, my son. The darkest hour approaches."

Collin shifted Maggie's sleeping form and held her more securely. The priest lit a torch hanging at the top of the steps. They climbed down a long set of stairs to a landing, then took another set, deeper yet, into a dank, earthen tunnel.

Collin knew they were beneath the old church, but he could clearly smell the rich mixture of life and rot coming off the bayou. "Where are we?" he asked with some trepidation seeping through his voice.

"Have no fear, my son, we are safe down here. This is where the sacred and blessed have been entombed in their crypts and where secret Masses were held when the Devil roamed our lands, devouring the faithful at will. I have been priest and guardian here now for nearly two centuries and have battled St. Germain for nearly all of that time."

"When did he…?"

The small priest spoke in a rush as they continued to walk. "When did the vile creature turn me? When I was still a young, fervent priest, excited with serving the Lord in this, my first and only Parish. The beast found my weakness and played upon it like a virtuoso on a violin. She was not unlike your own, Sleeping Beauty", he said, nodding at Maggie. "She was lithe of body and her beauty was nearly painful to behold, to my eyes. As a member of my small congregation, I saw her often and began arranging times where I could be alone with her. In her naiveté she never guessed my motives until…until it was too late. My love for her innocence and beauty soured like milk left under a burning sun. It stank with lust and greed to possess her every breath. Her name was carved into my heart and mind like the thrust of a keen blade. Deep and permanent. Mari, Mari. My doomed love."

Chapter 59

Collin thought he must have misheard, but with the second calling of her name by Father Patrice he knew without a doubt, he'd heard correctly. The Voodoo witch had another layer revealed.

Collin wondered what lay at the heart of the shrunken old woman that was left to be discovered. He'd already seen her display of powers, perhaps from realms too dark to be comfortable, yet needed to keep him and Maggie safe.

That thought brought him back to his current place, holding the woman he loved and needing to cleanse her of the touch of the vampire.

Remembering that St. Germain had already placed six bites on her, Collin was anxious to be assured there was no seventh anywhere on her body. "Father Patrice, Mari said you'd know how to cleanse Maggie of the touch of the beast. We need to move quickly. I don't know if St. Germain gave her the seventh bite, but she's been moaning out a stranger's name, like she was calling to him."

"A name? What was it?"

"It was "Jacques" and whenever she said it, it seemed to make her more restless and fall deeper into this sleep she's in now."

The priest's face, already drooping in extreme age, took on an animated look as he moved closer to Collin. Putting a cold hand on his arm said, "We must act now, my son. There is no time to lose. The Blessed Waters of Renewal are close by."

Father Patrice's sudden movement caused the torch he held to cast jumping shadows ahead of them. To his own eyes, Collin's shadow took on the form of a deformed creature as he rushed to follow.

For all his great age, the priest was extremely self-assured in his movements. Stepping quickly over piles of broken rock or around large pools of oily looking water, he never slowed his pace. The catacombs, as the priest referred to the secret tunneling beneath the church, appeared to encompass a great more land underground than the small church did above.

Collin, following on the heels of the priest's sandaled feet, asked him how far the catacombs extended.

He replied, "Almost to the banks of the bayou. They actually run directly under Mari's cottage. Shamefully, I admit to using my knowledge of these tunnels to meet with Mari when we became lovers. The only reason I wasn't sent to the prison monastery deep in the swamps, was because of Mari.

She'd been studying Voodoo magic in secret, even while attending Mass every Sunday and Holy Day. Like many of the Cajuns in New Orleans and every other Parrish, Christian beliefs were easily balanced with the pagan. Voodoo is as deeply rooted as a Cyprus tree, in the heart of many."

Maggie was becoming something of a burden to carry after nearly fifteen minutes. Collin hadn't eaten or slept in nearly twenty-four hours. He began to stumble or lose his footing, along some of the more difficult passages.

The torch Father Patrice carried high, like an Olympic runner, magnified the darkness outside of its singular, yellow glow. In passing, it momentarily illuminated the many alcoves holding the bodies of hundreds of parish members, along with the priests serving them over the long centuries.

Collin felt like an intruder on their final resting place and couldn't wait to see daylight.

"It's here," the priest called back to the struggling young man.

"This is the pool we call The Blessed Waters of Renewal."

Collin came abreast of the priest who gazed down at the still waters like he was viewing a miracle. "What now, Father? Does Maggie need to drink from it?"

"This will be her second baptism, my son. You must carry her into the pool until you can easily submerge her completely. Her head must be held down until she dies to the hold the beast has on her. You must not be tempted to release her from the water's grip, no matter how she struggles."

"My God, man, she'll drown in my arms! I can't do that to her!"

"Listen to me!   It is the only sure way of cleansing her of the vampire's own venom. When he bit into her, he injected his evil poison with every bite. We *must* destroy the venom to restore her to natural life!"

Collin walked into the pool. Knowing St. Germain had filled Maggie with an evil that flowed through her body made his guts twist with dread. He kept plunging deeper and deeper into the quiet waters, feeling the unexpected warmth begin to revive him as he moved.

Maggie was now completely submerged, except for her head. Collin noticed the old bites on her neck and breast when his large shirt floated open mid-way down. The bites were raw looking and there was some kind of yellowish fluid seeping out from them into the crystal waters.

Father Patrice called across to him. "You must submerge now, my son. Hold her down even if she fights for breath!"

Collin took a deep breath himself, reminding himself he needed to survive this ordeal, if he was to save her. Then he bent his knees and submerged, digging his shoes like shovels, into the soft bottom of the pool. He figured at least six feet of water covered them.

He watched Maggie for any response to her emersion, when her dark blue eyes snapped open, staring into his own. They were filled with horror and fear, but mostly a glaring hate. He thought, for a split second, the handsome face of Grayson Gerrard, the beast, floated in front of him.

Just as suddenly as it appeared, it vanished, to be replaced by the beautiful face of Maggie Newsome, the woman he loved and had to save.

She looked pleadingly at him, streams of tiny bubbles leaving her nose and distorting his view. He felt her struggle and begin to claw at him. He held her arms tighter to her side, pressing her closer into his chest.

She tried to thrash her long legs and kick away from him.

When he stopped her, she nearly succeeded in biting into his arm, but she was already losing consciousness.

Already drowning.

Chapter 60

As Mari hurried with uncanny energy through the shadows, the piercing screech of the Spirit Birds became more distant, until it faded completely and the night sounds of the Bayou took its place.

Mari knew Father Patrice would take Maggie and Collin directly to the catacombs and the Blessed Waters of Renewal.

She and Patrice discovered the pool when Paxton Parrish was no more than a backwater fishing and crabbing village. Fevers were deadly. Often, the sounds of a wailing mother rode the clammy night air, like a coon dog howling at the moon.

Mari left the gardens, heading directly to the great house. It looked as cold and empty as a recently robbed grave. Shaking off that premonition of death, she pulled open one of the four garage bays.

Fishing in a deep pocket, she pulled out the keys to the automobile Isabella gifted her with, two Christmases before. Mari kept her car stored at the Butler Plantation, since her tiny cottage offered no safe area to park such a large vehicle.

Mari always hated ostentation and didn't feel comfortable driving the conspicuous thing around the lower Parrish where she lived. Tonight though, she silently thanked Isabella for her outrageous gift and private driving instruction as she turned the engine switch.

She pulled out of the stall and in a few minutes was racing down the dark, lonely road toward the church.

She knew it was only a matter of time before Maggie would be unable to fight off the effects of the vampire's serum. It would move through her body, corrupting everything that made her human and mortal, until she was as void of life as the tomb.

Mari spotted a few lights scattered among the cottagers living close to their boats and rafts, along the muddy shore. The church of St.

Anthony de Padua was located close to her own tiny house, just a few minutes away.

She rounded a curve, driving to the end of a short block. Stopping in front of the modest church, she returned the keys to the depths of her pocket and pulled the iron ring on the heavy wooden door.

The church vestibule was silent. There were a smattering of candles struggling to push back the heavy darkness of the interior. Mari tried to shake out her damp dress, reaching a knotty hand once more into a pocket. When she pulled it out, there was another fire stone glowing back at her like the single eye of a Cyclops.

She went directly to the Sacristy and the secret trap door, having done this many times before. The carpet was rolled back and the door was left open. *They were in a hurry, but this was foolish*, she thought disapprovingly. There was a slight chance of a mortal discovering this hidden passage. Mari never chanced that, pulling it shut behind herself as she stepped onto the third step.

The murky passage emphasized the stone's radiance when she extended her hand. Mari carefully took the remaining steps onto the tunnel floor and into the secret catacombs just beyond.

As she moved deeper, she inhaled the scent of the rich earth with an underlying odor of decay swimming beneath the loamy smell. She hurried on her short, frail legs, popping something taken from her pocket earlier into her mouth as she moved. The dried tadpoles were guaranteed to give her quick responses and vitality.

Mari smiled to herself as a jolt of energy shot through her body. The Fire Stone reflected momentarily on her deeply creased face and her small yellow teeth. "That should do me," she muttered into the thick air swirling around her.

There was a light, brighter than her own, painting the walls of the slots of the many wall crypts. As she passed these, Mari spotted several skulls and some whole skeletons, their clothing long rotted away, showing yellowed arms crossed peacefully over empty chests. They all held a silver cross in skeletal hands, warding off any intrusion by the beast.

Has he ever found this place? Mari wondered, creeping forward. As if in answer to that unspoken question, a sharp cry rang out, reverberating in the confines of the catacombs. Mari saw some of the rotting bones actually shift in their open crypts, stirred by the deep vibration from the scream.

"He's come!" she hissed. No longer creeping silently, she rushed toward the wide opening straight ahead and the shimmering pool of water. There was heavy thrashing in the inky waters, as if some animal had fallen in and struggled desperately to save itself.

Mari guessed Collin held Maggie beneath the Blessed Waters. There would be a battle raging within the young woman, between her natural humanity and the evil slithering like a water moccasin through her body.

A voice cut through the continuous sound of agitated waters. "Deliver the woman to me now, or suffer the consequences, priest!"

Father Patrice's answer to this demand made the waters roil even more. "You are Devil Spawn and shall never be more than that in the sight of the glorious God! Your powers are like dripping candle wax here, useless and ugly. The girl will never be given up to you!"

Mari shoved the Fire Stone into her pocket, stopping at the limit of the priest's lighted torch. Instinctively, she wanted to call out to him, but she knew he already sensed her presence as did the vampire. The undead always felt the flicker that animated others of their kind. Other undead who moved in the land of the living, between natural and mutation.

She watched as the priest raised a hand over the small waves that formed from the movement below the surface. They lapped at his sandals as he stood protectively at the edge of the Blessed Waters.

Mari sensed the utter terror radiating from the young man below the waters, fighting to hold the girl against her will. *Against the will of the beast*, she thought and called to the juju necklace she'd placed around Maggie's neck earlier.

Nothing. She no longer wears it, Mari realized, changing her plan of attack. There would be no help from the charm and the girl would be totally exposed to the vampire's seductive powers.

With a muffled pop, the leg bone was back in Mari's hand. The tiny sound alerted the vampire as she knew it would, but by then she was charging him. A scuttling black spider, detecting movement in her web.

St. Germain scowled at the oncoming Voodoo witch, but without hesitation reached for the bone she held like a harpoon. Whatever destruction he endured would heal quickly. It burned through the dead-white flesh of his hand, exposing tendon tissue, down to the bones, then scorching them black, like a branding iron.

His scream was uncanny in its deafening effect.

Mari held on to the Voodoo-enhanced weapon but was unable to shake his hold.

"Patrice! The waters! Splash it upon his arm quickly!" she shrieked over the low roar of pain from the vampire.

The priest turned his back on the part of the pool where Collin still desperately held his breath and fought to keep Maggie submerged. Father Patrice frantically used both hands to scoop at the water, sending wide arcs of the dark water over the smoking hands of the vampire.

It proved more than he could withstand.

St. Germain cursed Mari furiously as he relinquished his hold on the long bone. Mari used the opening to drive the skeletal remains into the vampire's side. He threw his dark head back in a great howl of agony and frustration. Somehow, combined with his rage, the extreme suffering resulted in him rushing his tormentor.

The vampire grabbed hold of the bone once more, only this time with his uninjured hand as well. Using his enhanced strength, he managed to pull the bone and Mari to his oozing side.

Mari tried to let go of the bone, but it was too late. The vampire pulled her close to his mouth and the dripping fangs, clamping down on her throat and windpipe, immediately cutting off her air.

Though she too was of the undead, he knew the oxygen in her mortal life still fueled her continued existence in her half-life.

Within a few seconds, Mari's neck was crushed under the pressure of the jaws holding her and shaking her small body like a rag doll.

Chapter 61

Father Patrice stood frozen in horror at the sight of Mari's frail body dangling from the vampire's hand as he held her away from his mouth, red with her blood.

"You are a fool, Patrice! See the fate that awaits any who deny me what is mine!"

The vampire spat out Mari blood, wiping his stained face on his shirt sleeve, the red silk immediately turned black with the stain.

The priest backed away from the advancing beast. His sandals were suddenly wet as he stepped to the water's edge.

The beast stopped moving.

The priest knew the Blessed Waters would prove his undoing. He had to find a way to lure him close enough to force him into the pool.

As he frantically thought of how to ensnare him, St. Germain moved slightly to his right, a look of disquiet marring his perfect features.

"Maggie!"

Collin emerged from the center of the pool, streams of water running from his head and bare upper body. Rising like Neptune from the sea, but instead of a trident, he held the still body of his fiancé.

Maggie's short black hair looked almost pixie-like as it clung to the high cheek bones. Her eyes were closed and she looked peaceful resting against Collin's broad chest.

St. Germain studied the tableaux of the two while water sluiced off them back into the sacred pool.

"Bring her to me, mortal," the velvety voice of the vampire carried easily to the dripping man.

"I will die before you touch her again, monster."

"You call me monster, but I am your superior in every way. With me, Maggie will have everything her heart could desire, or dream to possess. All of the world will be as a plaything to her every whim."

Collin smirked, "Maggie isn't about playthings. You are even a bigger fool than I took you for."

St. Germain came closer to the water's edge. The torchlight fell directly on his remarkably handsome face, as smooth and unlined as a twenty-year old.

The vampire's mouth twitched at the insult. He seemed to be struggling to control his rising anger but continued to speak to Collin in soothing tones. "I have the power to give Maggie more than material wealth and a lavish lifestyle. I can give her immortality! Her beauty will never fade, her body never corrupt and fail her unto her death bed. What can you offer as priceless as these?"

Collin only took a second to respond. He looked down at the peaceful, lovely face answering, "Love. I can offer her love."

Father Patrice had been moving like the phantom he should have been two centuries earlier, before he fell into this half-life with Mari. He watched the vampire closely, remembering his incredible speed and strength. Patrice had succumbed to both when he was still only a mortal man. But that was in a past, too distant to dwell upon. Now, he had to entice the murdering beast into the Blessed Waters or force him there.

"You are afraid to enter a little pool, beast?" the priest called out to him. He was clearly mocking St. Germain, letting his cocky smile add to the fuel of his contemptuous words. Without stirring a ripple, the priest gradually moved deeper into the water, feeling it lapping against his shins. He noted how Collin had remained where he was. *Smart boy*, he thought relieved.

The only sounds in the hollow throat of the tunnel were the soft plop, plop, plop, of the water dripping off Maggie and Collin. The priest cut a quick look at the young woman, seeing with relief she was breathing normally, no longer gulping for air as when they first rose from her cleansing.

The beast barely noticed the wretched priest taunting him. His piercing gray eyes were fastened on Maggie, the water beaded like blood droplets on her smooth skin. The shirt she wore was badly torn, sticking like a second skin on the gently rising and falling of her breasts.

The man who could never die was overcome with his own arrogance and the desire for this beautiful woman that burned away all else. He always got what he wanted, no matter what. No matter who. Queens and dairy maids, actresses and char women, all had fallen into his embrace and his bed.

Maggie was no different, but she was destined to be his for his long eternity of walking this earthly hell.

Both the priest and Collin had been watching St. Germain closely, waiting for his move. Collin noted a change in his eyes. There was a new light radiating from them. It wasn't the look of life, but a deep red, a burning madness.

The vampire reached a decision. His face contorted with fury and an all-consuming lust for the woman he had to possess. He flew at the priest, ignoring the splashing waters around him as they reached his boot tops.

Father Patrice was quick to act. As soon as the vampire was within striking distance, he pulled a large silver cross from inside a full sleeve. He knew this was only a weak method of stopping him, but the Blessed Waters were unknown to the beast and Patrice counted on the combination to prove his destruction.

Collin gathered Maggie tighter in his arms, holding his place in the pool's center as a battle unfolded several feet away.

The gaunt priest showed amazing strength, taking the vampire by surprise as well, as he dragged him deeper into the pool.

St. Germain realized the water was almost waist deep and the thin silk shirt he wore was no protection. Unbelievably, an ash colored smoke bubbled up to the surface, rising like a silver cask around his torso. The Blessed Waters chewed at his once perfect body, attacking mortal flesh like a pool of piranha.

Collin was morbidly fascinated by the horrific scene unfolding before him when he felt a light touch on his cheek. Maggie's small hand held his face.

"Darling, it's…"

"Over at last," she finished.

In the horror of the moment, Collin turned them away from the screaming vampire, not wanting Maggie to witness such a nightmarish sight. When he looked back, the pool was empty save for him and Maggie.

He turned in all directions, searching the pool for the priest.

Maggie spoke softly, asking Collin to help her get out of the water.

"The priest has vanished, Maggie," he said after helping her out of the dark pool.

"Part of me is not sure he was ever really here." Collin studied the unbroken surface of the Blessed Waters. He wondered if the priest was conjured by his imagination, out of desperate need. But the Voodoo witch was real enough, so why not an undead priest?

Maggie broke into his mental dialogue.

"Collin, I…I wasn't certain I could come back to you. I wasn't certain I *wanted* to come back to you. Where I felt my love for you in my every fiber before Grayson, I felt…nothing. When you held me down in the water, I knew I was drowning. I knew you were killing that thing in me that blotted out all of my human feelings. I had to die to break his hold on my life, on my love. Thank you for saving me and for saving that love."

Collin took her into his arms again, only this time, she could wrap her own arms around him tightly, in response.

"Collin, look. There's a light coming in from above us," she said after seeing a shaft of light fall on the still waters.

They discovered another trap door, the long staircase leading from the catacombs and opening into a meticulously kept row of above ground mausoleums.

In the early light of dawn, they quietly watched the sunrise painting the domed tops of vaults for the dead in soft pinks and warm gold.

There was a vault standing at the end of the first row that caught Collin's eye. "That vault's door is open," he said, indicating its position in the long line with a jerk of his chin.

"What do you think it means, Collin?"

"It means we need to do one more thing in this dark drama, my love. Come on."

They cautiously approached the yawning face of the high grave site. Because of the high water table in the area, all graves had to be above ground so there was nothing unusual about this one, except the name engraved on the stone plate by the open door.   Father Patrice Xavier Santiago

Lived in the light of the lord

1720-

"There's no date for his death, Collin. And why is the crypt still open?"

As if in answer to the questions they both had, the heavy wooden door swung shut with a resounding force that shook the air around them.

They jumped back, startled by the sound as much as what had just occurred.

When they were sure nothing else was moving, they approached the front of the grave site and saw "1920" had been carefully etched upon the stone, completing the life and death story of the remarkable priest.

"No one will believe the dates, Maggie. If anyone even bothers to come to this old cemetery." He was reassuring Maggie that the good priest would not be disturbed in his own long sleep.

"Collin, I think we need to get back home before the locals spot us in our nearly naked state."

Hearing Maggie talk about home gave Collin a rush of sheer relief.

She was his for as long as they were blessed with life. He didn't know he could love her as much as he did in that moment.

They walked toward his auto sitting at the front door of the church. As he was helping Maggie into the front seat, something slammed into his side, knocking him to the ground.

Before he could regain his feet, Maggie was out of the vehicle and in a blur had grabbed his attacker around his neck and twisted. The snap of the vertebrae sounded like the crackle and pop of a log in the fireplace.

She let the inert body slip away from her, panting as she stood there watching it for any movement.

Collin was standing but couldn't move.

Maggie stood over a dead man, his face obscured in the shadow of the auto. She had moved with the same uncanny speed he'd seen in one other. The Vampire, Jacques St. Germain.

"Oh, my God, Maggie! What have you done?"

"He would have killed you, Collin! He's one of St. Germain's. I'm sure St. Germain ordered him to follow you."

Without another word, Maggie picked up the body and slung him over her slender back.

"Let's reopen the Father's burial chamber, Collin. I'm sure Patrice won't mind the company. No one will miss this creature since he's likely from the monastery.

Collin followed his beautiful finance, watching her lithe form as she returned to long rows of vaulted crypts. He stood aside after he opened the door to the mausoleum, watching numbly as Maggie placed the dead man next to Patrice's coffin.

Collin took her arm firmly as soon as they were out of the cemetery.

"I have to know Maggie. How can you move like you did with that attacker? It was as if I was watching the damned vampire again!"

"Collin, Mari and Father Patrice knew the truth, but you hadn't guessed it yet.

St. Germain had already given me the seventh bite by the time you rescued me and took me here." She waited, as the face she loved so dearly, reflected the gambit of emotions he was feeling. From fear, to anger, to concern and back to fear. All within a few heartbeats.

"He gave it to me when he held me up in that tower, before Mari's Spirit Bird took me. He hid it carefully, so it wouldn't be discovered until it was too late." Her eyes drifted down to her bare thighs. "It would have meant your death my darling because you were to be my first victim, my first meal! I would have been turned into another Leslie Porter Booth. I would be St. Germain's slave for a dark eternity, if not for the intervention of Mari and Father Patrice." She shuddered. "I had to be immersed in the waters to be cleansed, but like both Mari and the priest, it was already too late to save my mortal life. The beast had already done his worse to me. I was reborn under the Blessed Waters of Renewal, but reborn to be like Mari and Patrice."

Maggie studied his face closely for any signs of revulsion at this revelation.

"Please, don't be afraid of me, darling. Our life together is just beginning and I promise you a lifetime of my unending love."

Collin hadn't moved a muscle while she spoke, but now exploded into action. Rushing to Maggie, he grabbed her into his arms, hungrily kissing her mouth until he had to stop to take a breath. "Maggie, whatever you are now, it doesn't matter to me. I don't begin to understand about vampires and undead people who are living like normal humans. I have seen killer ghosts and gigantic Spirit Birds. I've been seduced by a vampire and seen you lying with her Maker. It's all a blur, just like the way I saw you move just now. But Maggie, what is all of that, when the true mystery still lies ahead." He pressed his lips against the top of her head. "Loving you as human, or immortal, just promise you'll always wait for me in the darkness ahead."

The End

About the Author

    Francesca is part of a large Italian family where she discovered early on that a love of reading was as much a part of her DNA as her mother's skill at baking. Growing up in a house filled with laughter, screaming, banging pots, fighting and loving family bonds, shaped her life and heart.

    Having moved from the east coast where she was raised between New York and New Jersey, Francesca left for the mid-west where she spent several years outside the Chicago area raising a family of three children, completing her college degrees and writing introspective poetry as a young mother.

    Francesca has worked in local television, a small city zoo, founded a non-profit tutoring agency for an inner-city neighborhood which eventually served local school districts, worked for an International Evangelical Television and Radio Station and for a non-profit organization serving challenged adults.

Francesca Quarto resides in a small town outside of Indianapolis, Indiana with her husband Patrick. She still has a great love of the written word and while she enjoys her E-Reader immensely, she still treasures the excitement of turning the next page.

Tell-Tale Publishing would like to thank you for your purchase. If you enjoyed this book, please show the author your appreciation by posting an online review. If you would like to read more by this or other fine TT authors, please visit our website:

www.tell-talepublishing.com

www.ingramcontent.com/pod-product-compliance
Lightning Source LLC
Chambersburg PA
CBHW051638180726
48284CB00006B/1775